The Sky Took Him

Books by Donis Casey

The Old Buzzard Had It Coming
Hornswoggled
The Drop Edge of Yonder
The Sky Took Him

The Sky Took Him

An Alafair Tucker Mystery

Donis Casey

Poisoned Pen Press

First Edition 2009

10 9 8 7 6 5 4 3 2 1

Library of Congress Catalog Card Number: 2008931492

ISBN: 978-1-59058-571-9 Hardcover

Poisoned Pen Press
6962 E. First Ave., Ste. 103
Scottsdale, AZ 85251
www.poisonedpenpress.com
info@poisonedpenpress.com

Printed in the United States of America

For Delores

Acknowledgments

[illegible] Robert Allen [illegible] help and support.

[illegible]

Acknowledgments

This book owes its existence to my Enid family: Dolores, Jean, LaNell, Gary, and Lorraine, and their spouses and myriad offspring. And of course to Butch, who brought me into the family. How lucky I am!

Thanks also to reference librarians Amanda Kashevarof and Carmen Porter Akin, late of the Garfield County Library System, for their help and support.

I must also acknowledge my own siblings, Carol, Chris, and Martha, and thank them especially for their help in finding and testing the old family recipes.

The Family Tree
September 1915

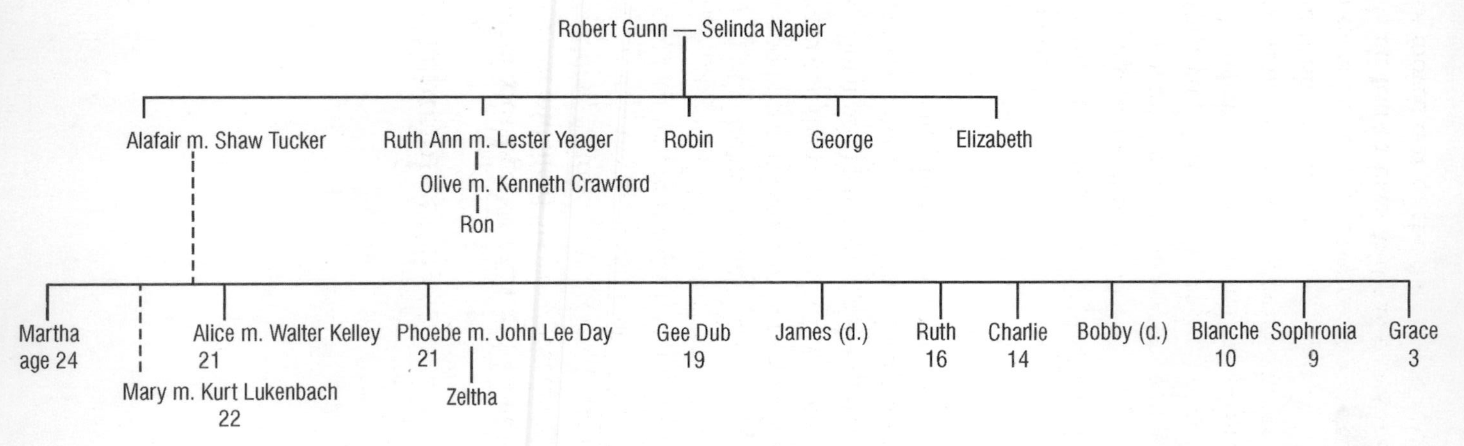

Monday, September 13, 1915

The train out of Muskogee was very nearly empty. Alafair Tucker settled into a seat and lifted her youngest daughter, Grace, onto her lap. Her eldest, Martha, unburdened herself of the luggage by cramming it into the overhead racks. She sat down opposite her mother and sighed, relieved to be off her feet at last.

"I have to go potty," Grace informed them grandly. Both Alafair and Martha burst into laughter.

Martha stood up and extended her arms. "I'll take her, Ma."

"No, you just sit there, hon. You've been toting the luggage ever since we left Boynton. Your arms must be about pulled off."

"I don't mind. I need to stretch. Grace probably doesn't have to go, anyway. She just likes to inspect the toilets in every new place she finds herself."

The three-year-old was affronted by the suggestion. "I do too have to potty!"

Martha nodded. "I know, sugar. And you'll have to go again when we change trains in the City."

"Y'all can go, but be sure and don't touch anything in there, Martha. Why, you don't know who all's been in there doing heaven knows what. And be sure and put plenty of paper on the seat." By this time, Alafair was admonishing the girls' retreating backs. "And wash your hands!"

Martha gave her a lazy wave of acknowledgment without turning. Alafair leaned back and gazed out the window as the train slowly moved out of the Muskogee station. It began to pick up speed as it left town and began the long, straight haul toward Oklahoma City.

After the girls disappeared, Alafair took an envelope out of her bag. She eyed her name written in a spidery hand on the front for a moment before she withdrew the creased and often read letter and began to peruse it for the dozenth time.

Dearest Alafair, *Sept. 5, 1915*

I hope this letter finds you well. I am writing to you because trouble has befallen us, Dearest Sister. As you know, my beloved Husband Lester has been suffering with a greevus illness for a long time now, and Doctor Lamerton has informed us just lately that poor Lester is not long for this world. I take comfort that long ago Lester accepted Jesus as his Savier and when his time comes he will be gathered to the bosom of the Lord.

Our sad vigil has been made worse because our son-in-law, Olivia's husband Kenneth, has undertaken to go on a trip to the No Man's Land in order to meet with an important client. I have come to rely so on Kenneth since Lester has been ailing, and his absence is distressing in this time of trouble. Mr. Beams and Olivia have done their best to keep the warehouse and shipping business running smoothly, and me and my serving girl Lu have been caring for my beloved grandson while she does so, as well as seeing to my poor husband's needs. I am plum wore out, and I am missing the help and comfort of Kenneth's manly presence.

I am distrait, Sister, as you can well imagine. I wish that Kenneth had not had to take hisself off on the eve of Lester's death. Lester has no family but ours, and he loves Kenneth like the son we never had. It will be mighty sad if he goes to meet Jesus before Kenneth returns. I have asked our Mother and Father to come from Lone Ellum to be with us, but they cannot come here for a while yet. I have also wrote to our Brother George and Sister Elizabeth, and I write to you, as well, Alafair, asking that you join us here in Enid for a spell, if you can. I expect you need not stray long from home. Lester is so weak that by the time you get this letter, he may already have gone to the gates of Heaven.

Please come, Dear Alafair, so Lester may see your welcome face one last time. I know this is a busy time on the farm, so if you cannot come, please join us in prayers for Lester's eternal rest.

Your Loving Sister
Ruth Ann Yeager

Alafair replaced the letter into its envelope and slipped it into her purse before she resumed staring out the window. She didn't look forward to the inevitably depressing visit with her sister, though it never occurred to her to demur. She knew from her own bitter experience that during a crisis, nothing could shore up a person like having her family around her.

Ruth Ann had been right about one thing, though. It was a bad time to leave the farm. Harvest was still going on, and school had started not long before, which robbed Alafair's husband Shaw of a large part of his workforce. Two of Alafair and Shaw's ten children were married with homes of their own, two had paying jobs in town, and one had just recently begun college. But of the seven who still lived at home, all but Grace were old enough to have their own responsibilities.

She stared absently at the brown country passing by. A long, dry summer was coming to an end, and everything looked tired and thirsty, drooping in the dusty heat. Still, there was a smell on the wind, a heaviness in the atmosphere which told Alafair that a change was on the way. Her half-Cherokee mother-in-law was predicting a very cold winter. The squirrels were storing nuts in August and the bark on the trees was particularly thick this year. Grandma Sally was seldom wrong about these things, and Alafair had already begun putting by extra fuel.

The train made a long turn to the northwest, and Martha's hat slid languidly from one end of the seat she had vacated to the other. Alafair retrieved the hat and placed it in her lap. She was glad that Martha had volunteered to join her on this trip. Not only was Martha an excellent traveling companion and good company, but having her along as a babysitter had made it possible to bring Grace. Though she was sure that her older children were perfectly capable of caring for the child for the few days that Alafair would be away, Grace was not quite three, and had never been apart from her mother for any length of time.

As happy as she was to have Martha along, Alafair was surprised that she would consent to take two weeks off from her job as secretary to Mr. Bushyhead, manager of the First National Bank of Boynton. She was even more surprised that Mr. Bushyhead would let Martha go for so long. In the three years that Martha had worked at the bank, she had made herself indispensable. That fact did not surprise Alafair in the least. Martha was the most naturally efficient person she had ever known.

Grace pounded down the aisle with Martha close on her heels, and threw herself across her mother's lap, full of news.

"It's beautiful, Mama. Martha put paper all around the seat." She was frantically pulling imaginary paper off a roll, hand over hand, and padding an imaginary circle with it. Alafair was amused. Martha must have lined the seat six inches deep with paper, if Grace's pantomime bore any relation to reality. "And then after I pottied, Martha lifted me up so's I could pull this long chain! It made this big 'whushhhh' and water come down and a hole opened up and we could see the ground. There was tracks going by like 'shupshupshup.' I couldn't hardly see them they was so fast!" She illustrated by flicking her eyes back and forth, then she hugged Alafair's knees. "I wasn't scared."

"She reckoned that she might fall in and never be seen again," Martha interjected, "but we finally came to the conclusion that she's too big to fit through the hole."

"Did you wash your hands?"

Grace nodded emphatically. "Yes a hundred times. We turned a iron handle and water came out of the faucet, but we didn't have to pump at all."

Alafair looked up at Martha, who had resumed her seat opposite. "You didn't use the soap that was in there, did you?"

Martha shot her an ironic look, then reached into her bag and pulled out a little wooden box, which Alafair knew contained a bar of her own homemade soft yellow soap. "You've ruined me, Ma, I hope you know. I'm unable to use a bar of soap unless I personally know who made it."

If Martha was teasing her, Alafair missed it. "You can't be too careful."

By this time, Grace had pasted her nose to the window and was engrossed in watching the country rush by at the blazing speed of fifty miles an hour. Alafair handed Martha her hat and sat back as comfortably as she could in the horsehair-padded wooden seat. She wished she had a pillow for her back. It was going to be a long trip to Oklahoma City.

She eyed Martha thoughtfully. "I'm glad you decided to come with me on this trip. I'm not much looking forward to it."

"I hope Grandma and Grandpa make it while we're there. I haven't seen them for a good long while."

When she was little, Martha had been particularly close to Grandpa Gunn. But for the past few years, Martha hadn't seen eye to eye with her opinionated and extremely self-assured grandfather on a number of things, and when she was in his company she tended to bite her tongue a lot. Alafair let the comment go. "I doubt if they'll make it to Enid before we have to leave. Maybe after things are settled with your aunt Ruth Ann, Grandma and Grandpa can come down our way for a spell. I wouldn't think Mr. Bushyhead much likes you being gone for such a long while. I had about decided that bank can't run without you."

Martha puffed a laugh. "It can't, hardly. Mr. Bushyhead and Uncle Jack may know all there is to know about loans and investments and the like, but neither one of them could find his way out of tow sack with a compass. Well, they'll appreciate me even more when I get back."

"Still, I'm surprised you'd want to be away so long, the way you enjoy that work."

"Mr. Bushyhead understood when I told him about Uncle Lester dying and Kenneth up and taking off and all."

"I know, honey. It's just that you've been acting like there's something on your mind lately. Is there something troubling you?"

Martha's gaze shifted away from the window to her mother's face. She smiled. "I figured you'd be asking me that before long. You can smell a troubled mind like a hunting dog smells a trail."

"Just with you kids. Is it Streeter McCoy?"

Martha's cheeks reddened. She was silent for a long minute while she considered her reply. Why, oh why, oh why was she surprised that Alafair had asked her that question? There was no keeping secrets from her mother. Aside from the fact that Alafair could apparently read her children's minds, she had a spy network that any government in the world would envy, the prime recruits of which included Martha's nine blabbermouth brothers and sisters. "What makes you think that?"

"Your Uncle Jack told Aunt Josie that Streeter McCoy has been coming around to the bank an awful lot for a man with no particular business to discuss. Said he shows up around noontime, checks his account, which ain't changed since the day before, and, 'oh, by the way, Miss Martha, if you're not doing anything for luncheon, I'm on my way to Williams' Drug Store for a bite, and I sure would admire some company.'"

Martha laughed, but she didn't look very happy. "Uncle Jack has too busy an imagination, Ma. There's nothing to be said about Streeter Donald McCoy, believe me."

The flush that colored her cheeks belied her words. But Alafair's mothersense would have detected the disturbance in the ether around her daughter even if Martha had been the coolest liar on the face of the earth. She opened her mouth to probe further.

When it came to her mother, however, Martha had some extrasensory abilities of her own. She executed a preemptive maneuver. "Kenneth picked a bad time to go on a business trip, didn't he?"

Alafair swallowed her question. She was aware of what had just happened, but it wasn't necessary to pursue this now. She was perfectly confident that a better opportunity would arise later. "Oh, I don't know. I know your aunt and uncle think a bunch of Kenneth, but that young'un never did have a lick of sense, to my way of thinking. I don't know what sort of 'business trip' he went on, but I'll bet you that he just couldn't stand being around all that sorrow and sickness one more minute and decided to take a little vacation from it. I swear, Olivia has the patience of a saint to have put up with his inconsiderate behavior these past couple of years."

"Well, he's affectionate to her, and a good daddy to that child. But he does take her good nature for granted, that's straight, and just between you and me, Ma, she's not as happy about his behavior as she lets on, if I'm reading her letters right. He's spoiled, is my opinion. Thinks the sun and stars revolve around him. Uncle Lester and Aunt Ruth Ann have never done anything to disabuse him of the notion, either. To hear them tell it, the sun shines right out of his posterior."

Alafair didn't know the word "posterior," but she got the picture. "Martha!" She tried to look shocked, but laughed instead, a victim of her love for a good phrase.

"Posterior," Grace repeated, without removing her nose from the window.

"Now see what you've done?" Alafair chided, trying hard to keep the laughter out of her voice.

Martha had brought along a book to amuse herself, but Alafair spent most of the trip gazing out the window while at the same time trying to keep an eye on an excited and energetic three-year-old. At the moment, Grace was bouncing up and down the aisles, stopping occasionally to engage some willing adult in animated conversation about herself and her first train ride.

A well-dressed elderly gentleman lifted the child onto his knee, the better to hear her story. He scanned the other passengers until he caught sight of Alafair's weather eye on the girl. They exchanged a smile and a nod before Alafair leaned her elbow on the arm of the seat, absently watching for any sign that Grace was beginning to bother the old man and his enchanted wife, who had taken the child's hand and leaned in close.

"You sure look to be enjoying that book," she observed to Martha, without taking her eyes off of Grace. "What is it?"

Martha didn't look up. "*Pudd'nhead Wilson.* It's by Mark Twain. I like just about anything of his I can get my hands on."

Alafair chuckled. "I like the title."

"His work is always a mix of funny and serious. This one is about a trial. It's real interesting. You should read it when I get done."

"Now, when would I ever get time to read a book, sugar?"

Martha finally lifted her eyes from the page and scrutinized her mother. "Oh, Ma, you wouldn't read a book even if you had the time, and you ought to. You know, you'll probably be sitting with Uncle Lester a bunch while we're there. Olivia wrote that he likes to be read to—maybe he'd enjoy this. You can read it to him."

"Maybe I ought. I'm such a bad out-loud reader that my voice would put him right to sleep." Her comment was offhand and absent, since she was still intent on keeping an eye on Grace's antics. Martha shook her head and returned to her book.

Alafair became aware that the train was slowing long before she could see any settlement. The look of the country had changed drastically once they had pulled out of Oklahoma City, from rolling wooded hills to the endless grassy expanse of the Great Plains. As they neared Enid, the wild sea of grass had been long replaced with vast wheat fields, newly plowed and planted at this time of year. Alafair awoke the drowsing three-year-old on her lap and began to pull on the child's shoes.

As soon as the train pulled to a stop, Martha stood and reached for their luggage on the overhead rack. The bustle in the car increased as the other passengers did likewise, adjusted their hats and coats, and began to move in a desultory line toward the exits.

Alafair sat for a moment to let the car clear a bit before she made her move, though Grace was pulling on her hand in a rush to get on with this adventure. "Look out here, shug." She lifted the little girl bodily and plunked her down before the window. "Did you ever see so many folks all at one time? And look yonder! There's your cousin Olivia waiting for us. Look, Martha. She looks good. She came to fetch us herself, and she don't look broke up. I'm guessing her dad is still alive and that Kenneth has showed up. That's a nice bonnet she has on."

She continued prattling on in order to distract the girls for a couple of minutes, but she wasn't really paying much attention to her own words. She was always awed in spite of herself whenever she came to Enid. Enid was one of the Oklahoma Territory towns that had literally sprung up overnight after the Cherokee Strip land run. On September 15, 1893, the prairie was devoid of habitation. On September 16, Enid was a fully formed town of five thousand souls. Now, as the town readied itself to celebrate the twenty-second anniversary of its founding, it boasted a population of nearly twenty thousand people and was the fourth-biggest city in the state, after Oklahoma City, Tulsa, and Muskogee. Alafair could barely imagine such a number, and since the Founders' Day Jubilee was in a couple of days, the population would be swelling with visitors from all around Garfield County, and in fact, the entire Cherokee Strip. The noise and perpetual motion of the busy town literally made her dizzy.

The car had emptied enough to allow easy movement, and the three of them picked their way through the humanity and onto the platform where a thin, dark blond, bespectacled young woman in a mauve suit with a matching hat was jumping up and down and waving to get their attention. "Aunt Alafair, Martha!"

Martha set one of the suitcases down on the platform and waved back. "Here we are, Olivia."

Olivia squeezed her way between a prosperously hefty couple and threw her arms around her aunt. "My, oh my, but y'all are a sight for sore eyes. Grace, I declare, look how big you are! What a pretty bow you have in your hair!"

Grace gave her a grin full of little white pearl teeth and patted the big floppy bow that Alafair had tied onto a hank of her thick, black, bowl-cut hair.

Olivia laughed. "Why last time I saw you, you were just a little baby."

"I'm two," Grace informed her. "On my birthday, I'll be three and we'll have cake."

"Four weeks to go," Alafair said. "Well, Olivia, we sure do appreciate you going to all this trouble to come fetch us off the train."

"It's no trouble at all, Aunt Alafair." She pushed her glasses up her long nose before she led them off the platform and through the station. "In fact, I have to admit I'm relieved to get out of there for a little bit. I want to help Mama as much as I can, but it's all so sad that Daddy's sick." Her voice caught but she took herself in hand and continued briskly. "It's a relief that y'all have come, especially with Kenneth away."

"Oh, I'm glad to hear Lester is holding on. I feared we'd be too late."

"Daddy's been doing a little better for the last week, a little stronger. Seems he doesn't tire quite so easy. But the doctor says it's just a temporary rally. He doesn't expect Daddy to last more than another few days at the most."

"But Kenneth hasn't turned up?" Martha asked.

"No, but he told us he'd be back in time for the Founders' Day doings, so I expect him directly. He must be really busy, though. He usually wires or telephones me once or twice when he's gone over a week, and I haven't heard from him."

"Are you worried?"

"My stars, Martha, I haven't had time to be worried what with trying to help Mr. Beams at the warehouse and take care of little Ron and Mama, too. I'm sure he's fine. Now, come on, you all, give me one of those bags and let's get to the house. Mama can't wait to see you."

Olivia led them through the station and down the steps to a sharp new 1915 model Oldsmobile roadster and began to pile their suitcases onto the back floorboard. There was still plenty of room for Alafair and Grace to settle themselves in the backseat. Olivia hoisted herself into the driver's seat, and Martha jumped in beside her after giving the starter a crank. Olivia stepped on the clutch and pushed the gear shift and they roared off, Grace squealing with glee and Alafair clutching her daughter and her hat in alarm.

"When are Grandma and Grandpa coming, Olivia?" Alafair was yelling over the noise of the wind and the engine.

"Not for a while, yet," Olivia yelled back. "Grandpa is leading a revival at Lone Elm this week, and next week at Mulberry. He's asked Elder Knox to preach for him at Mulberry, but the elder can't get there until after the revival's been going a day or two. Grandma and Grandpa probably won't make it here for ten days or two weeks."

Alafair grimaced and sat back in the seat. She had forgotten that this was the time of year for her father's quarterly revivals at some of the Franklin County Freewill Baptist Churches. She hoped her parents made it before Lester passed, or before she had to go home.

It was only a matter of blocks from the train station to Ruth Ann's house, but Olivia took them on an abbreviated tour of the town, since it had been so long since they had visited. From the station, she drove down Maine to Grand, where the office and warehouse of the Yeager Transfer and Storage Company were housed in an enormous three-story red brick building, which took up most of the block between Maine and Cherokee. She didn't stop, but shouted a running narration at them as they rattled over the brick streets and bumped over trolley tracks.

"We own four trucks, now, Aunt Alafair, and I expect we'll need to order another before the year is out. The building looks about the same as when y'all last saw it, from the front, but Daddy bought most of the block behind and almost doubled the warehouse space. That's where he put the refrigeration unit.

You wouldn't believe the machinery in there. I'll have to show you how it works, if we get a chance." She was enlightening her passengers at the top of her lungs, and Alafair began to wonder how long she'd be able to go on before her voice gave out.

"Anyway, now we can store perishables before shipping. We do a land office business in frozen chickens. Daddy added a big old cold storage unit right between the warehouse and the freezer, where people can rent chests and lockers just about any size, from a drawer to a walk-in. Why, with one of them, a family of two can buy a whole side of beef or a whole hog, have it butchered and wrapped, and have enough meat to last them the entire year. Then they can store it here and get to it whenever they want. It's really economical for city folks not to have to buy their meat fresh from the butcher shop every day or risk it spoiling on them." Olivia shifted and they sped off down the street with a jerk.

She ferried them west down Randolph, through the large town square and past the county courthouse and the Federal Building. A team of shirt-sleeved men were constructing a wooden platform near the street, from where dignitaries would preside over the upcoming Founders' Day celebration. They turned north on Washington, then up to Elm, where Olivia's parents' enormous white house sat right on the corner. The house was relatively new. Lester had had it built in '05, twelve years after he had made the Cherokee Strip run in '93. On the day of the run, he had staked his claim on a platted space right in the middle of an empty prairie, and on the next day he owned a lot near the center of town, by the railroad tracks. A week later, he had begun building a warehouse, and by the turn of the century, Lester was, if not rich as Balthazar, then at least more than comfortable. So, he had built a more than comfortable house for his wife and one beloved daughter. In fact, in Alafair's opinion, the three-story Victorian with the wraparound porch and five bedrooms was awfully big for what were now only two people. Alafair was in the midst of raising ten children in her perfectly adequate two-bedroom farmhouse, after all.

But, Ruth Ann had insisted that they needed all that space to entertain Lester's business and political associates, and Alafair had to admit that her sister did run what amounted to a high-quality bed-and-breakfast inn, what with all of Lester's social connections and Kenneth's big plans. Not to mention the continual parade of their Gunn relations who loved to take lengthy advantage of Ruth Ann's hospitality.

Ruth Ann herself was standing on the sidewalk, holding her infant grandson, little Ron, cradled in the crook of one arm. She had begun waving a white handkerchief at them the minute they rounded the corner onto Washington. Alafair broke into a smile when she caught sight of her sister.

Ruth Ann was barely a year younger than Alafair, and they had grown up practically in each other's pockets. In truth, Alafair hadn't realized her name wasn't "Alafairandruthann" until she was almost big enough to start school. As close as they had been when they were children, they had little in common, now, and saw each other seldom. Alafair felt bad about it. She'd always had the feeling that Ruth Ann had not been happy to grow up in her older sister's shadow, and had spent her life trying to be as different from Alafair as she could. She belonged to every woman's club and charitable organization in town. In fact, she ran most of them. Her husband was an important man, after all.

She looked well, Alafair thought, as the roadster pulled up the unpaved drive at the side of the house. Ruth Ann had always been just a slip of a woman, small, like their mother, delicate and neat, always decked out in the latest fashion. Today she was dressed all in beige, from the silk blouse with the frilly jabot cascading down the front to the beige stockings and pumps that matched her ankle-length linen skirt to a tee. The afternoon sun highlighted the reddish undertones in her chestnut hair.

When they first dismounted the roadster, the women had to stand a while and ooh and aah over four-month-old Ron, whom Alafair had never seen, and then exclaim for a bit longer over how big Grace had gotten. Then, while the younger women unloaded the luggage from the back of the roadster, Ruth Ann and Alafair, Grace and little Ron in arms, walked up the paved sidewalk past dozens of gloriously blooming rosebushes, then across the large covered porch to enter the house through the lead-glass-paned front door. To the left of the spacious entryway, a wide staircase wound its way past a stained glass window up to the second floor. To the right, the house opened up into a huge parlor with French doors in the south and in the east walls, both of which opened onto the shady, potted plant laden porch. Pocket doors on the parlor's north side led to the formal dining room, with its long, oval mahogany dining table and a grand bay window that overlooked the garden.

As Olivia was taking their hats in the foyer, a plump animal the color of soot trotted down the stairs to inspect the newcomers.

"Kitty!" Grace cried, and the creature did an immediate about-face and disappeared back up the stairs.

"Whoa!" Alafair exclaimed. "I declare, Ruth Ann. I thought that was a dog, he's so big! What happened to his face?"

"Why, nothing." Ruth Ann was slightly affronted at the aspersion on her cat's beauty. "That's Ike. I bought him from my neighbor, who breeds them. He's a Persian cat, Alafair. All Persian cats have pug noses like that."

"You paid money for a cat?" Alafair asked, so surprised that for a moment she forgot not to be rude. Fortunately, Ruth Ann didn't hear her, because at the same time, Grace said, "Where's the kitty?"

"He's particular about meeting folks, honey," Ruth Ann told her. "He'll introduce himself in his own good time."

Ruth Ann led them into the parlor, and Grace immediately wriggled down and began flitting around the room, curious about her new environment. She knew better than to touch anything, at least with her mother watching her, gimlet eyed, but she took good note of prospective playthings for later. Then she stopped in front of Alafair and spread her arms wide to take in the whole room. "It's beautiful, Mama."

"It sure is, sugar." Alafair looked up at Ruth Ann. "'Beautiful' is her favorite word, these days."

"Well, then, Miss Grace, I surely am glad you approve of the décor." Ruth Ann sat down and arranged the wiggly Ron on her lap. "I declare, girls, y'all must be parched. I've got some tea to going and a big pitcher of lemonade. What's your pleasure?"

"Lemonade sounds good."

Olivia strode through the room and toward the kitchen while withdrawing her hatpin. "I'll do the honors, Mama. You stay there and get to visiting with Aunt Alafair."

"I'll help you," Martha interjected. "Come on, Grace. You can carry the napkins."

After the girls disappeared through the dining room, Alafair sat down on the red velvet settee. Out of the corner of her eye, she could see Ike the cat peering at them from the entryway, assessing the situation. "Olivia says that Lester is doing better and that Kenneth is still out of town."

Ruth Ann shifted the baby to a sitting position and tried to put on a cheerful expression, but her pinched little smile looked more like a heroic effort not to cry. "Yes, Lester has had a rally, praise the Lord. He seems to have a lot more energy than he did when I wrote you a while back. His color is a little better, too. I was real hopeful when he got to feeling so much better, but the doctor told me it probably was but a temporary thing. Said he's seen this before in folks who are about to pass. Anyway, it's a mercy. Lester sure felt bad before, and now I feel like we've got him back for a little while, anyway.

"As for Kenneth, well, that poor fellow is just working himself to a frazzle, running hither and yon trying to take care of clients. Why, in the last couple of months, he's been to Woodward, Guthrie, Wichita, and all points in between. He's probably on his way home from Guymon or Buffalo right about now. I expect he'll be home by tomorrow or Wednesday, though."

"Yes, Olivia said he planned to be home by the time the Founders' Day Jubilee starts on Wednesday."

"I hope he makes it home soon. We really miss him."

"Does seem to be a bad time to go on a business trip," Alafair ventured.

"Well, he told Olivia that her dad would be happier to know that he was doing everything he could to make sure the company is doing as well as possible."

"He could have sent someone..."

The pug-faced cat had strolled into the parlor and was now sitting at Alafair's feet, staring casually off into the distance, his tail twitching on the floor.

"Lester asked him to take care of it personal. Besides, that boy doesn't trust anybody to do it as well as he can. And Lester sure appreciates his efforts. He's real concerned that Olivia and us are taken care of proper. Anyway, you'd better catch me up on your bunch. Martha looks good. She looks more like you every time I see her. Is she still working?"

"Yes, she loves her job. And she's really saving money for her future."

Ike leaped up into Alafair's lap and practically knocked the breath out of her. She laughed as he settled himself on her knees. "Oof! This cat must weigh twenty pounds! Are you sure this is a cat and not a horse?"

"Why, look at that! He likes you, Alafair. He generally takes a long while to warm up."

"I'm flattered."

"How's Gee Dub liking A&M?" Ruth Ann returned to the subject.

"He just started the term at the first of the month, but the way he writes, he likes it fine. He's like any young fellow away from home for the first time. It's all a big adventure for him. Me and Shaw sure miss his shining face, though. I was kind of hoping we might be able to catch up with him on this trip, but he's so busy with his studies—and whatever else he's into that he's not telling his ma—that I don't expect it'll happen. Yesterday was his birthday, you know. He's nineteen years old."

"You don't say! That just don't seem right."

"That's for certain."

"How about Phoebe and her husband, and that baby girl of theirs?"

"Oh, they're fine. Just working like ants. John Lee is putting a bedroom on their little house. It's a big dusty mess, and Phoebe and the baby spend a lot of time over to our place. Baby Zeltha is cuter than a speckled pup, and real sweet-natured. Grace thinks the baby is her own personal real live doll. She's not walking yet, though, and she's just turned one. Phoebe frets about that some, but I told her they walk and talk when they get around to it."

"How about Alice? Any new grandchildren on that horizon?"

"Not yet. Tell you the truth, I don't think Alice is in any hurry for a family. She's too busy keeping Walter happy. They go to more socials and gatherings and parties than anybody has a right to. Throw their own, too. Makes me tired just to hear about it. She wouldn't say it to me, but I hear from Phoebe that if Alice doesn't come up with things for Walter to do, he's liable to go off on his own for a night on the town. I have a feeling she's worried about her figure, too, if she goes to having babies. Of course, it'll happen sooner or later, and they'll wonder why they didn't just go ahead and do it right away."

Ruth Ann snorted a laugh. "You'd better not mention to Daddy that Alice is holding back from a family."

Alafair laughed, too. "I'm not witless, Ruth Ann. Mary plans to marry in a few months, after her second year of teaching is done, and to hear her tell it, her and Kurt will be having as many kids as they can as fast as they can. That should make Daddy happy."

"She's still planning on marrying that German fellow?"

Ruth Ann's tone gave Alafair pause, and she raised an eyebrow. "Yes. Does that worry you?"

"Well, with all the awful things the Huns are doing over in Europe right now, I half expected she'd reconsider."

"That has nothing to do with Kurt..."

Ruth Ann plowed ahead as though Alafair hadn't spoken. "And after all those innocent people died on the *Lusitania* last spring! Why, they didn't have no call to go sinking a passenger ship, and especially one with Americans on it. And Mr. Wilson making such an effort to stay out of it! You'd think the Germans would be grateful to the president, but they keep shooting at one ship after another. Why just today I was reading in the paper that they tried to torpedo a ship called the *Arabia* or the *Orbia* or some such..."

"I can promise you that Kurt didn't sink any ships." Alafair raised her voice to be heard over her sister's rant. "It'd be mighty hard for him to do that from Oklahoma, wouldn't it?"

"But what if we get into the war?"

"We won't. Mr. Wilson promised to keep us out of it, and the president of the United States would never lie, would he? Kurt's an American citizen now, anyway, and a real good boy. He told me he didn't want to have anything to do with Germany any more."

Ruth Ann didn't seem to want to be swayed by Alafair's reason. "But if the Germans are really doing those things in Belgium that we're hearing about, what does that say about them? Aren't you worried about the young fellow's character?"

Alafair felt herself growing exasperated. Talk of the war always upset her, and she certainly didn't want to hear her own sister cast unfounded aspersions on her future son-in-law. "I don't want to hear that kind of talk, Ruth Ann. Just being German or French or American, for that matter, don't make you one way or another."

"But..."

"Besides," Alafair cut in, "I believe you told me years ago that Yeager is a German name. You're not thinking that Lester's blood is tainted, are you?" The comment made her feel a little perverse, but that didn't prevent her from saying it.

Ruth Ann bit her lip. Apparently she had forgotten that fact. "All right, I'm sorry. You're right. You know how feelings are running high since them ships were sunk, and I expect I'm a bit on edge these days, anyway. I hope you won't hold my unruly tongue against me."

"I'm used to it, Sister. I wouldn't recognize you if you didn't just say the first thing that popped into your head. You just wait 'til you meet Kurt, though. You won't have any bother about him being in the family after that. I hope y'all will be able to come to the wedding."

"When is it, again?"

"Late May, right after school is out." She shifted the cat in hopes of restoring circulation to her lower limbs.

Ruth Ann looked down at her hands. "I'd like to come, but of course who knows what will be happening with us by that time? We'll be there if we can. I sure hope Mary will be happy."

"If anybody is built for happiness, it's Mary."

"I know it. And the rest of them? How's that namesake niece of mine?"

"They're all back to school. I think this will be Ruth's last year. Over the summer, she did some special study with Miz Davis, the high school teacher, and it looks like she'll be graduating early. I'm so proud of her, I could bust. So far, every one of them has finished school. Our kids sure have better opportunities than we did, Ruth Ann, and they're smart enough to grab hold of them."

"Well, we couldn't have gone past eighth grade even if we'd wanted to, Alafair, unless we had moved to Fayetteville."

Alafair nodded, thinking that they had been too busy helping out on the farm, anyway. "Shaw was sure sorry he couldn't come, but the cotton and the head feed has to be got in, and then Mr. McBride's fall apples will be ready to pick. Besides, the county cooperative has offered to take as many trained mules as he can supply, to sell over in Europe, so he's spending every spare minute getting yearlings broke to harness and saddle. Charlie, Blanche, and Sophronia rush home from school and head out to the field to help however they can, and Ruth is running the house while Martha and me are gone and Mary's working."

"I sure am glad you and Martha could make it. Our sister Elizabeth and brother George will be here when they can break away, but I doubt if they'll be here before…"

Alafair put her hand on Ruth Ann's knee. She didn't need to comment. Instead she asked, "I noticed you didn't mention Robin in your letter. Weren't you able to get hold of him?"

Ruth Ann shrugged. "Didn't know where to write."

Alafair was not surprised. Their prodigal younger brother seldom stayed in one place long enough to receive responses to his sporadic letters to his relatives.

The fat cat slipped out of her lap and hit the floor with a muted thud. He disappeared from the room just as Grace clattered into the parlor with five lacy white cotton napkins clutched in her hands. Olivia followed close behind with a doily-covered wooden tray of molasses cookies, as did Martha, with her own tray full of tall, frosted glasses of iced lemonade. The food service was temporarily delayed by the fact that Grace had to carefully arrange napkins over the laps of her mother and aunt. The two young women stood by patiently, though, and once she was properly swathed, Alafair eagerly helped herself to a cool glass and a chewy cookie.

After their elders were served, Martha and Olivia sat down, allowed Grace to have a care for their skirts, and helped themselves.

◇◇◇

After refreshments, Ruth Ann led Alafair and Martha up the staircase to the second floor and down the long hallway to the master bedroom at the end. Lester was ensconced in an enormous double bed, the headboard of which had once been centered in the alcove formed by large bay windows. The bed had been turned around at an odd forty-five-degree angle, which enabled Lester to see both the bedroom door and out the windows into the garden.

"Look who's here, sweetheart," Ruth Ann said.

Lester was propped up on half a dozen feather pillows and covered with a quilt, in spite of the warm weather. He smiled at the women as they entered the room.

Alafair could tell at a glance that he would never leave that bed again in life. The faded and desiccated body that now housed Lester Yeager's spirit bore little resemblance to the robust frame he had inhabited since Alafair had known him. He looked like he had aged an entire lifetime since the last time Alafair had seen him. It occurred to her that Lester was coming to the end of his life after only forty-eight years—not much older than Shaw. Martha, close by her side, said nothing, but Alafair could feel her stiffen when she laid eyes on her uncle.

"Alafair," Lester said. His voice creaked and rustled like dry husks.

"I declare, Lester."

That was all Alafair said, leaving it to Lester to interpret her comment as he would. Martha glanced at her mother, relieved. She had rather expected that Alafair would ask him how the dying was coming along, or something equally blunt. Of course, the visit was young. She sat down next to her mother in the chairs next to the bed, still braced for anything.

As they sat, Alafair glimpsed a slight figure perched on a padded stool in the far corner of the room, so still and quiet that she was practically invisible in the shadows. Alafair had seen her sister's Chinese cook and housekeeper, whom she called Lu, many times before. In her letter, Ruth Ann had called Lu her 'girl,' which she definitely was not. It would have been hard to guess her age. Her thin hair, which she wore in a kind of a bun right on top of her head, was completely gray, though her delicate face with its oddly crooked little nose was entirely without wrinkles. She could have been any age from forty to one hundred and forty. If Lu was five feet tall, Alafair would have been surprised. Every time Alafair had seen her, she was wearing a plain, dark-colored, Western-style dress. Today's version was a gray, sacklike affair with a wide white collar, which was mostly covered by a flowered bib apron.

Lu was the first Asian person Alafair had ever seen, and the only one Alafair had ever spoken to. She had been with Ruth Ann and Lester since Olivia was a small child. Alafair had never quite known how she had come to be in her sister's employ. All she knew was that Lester had come back from a trip to California with the woman in tow and presented her to his wife as the answer to all her household needs. And according to Ruth Ann, so she was—the perfect nursemaid, chef, housekeeper, gardener, and lady's companion, rolled into one tiny Chinese package.

Alafair had been curious about the woman for a long time, but Ruth Ann had never seen fit to properly introduce them. As far as she knew, Lu was the only Asian person in Enid, and she wondered sometimes if the housekeeper had any family or friends. She didn't really know what kind of relationship Lu had with her sister. Ruth Ann never made any bones about the fact that Lu was actually the one responsible for the efficient way things ran around the Yeager household, but neither did she seem to treat her as anything other than a trusted servant. For the past many years, the woman had just been there, in the background, a fixture in the household, like the furniture.

Now, Alafair imagined that Lu was efficiently overseeing Lester's departure from the world. Before turning her attention back to the invalid, Alafair nodded at the tiny, silent woman and received a nod in return.

"Well, how are you doing, Lester?"

"'Bout like you'd expect, Alafair. Could be worse, though. The laudanum the doctor gave me still manages to take the edge off. Seems to be taking me a long time to get this dying business done. Since there's no getting around it, I'd just as soon be getting on with it."

"Now, don't be in such an all-fired hurry. There's a bunch of folks who are going to be mighty sad to see you go."

Martha glanced at Ruth Ann, who was sitting in a chair next to her with her hand placed comfortably on Lester's knee and a wistful smile on her face. All this talk of her husband's imminent demise didn't seem to be upsetting her unduly, or if it was, she was hiding it well.

Lester managed a weak laugh. "Oh, I know it, and I'm not all that eager to leave them, either." He smiled at Ruth Ann and shot a brief glance toward Lu's shadowy corner, which interested Alafair no end. "Now, where's that little imp Grace? She's probably grown out of all recognition since I last saw her."

"I expect she has, Lester. She's downstairs with Olivia and the baby. Maybe I'll bring her up tomorrow morning for a few minutes, when you're rested, so you can get a look at her."

"I'd like that. So how're Shaw and the kids?"

While she filled him in on the news, Alafair studied her brother-in-law's face and determined that Ruth Ann had not been exaggerating when she said that Alafair would not be away from home long. Lester had always been a hardy man, middle-sized but beefy and muscular, but this withered gray creature bore little resemblance to the man Alafair had known for so many years. Ruth Ann joined in the conversation, chipper as always, but Alafair was quite aware of the strain underlying her sister's upbeat attitude. Lester seemed entirely prepared for the inevitable. Whether or not Ruth Ann was, Alafair couldn't tell. She decided she was glad she came, for Ruth Ann's sake if for no other reason.

It didn't take long for Lester to reach the limit of his visiting strength, but when the women stood to leave him in peace, he grasped Alafair's hand.

"Come back up and visit with me a spell more after dinner."

"We don't want to come trooping up here every hour and tire you out, Lester."

Another glance at the shadowy corner. "Well, if you was to come up on your own for a bit, I reckon I could handle that."

Ruth Ann leaned forward. "Lester…"

Lester shook his head. "It's all right, Ruth Ann. I'm sure Olivia and Martha will want to get caught up, and you and Lu could use the break. I get mighty bored up here just waiting to cross over. A fresh face will perk me up. Alafair can do the talking."

"I expect Lester wants to get you alone so he can worry to you about me and Olivia." Ruth Ann and Alafair had hung back in the hall and allowed Martha to go upstairs to the third floor and inspect her room. They were standing head to head as they speculated on why Lester would ask to see Alafair alone after supper. Ike the cat had reappeared and was weaving around their feet, looking for attention.

"I imagine you're right," Alafair agreed. "He needs to be sure everyone he meets with before he goes will be watching over you. That's a good thing, Ruth Ann. I'll be proud to let him bend my ear about it."

"Oh, Alafair, what am I going to do without Lester? This big old house, and just me and Lu. I've been trying to get Olivia and Kenneth to move in here after...well, when I'm rattling around on my own. Kenneth wants to do it; raring to go, in fact. But Olivia don't seem to want to. I don't know what's bothering her about it."

"Maybe Martha can find out what's on her mind." Alafair felt Ike rub along her leg and watched him trot away down the hall, tail high.

"Yes, maybe she can. You talk to her about it, will you? I'm so glad y'all are here, and I can hardly wait for Mama and Daddy and our brother and sister and their folks. I need my family with me right now. You don't know how you help me."

"We'll help you the best we can, Sister. You know that."

"Yes, I know you will, Alafair. Thank heavens for y'all."

Grace must have heard Alafair's voice from downstairs, for she came pounding up the stairs to inject herself between them, and the two women paused to listen to a couple of minutes of chatter as the child related her adventures with Olivia and the baby in the parlor.

When she could at last get a word in edgewise, Ruth Ann jumped in. "Come let me show you your bedroom. I had Lu put your things in this corner room, here at the other end of the hall. It's a nice sunny room, and there's a little couch that we've made up for Grace. It's real comfortable."

Before Ruth Ann had finished telling her where they were going, they were standing in the middle of a bedroom that was as large as the entire parlor of Alafair's farmhouse, and she unconsciously shook her head.

It was a nice room. While Grace caromed from one delightful corner to the next, Alafair gave the place a thorough once-over. Tall windows in the south and west walls flooded the room with warm afternoon light. A long streak of sun fell across the cheerful broken star quilt that covered the high, carved, four-poster bed. A small daybed/couch had been made up at the foot of the bed for Grace. A mirrored dressing table sat next to the wall between the windows, with a little sateen-covered stool before it. A comfortable rocker, an upholstered side chair and reading table, and a tall armoire completed the furnishings. To keep bare feet from being chilled, two or three large scatter rugs graced the polished wooden floor.

The furniture was a suite, all made of dark mahogany, and ornately carved. Not like Alafair's furniture, every piece of which had been acquired in its own good time over the years, made by Shaw or some other relative, handed down from grandparents and parents and older siblings, even rescued from the trash heap in the early days, and yet still in use. In her organic home, nothing went with anything. Every single stick of furniture was an individual with its own character. Much like the people who lived in the house.

Still, once in a while luxury is a good thing, Alafair thought. She sat down on the bed. "It's just lovely, Sister."

"Martha is right above you in the attic bedroom, Olivia's old room. I figured the young lady might appreciate a room to herself for a change. If George or Elizabeth gets here before y'all leave, Martha can move in here with you. Mama and Daddy will be down the hall, when they come. I've got me a bed set up next to Lester. The facilities are directly across from you, next to Mama and Daddy's room. Well, I reckon you must be plumb tired from your trip, so I'll leave you to rest. I'm going to go sit with Lester for a while. Lu has a big supper planned for us, so I hope y'all are hungry."

"I can always eat, and a rest would be welcome. I expect Grace could use a nap right about now, too…"

"No, Ma, I'm not sleepy!" Even as she said it, Grace was climbing up on the intriguing pink-covered daybed. Alafair sat down next to her and began to remove the girl's shoes.

"I wish Daddy was here, Mama."

"So do I, cookie."

"Daddy and Fronie and Charlie. Not Blanche, though. She called me a poop and I don't miss her." Grace snuggled down as her mother gave her a stuffed bear that Ruth Ann had thoughtfully provided, as well as her own worse-for-wear rag doll. "Well, maybe I miss Blanche, too. And Ruth, too."

"I know you miss everybody, sugar. You can visit them in your dreams."

"Yes," Grace agreed, serious. "I'll see them in the sky and tell them all what happened when we rode the train." Before Alafair had the chance to see that the dolly was well and truly tucked in, Grace was asleep. Alafair looked up at her sister and winked.

"She'll see them in the sky?" Ruth Ann said.

"That's her words for where she goes in her dreams; up in the sky. Same as heaven, I think. When you wake up, you come back to the ground."

Ruth Ann laughed. "I declare, little ones have the most precious way of putting things. Well, you rest as long as y'all want, Alafair. I'll come wake you when supper is ready, if you're not down by then."

◇◇◇

Alafair had intended to do a little unpacking before looking for a chore that needed doing, but after Ruth Ann left, she sat down on the bed, enjoying the quiet and inspecting the amenities. She wondered briefly what her family was doing right at this minute. Shaw was probably just on his way back to the house for supper, along with son Charlie and Mary's intended, Kurt. Maybe even their son-in-law John Lee, if Phoebe and the baby had decided to visit.

Alafair knew exactly what would happen when Shaw and the boys trooped into the house through the back door. All the girls, no matter what age, would descend upon their father with cries of "Daddy's home!" They would smother him with hugs and kisses, which he would return with warm enthusiasm. Alafair wasn't there for Charlie to kiss tonight. The realization disturbed her a little, until she decided that Mary would probably take that duty upon herself. She'd pursue her protesting brother around the house for a messy smack on the cheek. She smiled when she thought that Mary's fiancé Kurt probably wouldn't protest very much at all, in spite of the close and narrow gaze his prospective father-in-law would be giving him. Mary had more than likely cooked up a giant feed for them all after she got home from her teaching. She liked to eat, and never had known the meaning of the word "restraint."

She felt a sudden pang of loneliness for Shaw. This was not the first time they had been apart during their twenty-five-year union, but it was a rare enough occurrence that it jarred her when it did happen. Truth was, she wasn't particularly pleased about sleeping in someone else's bed. She liked her own bed, her own things around her, and she wasn't looking forward to sleeping alone.

Well, the likelihood was that Grace would want to sleep with her tonight instead of in the little bed, even though it was a novel place for a nap, made up very prettily with a pink lacy coverlet that obviously delighted the child. Still, Grace was not one to let an opportunity go by. Even if she started out under the lace, she'd end up with her mother before the night was very far along.

I ought not to allow it, Alafair thought. She knew that once she let Grace sleep with her, she'd have a devil of a time getting her back into her own bed when they got home. She knew she would allow it, though, and be grateful for the company. She wondered briefly if Martha would consider moving in here with her, but decided that Martha was probably overjoyed to have some unaccustomed privacy.

Alafair removed her shoes and lowered herself onto the bed. She folded her hands over her stomach and stared at the curlicues in the white, stamped tin ceiling until she began to drift between wake and dreams. Her mind floated back to Ruth Ann's troubles, and she began to conjure up possible ways to be of help. Lester seemed to have stepped back from death's door for the moment, and she wondered if she would be able to stay here until he actually passed over. Well, her parents would be here in a few days, and she expected they would stay as long as necessary.

She still felt mildly annoyed at Kenneth for choosing to go out of town instead of sending someone in his place. Not now, when his wife and mother-in-law surely needed his support. Putting the business before family seemed downright absurd, as far as she was concerned. But neither Ruth Ann nor Olivia seemed bothered by it, she admitted to herself, so she guessed she had no call to get all fretted over it.

She turned over on her side and closed her eyes. If I had him here, though, she thought, I'd give him a piece of my mind.

Alafair sat bolt upright, shocked wide awake. She had dreamed that Kenneth was standing in front of her, beside the bed. He looked like he had the last time she had seen him, his hair shaved close, a little mustache over his lip. Nice looking, though maybe running a little bit too much to fat for such a young man. He seemed pale; blue, almost. She hadn't heard him speak, but she sensed that he wanted to tell her something. The only other soul in the room was Ike, lying next to her on the bed. She chuckled at her vivid dream, and then took a couple of breaths to calm her racing heart.

"When did you come in here, you big old thing? The bed is no place for cats." She hoisted him off the quilt and set him on the floor. He looked up at her, his yellow eyes full of indignation, and padded out of the room.

She didn't think she had gone completely to sleep, but the angle of the sun coming through the window had changed quite a bit, so she supposed she must have. The breeze had freshened and cooled, and she could see a few large white clouds floating by. The weather was about to change.

The little daybed was empty. She was surprised that Grace had not wakened her, and she got up to go find her, slightly worried that the child was making a nuisance of herself. She met Ruth Ann in the hall.

"I was just coming to get you, Alafair. Supper is about ready."

"Gracious, I was a bunch more tired from the trip than I thought. I didn't even hear Grace get up. I hope she ain't down there pestering everybody half to death."

Ruth Ann led her down the stairs. "No, she came down with Martha about half an hour ago. They're out in the yard with Olivia and the baby, playing."

Alafair intended to offer to set the table, but as soon as they went into the dining room, she saw that her offer came too late.

Ruth Ann had broken out the good china for the occasion, as well as linen napkins and her wedding silver. A beautiful rose centerpiece decorated the table.

"Are those from your own bushes, Ruth Ann? They're an eyeful!"

Ruth Ann looked properly proud. "Thank you. I can't tell you how much time I spend on those rosebushes, but they've turned out so nice that it's worth it. I ought to be ashamed to say it, but I like to make the other ladies in the garden club jealous."

Alafair didn't comment. She didn't have the leisure to spend hours a week on landscaping, but she couldn't bring herself to think of something as lovely as roses as a waste of time. Instead she said, "Looks like you've planned quite a spread."

"I expect you didn't have a very good dinner on that train, and besides, it's not every day my big sister comes to visit. I think Lu has done herself proud tonight, too, judging from what I saw in the kitchen a minute ago. I told her I'd take care of the serving, since we're all family, here. She's gone upstairs to take a little broth to Lester and sit with him while we're eating. Let's you and me tote the food out, and then we can call the girls."

Lu had indeed done herself proud. A giant pork roast had already been removed from the oven and was sitting in its roasting pan on the back of the stove, along with a casserole dish of mashed squash. Ruth Ann pointed to something incredibly fragrant which was simmering in a pot on a front burner. "Ladle up that soup into the tureen over on the cabinet, Alafair. There's a green bean salad under that dishtowel and some succotash in this pot here. If you'll take that off the fire and put some cream and butter in it, I'll make gravy for the roast. I think we can serve up the squash in its dish. Lu already put butter and syrup in it when she mashed it up, but I think a chunk of butter on top wouldn't do any harm. There're potatoes in the oven that will be done browning in about five minutes."

As she carried dishes from the kitchen to the table, Alafair thought it was a good thing that they hadn't eaten very well on the train, because it was going to take an army of starving people to make a dent in this meal. By the time Ruth Ann left to call the girls, they had loaded the table with the tureen of gumbo soup, the huge pork roast with gravy, bowls of creamed succotash, browned potatoes, a warm bean salad, buttery orange squash, as well as pitchers of sweet tea, milk, and pots of coffee.

After they all were settled around the table and the meal was properly prayed over, the Tucker females dug into the food like it was their last day on earth. Apparently, the trip had sharpened their appetites as much as it had tired them out.

"This roast is delicious, Aunt Ruth Ann!" Martha exclaimed. "Why, it's so tender that it just about melts in my mouth. You must have been cooking this since yesterday."

"Thank you, honey, but I can't take credit for the cooking. Lu fixed this all up herself. Pork is her specialty, in my opinion."

"Do you expect she learned to cook like this in China?" Alafair asked.

"I don't know where she learned about American cooking, but I expect it was in San Francisco. I don't know anything about Chinese cooking, but I know that Lu likes to fix up some mighty odd things for herself."

"She likes rice," Olivia interjected. "I swear she eats rice three times a day, every day of the world." She sat up straight after checking on the baby in his bassinet beside her chair. "When I was little, Lu used to let me taste some of the things she made for herself, if I asked her about it. I'd always end up making a horrible face and spitting it out, and she'd laugh and laugh. Actually, some of it was pretty tasty, but I liked it when she laughed, so I'd carry on no matter what I really thought."

"Does she have any family around here?" Alafair wondered.

"She has a couple of grown sons, and I think some grandchildren," Ruth Ann said. "One or the other of them will come visit her every once in a while. I usually don't even know it till after they're gone. They all live down in the City. Moved out here from California a while after their mother did, I think. One of her boys is a teamster for some oil equipment company. He's delivered a load up here to the warehouse a few times."

"Do you suspect she gets lonesome with no other of her own folks around to talk to?"

Ruth Ann shrugged. "I don't know, Alafair. If she does, she keeps it to herself."

Olivia seemed to be equally uninterested in the question of Lu's social life. "Aunt Alafair, why don't you and the girls walk around town for a while in the morning? They'll be setting up the carnival and the tents and bandstands for the fair all day, and y'all could do a little shopping, as well. Then, when you come back, maybe Mama and me can walk around some, ourselves."

"Now, Olivia," Alafair interjected, "I came here to be of help to your mother, not have a holiday. But if you want to take your mother around, that'd be..."

Ruth Ann cut her off. "Oh, Alafair, there's no need at all for you to stay cooped up in this house every minute of the day. I'll feel a whole lot better about taking advantage of you if you'll get out with the girls for a while tomorrow, and go to the Founders' Jubilee some, too, when it gets going. Then you can spell me with Lester later, and maybe Martha can watch Ron, and Olivia and I can get out a bit. I'd like that a lot better."

"Well, all right, if that's what you would like, Sister."

"I'd enjoy doing some shopping, Mama," Martha said. "I withdrew some money from my bank account just so I could buy a few things while we're here that I can't get in Boynton.

I'd like to buy some presents, while I'm at it. It's not every day I get the opportunity to shop in a department store, and I could use a new dress or two for work."

Alafair shrugged her acquiescence. "Grace needs some new shoes."

Grace straightened on the several pillows upon which she sat and clapped her hands in delight. "I want shoes! I want pink shoes!"

"I don't think shoes come in pink, sugar, but we'll find you some nice ones."

"I was noticing that the wind has shifted in just the past couple of hours," Olivia observed. "I'm wondering if it might actually rain."

Ruth Ann spooned more mashed squash onto her plate. "We could sure use it. I swear I'm about to wilt in this heat, and it's hard on Lester, too. Of course, rain coming in on top of this dry heat is just the right combination for a bad storm. I hope Kenneth gets home before it comes a gully-washer."

"Me, too," Olivia seconded. "Well, if he's on the road and gets a notion there's a storm coming, he'll probably hole up for the night in Woodward or Slapout or somewhere and come on in tomorrow morning."

"So you're expecting Kenneth is already on his way home?"

"Oh, I imagine so, Aunt Alafair."

"Funny. I just had a dream about him."

"What kind of a dream, Sister?"

Alafair shrugged. "You know how dreams are. Nothing that made any sense. Mercy, this squash is delicious! I don't believe I've ever tasted squash done like this before."

"This is winter squash, Alafair," Ruth Ann told her. "I grew it myself in the back garden. It's just coming in right now. Lu bakes it in the oven then scoops it out of the peel and mashes it like potatoes with a little maple syrup and butter."

"And nutmeg," Alafair said.

Martha put down her fork and eyed Alafair with something on her mind that had nothing to do with squash. She was less inclined than the rest of the company to so readily dismiss the fact that her mother had dreamed of Kenneth.

After eating too much dinner, they practically foundered on dessert, but none of them intended to do dishonor to Lu's lovely white cake topped with peaches and cream. When Grace began to alternate between whining and drooping with fatigue, Alafair gave up and took the child upstairs, leaving Ruth Ann and the younger women to coffee and conversation.

Grace was quite intrigued when Alafair cleaned her up in a bathtub with running water, but by the time her mother dried her off with a big cotton towel and put her into her flour-sack nightie, she was nearly asleep on her feet, and Alafair carried her back into the bedroom.

Just as Alafair had predicted, Grace wanted to sleep in the big bed with her, and she didn't argue. She tucked the girl under the sheets and together they sang "This Little Light of Mine," as they did every night. Alafair usually finished the bedtime ritual with a Bible story, but Grace was asleep before she could even mention that young David was a shepherd boy. She gave her little angel a kiss before she walked down the hall to fulfill her promise to see Lester for a few minutes after supper.

Alafair knocked on the bedroom door. There was a moment's pause before the door seemed to open itself, and Lester gestured from his bed for her to enter. Alafair took a step into the room and blinked when she saw the minuscule Lu, half hidden behind the open door, her hand on the knob. Alafair had heard that servants were supposed to be unobtrusive, but Lu had practically perfected the art of invisibility. She nodded her usual silent greeting to the woman, who nodded back before she padded out of the room.

The windows were wide open. A pleasant breeze intermittently billowed the curtains. Alafair was surprised, since the wisdom of the day dictated that a dying person was best served by passing on in a dark, close room.

The breeze felt wonderful to her, but Lester looked as though he had no blood left to warm him. She walked over and looked out into the evening. She could barely see Ruth Ann's cat nosing around the bushes in the backyard. She put her hands on the sill to close the window, but Lester said, "Leave it open, Alafair."

She looked back over her shoulder at him. "Aren't you cold?"

"I'm about smothered with covers. I like the air. Makes me know I'm still breathing."

"Are you up to this visit? Your voice sounds stronger than it did this afternoon. How are you feeling?"

"Well, I'll tell you why I'm looking to get on with it. If it don't hurt like fire, I'm asleep or bored, or dreading the next spell. Ruth Ann helps a lot by reading to me. I swear she'll wear her throat out, but it does help."

Alafair took a seat next to the bed. "Martha brought along Mr. Twain's *Pudd'nhead Wilson* to entertain herself on the train. She mentioned that you might enjoy for me to read to you."

Lester brightened at the suggestion. "Why, yes, I enjoyed that book particular when I was a youngster. Lately Ruth Ann's taken to mostly reading to me out of the Bible, trying to get me ready for heaven, I reckon. But if I'm not ready now, I never will be. Besides, I heard it all before. I'd rather she'd read me some Robert Louis Stevenson, or that Kipling. My last chance to travel to exotic climes, don't you know."

Alafair patted the desiccated hand that lay on the quilt. "Pretty soon you'll be able to see all the exotic climes you want, if that's your fancy."

"Now, that's a nice thought. But never mind that now, Alafair. I reckon your dad will have plenty to say on that subject. I want to talk about Ruth Ann and Olivia."

"Ruth Ann expected that's what you had on your mind. They'll miss you terrible, Lester, but they'll go on. You can't be troubling your rest with that now."

"I know. I fixed it so that Ruth Ann will be taken care of. She gets the house and enough money to see her through the rest of her life. I love Ruth Ann. She's been all I could want in a wife, but I know she's not the most practical woman ever born. She's just too blamed good, is what. Never thinks a bad thought about anybody, never expects that anyone would want to take advantage of her trusting heart. Now, Olivia's got a good head on her shoulders, just to be twenty-one. I reckon being an only child has made her older than her years. I've already told her to watch over her ma, and make sure she don't get led astray by some unscrupulous banker or the like. But it's the business I'm worried about."

Alafair was surprised. How on earth could she possibly help him with that? "Kenneth has been your partner in the business for some three years now. Surely Kenneth knows how…"

Lester cut her off. "Kenneth means well, Alafair. But he's young and inexperienced. I don't want him and Olivia to have the burden of the whole business on their shoulders for a while."

"He's not much younger than you were when you started the business, Lester. Besides, that's how you learn. You jump in there and sink or swim."

"Maybe. But I want to make dang sure they don't sink. I'll do anything to make sure my girl and that baby are taken care of proper."

"Like what? You can't run things from heaven, Lester, no matter how bad you want to."

Her comment caused him to puff a little laugh. "Are you sure?" he asked wistfully. "All right, maybe not. But I've been thinking on how I can protect them best I can before I go. I'm leaving controlling interest in the shipping company to your brother George. I trust George. He's a good honest man. He wouldn't try to cheat Olivia and Kenneth out of their due, and he'd be a good teacher for Kenneth. I told my lawyer to fix it so that George can sell them his share any time after five years from my death, whenever he thinks Kenneth is ready."

"George is a good businessman, but he lives in Arkansas. I'd be surprised if he'll want to pull up stakes and move out here to Oklahoma so he can manage Yeager Shipping and Storage."

"I know he won't. We've already written back and forth about it at length. But I'm fixing it so that Kenneth won't be able to make any big decisions about the business without George's approval. I instructed that the youngsters have to send statements to him once a month and he's agreed to check them over, as well as to come out here a couple of times a year and give the place an eyeball. I've done my best to teach Kenneth what he needs to know, and he is full of gumption and big ideas. But he's inclined to be rash, sometimes. He needs time to grow some sense. Olivia could run things, though, and do a real good job at it. What I'd really like is to leave the whole thing to her, lock, stock, and barrel. But Kenneth is her husband, so even if I did, it'd be his anyway."

"What does Olivia have to say about this?"

"She doesn't know about it. Nobody does, except Russ Lawyer, my lawyer."

"Your lawyer is named Mr. Lawyer?" Alafair was unable to let this delightful piece of information go by without comment.

"Afraid so. Fortunately for him, he's a good one."

Alafair returned to the point. "Olivia's got a little child to raise. She might not be interested in running a business."

Lester smiled. "I know my girl. My darlin' girl, sweet as maple syrup. She won't admit to it, but she's a businesswoman at heart. Ruth Ann would be happy as a clam to take care of Ron while Olivia takes care of the warehouse. Kenneth prefers the socializing side of it, anyway. Likes to play the big tycoon and woo the customers."

"Why, it sounds like you've got it all figured out, Lester. What is it you want me to do?"

"I just want somebody else to be in on my plans. Russ Lawyer has been my friend since '93. He knows the situation and what my wishes are. I always thought you and Shaw had good sense, and if he had come with you, I'd be telling him this as well. But since he didn't, I guess it's just you. Y'all aren't named in the will, so there's no conflict for you to know this. I reckon Kenneth won't be happy about my leaving such a big chunk to George. He might even want to contest the will. Now, Olivia, she'll go along with whatever I want."

"You really think Kenneth would make trouble?"

"I just got a feeling, Alafair. I just got a feeling."

Alafair wasn't inclined to dispute the feelings of a man who was already halfway to heaven. She figured that as the world of the flesh dropped away from a person, his ability to see the truth of things improved.

She nodded. "Well, I don't know what I'd be able to do about it, Lester, but I promise I can at least bear witness to your wishes."

"That's all I ask, Alafair. Thank you." Lester managed a wry smile. He looked uncomfortable, pinched.

"You think you're needing some of your medicine, Lester?"

"If you please. It's through that alcove, there, on top of the chiffarobe. Ruth Ann keeps it way over there. I think she's afraid I'll take a notion to down it all at once and get this durn business over with."

Alafair retrieved the square brown bottle from the top of the chest in the dressing alcove, along with the tablespoon beside it. She sat back down in the chair beside the bed before she started to remove the cork, but Lester stopped her with a gesture.

"Never mind, Alafair. I can manage it on my own. I'd rather wait a bit before I dose, anyway, 'til I really need it. Lasts longer that way." He eased back down on the pillow, closed his eyes and sighed.

Alafair didn't argue with him. She thought he deserved to manage his own death however he saw fit. She put the bottle and spoon on the bedside table. She intended to slip out and leave the man to his rest, but when she stood to go, she saw that his eyes were open and he was looking at her. She resumed her seat and leaned close.

"While I'm here, will you let me help Lu with your nursing, Lester? Howsoever much time Ruth Ann spends keeping you company, I know she can't quite bring herself to tend to…the harder things. Lu might could use the help. I've nursed folks through the end before, you know, and I have more kids than anybody has a right to. There isn't much I haven't seen."

"I appreciate the sentiment, Alafair, but allow me my last little bit of dignity."

Alafair nodded. "Whatever you want. But your dignity is in you, Lester, and this ain't going to touch it. Truth is, if you let me help, you'd be bestowing an honor on me, and I'd feel more useful."

"If you can help Ruth Ann through this, then you'll be more than useful. Babysit me, let Ruth Ann get out of the house a while, maybe go to the big Founders' Day do and have some fun for a change. But I'll ask Lu if she'd like you to spell her now and then."

"Tell her I understand if she'd rather handle it herself. I don't want to make out that she ain't doing a good job."

"Y'all can work that out between you."

"I swear, I have no idea how to talk to Lu. It's like trying to talk to someone from the moon."

"Well, I've known Lu for dog's years, and you can talk to her like you talk to anybody else. She's plumb full of sense. Knows all kinds of strange Oriental doctoring and dosing that's helped me a heap. Though I'm not saying she don't get the strangest notions from time to time."

Alafair chuckled. "Sounds like a woman after my own heart."

The curtains billowed out and a rush of sweet, damp air cooled the room. Alafair straightened and took a deep breath. "Smells like rain."

"We sure could use it," Lester said, but his reply lacked conviction. His voice had weakened considerably in the last few minutes. He looked a bit green, Alafair thought.

"I'll fetch Ruth Ann now, Lester. You rest now."

He didn't reply.

A light rain had begun to fall when Alafair left Lester to his wife and retired to her room. In spite of the nap she had taken in the afternoon, she was so tired that she could hardly focus her eyes. It was all she could do to keep from falling on top of the bed fully clothed and sinking into oblivion. But the journey had left her feeling grimy enough that she determined to drag herself into the bathroom and take advantage of running hot and cold water to wash herself all over before crawling between the crisp white sheets.

She shot the lock on the bathroom door and removed her clothes while the tub filled with lovely hot water all by itself. She took a moment or two to inspect Ruth Ann's intriguing collection of soaps, creams, and lotions before choosing a paper-wrapped, milky white bar that smelled of roses. She stepped into the big, claw-footed tub and lowered herself gingerly into the comforting embrace of the steamy water, sank back, and almost instantly fell into a stupor.

Every muscle in her body melted with relief, but she was too tired to be able to govern her unruly brain, which couldn't stop worrying over her sister's troubles. What can I do to help, her mind repeated, over and over. What can I do to help? Her eyelids fluttered. That blamed Kenneth, she thought. Big healthy galoot, owes everything to his in-laws, and can't keep home long enough to be their support in time of trouble. If Shaw were in such extremity, God forbid, my sons and sons-in-law—well, most of them—would be falling all over themselves to see I was taken care of.

She was thinking of Kenneth. In fact, she could almost see him, standing at the end of the long, narrow bathroom with his back to her, gazing out the window at the street below. If I could talk to him right now, she was thinking, I would say, "Come home. Your family needs you. It's not too late."

He turned his head just enough that she could see one eye. The expression on his face was distracted. He shuddered, and wrapped his arms around himself. He began to break up, like a windblown mist, blue and insubstantial. *I want to, but I'm so damn cold I can hardly move.*

◇◇◇

A giant flash of lightning and crash of thunder rattled the walls, shocking her awake. Her eyes flew open and she bolted upright, splashing bathwater onto the floor.

Alafair hadn't realized that she had fallen asleep, but she figured she must have, because the water was barely warm.

She rubbed her eyes with her palms, and managed a chuckle. "That's what happens when you get too tired," she said aloud. "You have crazy dreams and nearly drown yourself."

Tuesday, September 14, 1915

Martha hadn't intended to sleep late on Tuesday morning, but she had had a restless night, and the sun was well up by the time she finally managed to rise. Thunderstorms had raged off and on all the previous night. Her unfamiliar room was situated all by itself at the top of the house, too close to the thunder and lightning for comfort. It was a shame, too, because she had really looked forward to having a room all to herself. She hadn't anticipated missing her sister Mary's comforting presence in the bed with her.

The rain was abating by the time Martha was dressed, and she walked over to the gable window and pulled back the curtains to get a first look at the day. Low clouds were still scudding across the sky, and the wind was damp and blustery, but it was lovely and cool and fresh after such a long, bedraggled summer, and she took a deep breath. She stood at the window for a few minutes, looking up and down the tree-lined street below and planning the upcoming day.

She expected that most of the day would be spent helping Olivia in any way that she could, probably by babysitting little Ron and Grace and giving her cousin the opportunity to go to the warehouse and confer with manager Mike Ed Beams for a while. This would relieve Aunt Ruth Ann to tend to Uncle Lester, and Lu to attend to the house, and Alafair to attend to Ruth Ann, Lester, Lu, and the house.

But Martha did hope she would be able to do some shopping with her mother and sister today, and she expected that the best way to accomplish that was to spirit them away as soon as possible after breakfast, before Alafair had the opportunity to get involved in something.

Alafair had tentatively agreed to take a little time for shopping, but Martha knew that if she didn't broach the subject quickly, and vigorously insist that she keep her bargain, her mother would find some reason to demur.

And this time, at least this one time, Martha wasn't going to let her. She stared down at Aunt Ruth Ann's roses and sighed. Alafair worked too hard for Martha's comfort, and it seemed to her that her mother never did anything just for the pleasure of it. And, in the past year or so, she had been noticing new lines that were appearing around Alafair's eyes and mouth, and the gray streak in her hair was becoming more and more noticeable every day. Alafair didn't seem to be in the least aware that she wasn't getting any younger, either. She did insist on roaring into every situation like a locomotive, and never paid the least attention to Martha's suggestions that she let somebody take care of her once in a while. It had been worrying Martha for some time now.

She was still gazing into the street, planning her strategy for getting Alafair out of the house, when it suddenly dawned on her what she was looking at.

There was a motorcycle parked next to the curb in front of the house.

Martha straightened like she had been shocked. She only knew one person who rode a motorcycle.

"Oh, surely not!" she said aloud. After all, there were motorcycle races planned for the gala tomorrow, and it was likely that every motorcyclist in western Oklahoma and Kansas would make his way to Enid for the chance to compete.

But even as she rationalized its presence, she knew exactly why that particular motorcycle was parked in front of her aunt's house. Sudden wild emotion shot through her—fury uppermost, as well as healthy portions of disbelief and amazement. She turned and stalked toward the staircase, totally ignoring the thrill of joy that was bubbling up against her will.

◇◇◇

Martha stood stiffly in the doorway and eyed the unexpected visitor. He was sitting in the parlor, talking to her aunt, as calm and friendly as you please, with one leg crossed jauntily over the other and one arm stretched across the back of the settee.

"Streeter McCoy!" she blurted. He looked over at her. A delighted smile lit up his face, and he stood.

His fine, thinning hair was the color of ocean-washed beach, his eyes were a sparkling gold-brown, and his face was covered with a faint spray of golden speckles like grains of sand. He was a big man, not fat at all, but generously proportioned. He was dressed in a three-piece charcoal gray serge suit and a crisp white shirt, set off by a burgundy tie with a subtle gray stripe. He looked prosperous. He looked good. Martha felt her cheeks flush in spite of her steely intention to remain cool. The unruly nature of her emotions irritated her no end.

"What are you doing here?" she snapped.

Her ill-natured greeting didn't seem to bother him. "Howdy, Martha. I have some business here in the Strip, and I came up on the train late last night. Your uncle Jack Cecil told me you had accompanied your mother to Enid and were visiting Mrs. Yeager, so I thought I'd drop by and pay my respects."

Martha glanced at Aunt Ruth Ann, who had stopped petting the cat in her lap and looked shocked at her niece's lack of manners. Martha had the good grace to blush. "That was kind of you."

"Mr. McCoy and I were just talking about the thunderstorm last night," Aunt Ruth Ann said. "He tells me that lightning struck the high school building. About a wagon-load of brick was knocked off the southeast corner of the building, but nothing else was damaged."

Martha barely heard what her aunt was saying. "Is that so?"

Taking no note of Martha's pique, McCoy turned back to Ruth Ann and affably continued their conversation about the weather. "The rain must be a great thing for the farmers."

Ruth Ann nodded. "Indeed. The ground was so baked that it was too hard for plowing, and the heat was drying things up generally. We had a big old wheat harvest, but it was late for lack of rain. And the layers of dust on the roads have made automobile driving mighty unpleasant."

McCoy was chipper. "Well, after the sun shines in true Oklahoma fashion for half a day, the roads will be in fine condition for country driving."

Martha must have made some little noise of disdain, for Aunt Ruth Ann looked up and patted the settee. "Martha, why don't you sit down here and keep company with Mr. McCoy for a spell while I go upstairs and give Lester his medicine?"

Martha steadied herself before she walked into the room and perched on the edge of a chair. As she passed on her way out, Ike clutched in her arms, Ruth Ann gave her niece a look that said, "now, be nice." Martha bit her lip. McCoy waited until Aunt Ruth Ann was gone before he sat back down himself.

He smiled. "Well, Martha. I gather you're not overjoyed to see me."

"Oh, I'm sorry, Streeter. It's not that, really. It's just that the reason I came with Mama on this trip in the first place was to get away from you for a while."

He emitted a pained laugh. "You never were one to beat around the bush, and that's the truth. But that does sting a mite."

"Don't go acting all hurt, now. You know what I mean. What on earth are you doing here, anyway? Do you really have business? You didn't come all the way to Enid just to see me, I hope. If you can't do without my company for a couple of weeks, then I despair of you, Streeter."

McCoy sat back in his seat, spread both arms over the back, and crossed his ankle over his knee. The posture of a confident man, Martha thought.

"You certainly have a high opinion of yourself, Miss Tucker." His tone was light and teasing. "The fact is, I make three or four trips a year to our field office up here. I happened to be here a couple of years ago during the Founders' Day festivities and had such a good time that since then I've timed the trip to coincide with the celebration. I've entered the motorcycle races this year. Brought my new Harley with me on the train. So I was particularly looking forward to this particular trip. Especially when I heard that you happen to be here. I thought we might take in some of the sights together. But if my presence is so repugnant to you, I shan't impose myself."

Martha was hardly abashed. "That's a convenient tale, Mr. McCoy. To tell the truth, due to the reason we're here, which is my uncle's imminent death, I expect I'll have neither the time nor the inclination to indulge in any outings. I'm afraid we'll just have to wait until I get back home to socialize."

McCoy's expression became more serious and he sat forward. "I'm sorry, Martha. I wasn't thinking to bother you. Please don't give it another thought. I really do have to check the books in the field office, anyway. I'll talk to you when you return home." He allowed himself a smile. "It is nice to see you, though."

He was so sincere that Martha felt herself softening, but just as she opened her mouth to say something conciliatory, Alafair came down the stairs with Grace in tow. Grace skipped into the parlor and flung herself into Martha's lap, but Alafair stopped dead in the entryway when she caught sight of McCoy. He looked up at her and stood.

"Well, as I live and breathe, if it isn't Streeter McCoy!"

"How do you do, Mrs. Tucker?"

The sly smile that played around Alafair's lips knocked every bit of give out of Martha's attitude. She stiffened. "He's in town on business, Ma, and to make a good try at breaking his neck by racing that motorcycle of his at the Founders' Day Jubilee.

And he was just leaving." She stood up as well, hoisting Grace in her arms.

Alafair held her tongue. She could tell by the hectic color of her cheeks that Martha was not happy about having to deal with her feelings about Mr. McCoy right at the moment, but she was rather glad to see him, herself. She knew better than to convey that sentiment to Martha.

McCoy shot Alafair a glance. "Well, I guess I've been given my walking papers, Mrs. Tucker, so I'll say good morning to you all."

"It was nice to see you, Streeter."

But McCoy wasn't quite ready to give up. He turned back to Martha. "I have to work for a while this morning, but the office is right on the square. I'd certainly like to take you all to luncheon."

Martha didn't give Alafair the chance to respond. "I appreciate the offer, but I've talked my mother into taking a couple of hours to go shopping with me this morning; and I'll be having dinner here with my family. Besides, Streeter, I don't know if it's appropriate to be going off to enjoy myself with my friends, under the circumstances. Perhaps we'd better put that luncheon off until after I get back to Boynton."

"I understand. However, I do think it would be a shame for us to both be in town and entirely miss going to the event together. Maybe I could escort you and your mother to see the parade in the morning, and perhaps once around the carnival. I'm sure Grace would enjoy the whole spectacle immensely. Your cousin or your aunt might enjoy a brief respite, as well."

"Well..."

McCoy forged ahead. "And if that doesn't suit, I'll be entering at least one of the motorcycle races on the fifteenth and maybe on the sixteenth as well. Surely you could break away long enough to cheer for me on at least one of those occasions."

Martha tried to maintain her ill humor, but a chuckle escaped her. "You are persistent, Streeter. I'll say that for you."

"Then you'll consider it?"

"Oh, all right, since you're already here in town. I think the parade starts at eleven in the morning. If you'd like, come pick us up at nine. We can walk around a bit before the parade. But then you'll have to bring us back here straight away afterwards."

"Who is 'us' that are going to this parade?" Alafair interjected.

Martha slid her mother a look that was sly and innocent at once. "Why, you and Grace and me, of course, Mama. Maybe Aunt Ruth Ann, and Olivia, and little Ron, too. Anybody we can roust up."

Alafair opened her mouth to protest, but Martha cut her off.

"Aunt Ruth Ann said you should take a break or two while you're here, Ma, and then let her do the same. And remember, you're here to do whatever Aunt Ruth Ann wants of you."

Alafair would have refused outright, but McCoy gave her a pleading look, and she reconsidered. She expected he thought that Martha would not consent to spend any time with him otherwise. She also knew very well that he was right. "Well, Streeter, I guess we'll be seeing you tomorrow morning, then."

◇◇◇

"Mama, come look at this cunning dress." Martha held up a dark green cotton frock on a hanger and held it up to herself for Alafair to judge. It fell just below the middle of her shin and had a two-inch, pearl-gray belt under the bosom. The V-neck was set off by a shawl collar with a wide pearl lace trim.

Martha turned to look at herself in the mirror and caught sight of Alafair standing behind her with her arms folded over her chest and a critical look on her face. But the buxom saleslady who had been hovering about ever since they had entered the door of Klein's Department Store was filled with enthusiasm. "Oh, Miss, look at those colors! How they compliment your complexion!"

Grace, who had been amusing herself by running between the clothes racks, popped her head out from between a couple of coats long enough to bleat, "I like it."

"I'm sure you do, Grace." Martha's eyes narrowed as she scrutinized her reflection. "Oh, I don't know. I like the green, but I'm wondering if it doesn't make my complexion look even more olive than it is."

"I don't think so, Miss. However, we do have a complete line of whitening products for the well-bred lady."

Alafair, who had pretty much kept her counsel on this outing up to now, finally offered her opinion. "There's sure no use to spend money on such a thing as a whitener, sugar. Your skin is still young and full of just the right kind of color. And if you'd just start rinsing your face in buttermilk at night, like I've been telling you, you'll never have to worry about getting too brown."

Martha smiled but didn't comment. Her mother had a home remedy for everything under the sun. Many of them were quite effective, whereas others…Alafair had bathed her face in buttermilk every evening for as long as Martha could remember. She eyed her mother's sun-brown face and came to her own conclusion about the efficacy of dairy products as whitening agents, especially for someone with as much Indian ancestry as she had. She shot the saleslady a glance, returned the dress to the rack, and chose another.

"Mama, I want you to try on this frock. I think this would suit you to the ground."

"Now, honey, I'm not buying something I can make up for myself and probably fit me twice as well. Just be a waste of money for me."

"You don't have to waste a dime. I'll buy it for you."

Alafair was taken aback by the offer. "Oh, gracious, no, darlin'. Store-bought clothes are well and good for a young working woman like you, who has to look stylish every day of the world, but I never go anywhere. Besides, you should be saving your money for your future."

"You just let me worry about my future. I live at home and don't pay a plug nickel for a bed and three square meals a day. I want to. It'll make me feel good to get you a new dress."

"I'm not letting you spend your hard-earned money on a present for me."

"Ma, you're a wonderful giver, but you need to work on your receiving. It'll be good for my soul for me to buy a present for my mother out of the goodness of my heart."

Alafair bit her lip. Clearly she hadn't thought of it this way before.

Martha tried not to laugh. "Now, I'm getting fretted with you, here. Quit fighting with me and try on this dress I like so much, and a hat to match it, too. That ought to teach you to just give in graciously when somebody tries to give you something."

"Oh, but it's too nice! Where will I ever wear something as nice as this?"

"How about to Mary's wedding?"

"I was planning on my good blue serge suit for that. I wore that to Phoebe's wedding and Alice's, too."

"Are you planning to wear the same outfit to all your kids' weddings? When Grace gets married in the 1930s you're going to look mighty funny in your raggedy old 1900 suit."

"Oh, mercy, girl, all right! You're about to wear me out."

"Well, praise be. At last."

"Did I hear you mention a wedding? Are you about to be married, Miss? How wonderful."

Martha blushed to the roots of her hair. "Certainly not. We're talking about my sister's wedding. My mother and I would like to find some new clothes for the occasion."

"Oh, this is a lovely dress you've picked out."

"I think so. Don't you like it, Mama?"

Alafair bit her lip and fingered the material. It was nice, she had to admit. But five dollars for a dress!

Martha could read her mother's expression like a book, and she knew exactly how to soften that recalcitrant expression. "Daddy'll love it."

Alafair crumbled. "All right, then. Is there somewhere I can try this on, Miss?"

The saleslady took Alafair's arm and quickly steered her toward the dressing rooms at the back before she could change her mind.

Grace had about reached the end of her patience with this enterprise. She seized Martha's skirt in her fist. "Let's go, Martha!"

Martha started. "I declare, Grace, do you suppose there's someone in this store who didn't hear you? You're like to wake the dead." She sat the girl down in a chair and pulled a little picture book from her bag. "Here, punkin. Let's read your book while Mama tries on some new dresses. You can tell us which ones you like best."

Five minutes and five verses about the adventures of Kewpies later, Alafair emerged, smoothing the seat of the full skirt, and gave Martha an uncertain look. Grace gasped and clasped her hands before her rapturously. "Oh, Mama, it's beautiful! You look like a real woman!"

Alafair grinned at the child's reflection. "That's mighty high praise, puddin'."

Martha stood and plunked Grace down in the chair before she walked up to her mother and nodded.

"Oh, lovely," the saleslady said, causing Alafair's cheeks to pinken with self-consciousness. "Notice how much fuller skirts are this year, and the hemline is coming up, as well. It's not only attractive, it's wonderfully comfortable, too, don't you agree, ma'am?"

"Better than those narrow styles where you could hardly take a normal step. Not that I ever owned any of those." Alafair walked to the tall mirror on the wall and eyed the frock. "Now, what on earth would you call this color? It ain't exactly purple but it isn't red either. Looks pretty much like a plum to me."

"Exactly right, Madam," the saleslady exclaimed. "This color is called 'plum,' and it suits your coloring perfectly."

"I like it," Martha stated. "Now, admit it, Ma. It looks real good on you, too. You'll be able to wear this to any dress-up occasion. You'll just get a ton of use out of it."

"It is mighty fine. Mercy, it's almost too fancy. I feel like a queen or a duchess or something."

"Everybody should own at least one dress that makes her feel like a duchess. That's what I say."

Alafair laughed. "Now you sound like Alice. In fact, why couldn't I get Alice to make me a dress that looks like this? Why she could tailor me a pretty frock like this with her eyes closed, and it'd only..."

"Mother!" Martha cut her off. "You're just determined to deprive me of the pleasure of buying a nice outfit for you."

"Well, when you put it like that..."

Martha gave the saleswoman a harried glance, and she smiled back knowingly. She had been through this a hundred times. The entire state of Oklahoma was full of thrifty women for whom buying a new dress was anathema.

Alafair looked at herself in the mirror from every possible angle, as Martha and the shopgirl oohed and aahed. She did like the way she looked. *If I had money to burn...* she thought. Suddenly she became aware that the reflection of the chair behind her was missing something. "Where's Grace?"

"She was right here half a second ago. Grace!"

Grace appeared from behind the racks when she was called, with eight brightly colored purses arrayed up and down her little arms, not at all abashed and in fact looking very pleased with herself. She pranced up to the mirror beside Alafair and spread her arms grandly, the better to admire each handbag.

"Grace!" Alafair exclaimed, intending to scold, but Grace looked so happy with her achievement that she laughed instead. "I think you have more than enough bags to be carting your things around in, there. Why don't we put some of them back?"

Martha relieved Grace of one of the bags. "Look, Mama, this little sateen one would go just perfect with that dress." She turned to the saleslady for backup. "Don't you think?"

"Absolutely."

"I refuse to let you bankrupt yourself..."

"Not this again! I'm about to tear my hair out, Ma. I promise that the more you protest, the more I'm going to buy for you."

When they finally left Klein's, they were in possession of two dress boxes, two hatboxes, and a child's shoe box which had once contained a pair of patent leather Mary Janes. It now carried Grace's old high-tops, since once the shiny shoes had been slipped onto her feet she had vociferously refused to allow anyone to remove them. The sky was still overcast and spritzing rain, and they stayed under the storefront canopies as they walked down the street. Alafair had to keep a tight hold on Grace's hand to keep her from running into walls or walking into the traffic, since the child couldn't take her eyes off her new shoes.

"I'm not ready to go back yet, Ma. What say we duck into the City Drugstore here and have us some ice cream to celebrate our fancy new clothes?"

"Gracious, Martha, haven't you spent enough money today?"

"I worked hard for it, Ma. I reckon I can spend it however I want. And right now I want a strawberry sundae."

"I want ice cream, Mama," Grace piped up, without taking her eyes off her feet.

"Oh, all right. Far be it from me to stand between you and financial ruin. Besides, I could use a sit-down."

They piled their packages on the floor at their feet and hoisted themselves onto the stools at the soda fountain with Grace between them. A light rain was still falling, but out the front window, they could see the workmen finishing the wooden dais on the courthouse lawn. The entire square was abustle with preparations for the celebration tomorrow, and they had stood in front of the drugstore for a few moments before they had come in, just to watch all the activity across the street. One entire side of the square had been blocked off to traffic already, and carnival rides and sideshow tents were being set up. Grace was beside herself with excitement when she saw that half a dozen Cheyenne tepees were going up on an expanse of lawn in front of the Federal Building.

Alafair managed to distract her with the promise of ice cream. The teenaged soda jerk made a show of creating their sundaes, and even Grace's single scoop of vanilla was grandly topped with a cherry. The three of them were well into their treats when Alafair made a careful approach to a tender subject.

"Ain't it a coincidence that Streeter McCoy should just happen to be in town this week?"

Martha nearly choked on her disdain. "You and I both know perfectly well that his being here is no coincidence."

"Well, that's flattering, then, isn't it?"

"Not very. It's not very flattering that he won't listen to me and take no for an answer. Like I don't know my own mind. Like he knows what's best for me better than I do. Or that he only cares what he wants. Maybe that's it."

"Whoa, hang on there, shug," Alafair cautioned, as she reached over to wipe ice cream off of Grace's chin. "I think your hat's about to blow off."

Martha sputtered, outraged and amused at once. "Well, I just don't understand him. He doesn't look stupid."

"Anything but, I think. And that's probably the kink in these here works."

Alafair was about to inform her of everything she had been doing wrong and what she should do instead, Martha thought. She made an effort not to roll her eyes. If she said nothing, would her mother drop it, she wondered?

Alafair speedily relieved her of that hope. "He's smart enough that he can see not to take your words at face value. You're telling him you don't care for him, but your eyes are saying something else."

"Oh, Ma, that's the kind of talk fellows use to talk girls into doing something they don't want to do. 'Your lips say no, but your eyes say yes.' Besides, what my lips say is all that matters."

"That's true enough. But Streeter senses that you're so pulled in two about it that he has hope you'll change your mind. And believe me, I'd never say this to anyone, especially to Streeter, but you can't fool me, darlin'. You really do care for him. I see how you look at him, plain as day. Are you really going to let him go? You'll be sad the rest of your life if you do."

Tears started to Martha's eyes and she looked away quickly. She didn't know why Alafair's blunt speech had taken her by surprise. That's what Alafair did, after all. She regrouped quickly. "Maybe, Ma. But I've got to face the fact square that I have to make a choice. If I marry him, or anybody, my life will change out of all recognition. I like my life. I like working."

"Can't you work and be married, too, at least until the babies start to coming?"

"You know very well how it is. Besides, once Streeter started coming around the bank so much, Mr. Bushyhead told me straight out that if the two of us got together, he sure would be sorry to lose me."

"Maybe he don't know you'd like to stay on."

"He knows. He just doesn't approve of married women working for money. Men, they all stick together. You think he'll change his mind?"

Alafair thought about this for a minute. Her approach had always been to deal with life as she found it, not as she wished it to be. She sighed. "Sometimes it seems like people change, honey, but most of the time it just takes them a while to show what they're really like. Generally, people don't change very much."

"Don't, can't, or won't. Doesn't it take somebody to stand up and say, why are things like this? This isn't good. Let's try this."

"More ice cream!" Grace demanded, and Alafair, who would normally have never countenanced more ice cream, absently spooned some of her sundae into Grace's dish. "It does take somebody to do just that," she said to Martha. "But the first people who do generally get slapped down hard. They're braver folks than I am. Besides, what do you propose to do? You can't change the way God made the world. But what higher calling is there than to make a home and raise a family? What could make a woman prouder than that?"

"Nothing, for some women. But maybe other women are more suited for something else. You know as well as I do that it's a bad thing to be married to someone whose heart isn't in it. Even worse to be raised by her."

Alafair thought about this for a minute. "Well, you don't have to have babies, I reckon," she said at length.

A long stunned silence, broken only by Grace's slurping, followed this pronouncement.

"Well, knock me right off this stool!" Martha finally managed. "How do you propose I go about that?"

Alafair gave her daughter an ironic look.

Martha shook her head. "That wouldn't be much of a marriage then, would it?"

"There's more than one way to skin a cat."

"Whatever do you mean, Mother?"

Alafair glanced around to make sure the soda jerk was well out of earshot. "Wasn't it you who was just reading to me about Miss Emma Goldman's lectures to women?"

Martha was speechless. She had not until this moment realized that her mother knew what the words "birth control" meant. And even if Alafair did know, the fact that she was apparently advocating the idea was so far removed from Martha's understanding of her mother's values that she could hardly credit her own ears.

"Ask your Grandma McBride about it," Alafair added. "She learned a bunch at her Cherokee mama's knee." She turned back to her sundae. "We'd better get cracking. I want to help Ruth Ann with Lester before the morning gets too far gone. And you can crank your mouth shut, now. You're twenty-four years old. It'd be pretty silly of me to still be talking to you like you're ten."

After they returned to the house, Alafair put Grace down for a nap. As soon as the girl was asleep, Alafair picked up the Mark

Twain novel that Martha had pressed on her and walked down the hall to relieve Ruth Ann at Lester's bedside.

She could tell by her sister's face that Lester was having a bad day. Ruth Ann looked drawn and pale as she gave her report on Lester's condition, Alafair thought. She determined to try and spend some time alone with Ruth Ann this very afternoon, if she could manage it. Sometimes just having someone to talk to honestly made it possible for one to bear the unbearable.

She sent Ruth Ann out with instructions to eat something and walk downtown to see the carnival preparations, then sat down next to Lester's bed with the book in her hand.

Ike was on the bed, scrunched up very close to Lester's frail form, and for a minute, Alafair and the cat regarded one another. She didn't know what to think about this cat. On the farm, a cat was definitely not a house pet, and certainly not a member of the family, like this creature seemed to think he was.

She didn't try to talk to Lester. His breathing was labored and his eyes were pinched closed. Ruth Ann told her that he had held out as long as he could before he allowed her to give him a dose of laudanum just a few minutes earlier. Alafair expected the narcotic would take effect shortly and allow Lester to sleep. She leaned forward to lift Ike off the bed, and was surprised, then, when Lester opened his eyes and said, "Leave him be, Alafair."

She sat back. "I'll swan, Lester, you gave me a start! Can I get something for you?"

"No, I don't need anything," he croaked.

"I brought that book by Mr. Mark Twain. Shall I read to you?"

"I was just hoping you'd talk to me a mite."

She lowered the book into her lap and leaned back. "Well, me and my girls did some shopping today. Martha was in the mood to spend some money, I reckon. I never seen so much spent at one time in one place in my life. I tried to talk her out of it, but you know how independent young ladies are these days. The more I protested, the more she insisted. I must say, though, that thanks to her foolishness, me and Grace have got ourselves some fine new duds."

Lester made a huffing sound that could have been a chuckle, and Alafair drew a breath to continue. But Lester had another topic on his mind.

"Kenneth back yet?" he said. His hand crept out from under the covers and rested on Ike's back. The cat's eyes closed.

Alafair blinked at the unexpected question. "No. If Olivia has heard from him, she hasn't said anything to me about it. I got the impression she thought he'd be back today, but she doesn't seem worried. Is Ruth Ann fretted about it?"

"She mentioned it once or twice this morning."

"Well, I reckon he's making a pretty long trip. One day is neither here nor there. Besides, the day ain't over yet."

"That's what I told her, but she's given to worry, as I'm sure you know."

Alafair smiled. "Well, don't *you* be worrying, now. I'll try to set Ruth Ann's mind to rest about things later."

Lester nodded and Alafair fell quiet, expecting the invalid to drift off now that he'd spoken his mind.

"I despair of that boy, sometimes." Lester's whispery voice barely disturbed the silence. Alafair looked up.

"You must be feeling a little better," she observed. "Is the laudanum helping?"

His thin shoulders shifted against the pillow in a shrug. "Olivia tell you how the young'un appropriated some business funds that he figured was just laying around doing nothing, and bought himself some land?"

Alafair was surprised. "No."

"He's sinking himself a wildcat well. Went in partners with a driller from over Osage County. Name of Nickolls. Met him once. Kind of like him. But I was riled that Kenneth practically stole that money from the business."

"I reckon!"

"I fixed it so he can't have access to the Yeager funds without my or Mike Ed's countersignature."

Ike obviously didn't care for the direction this conversation was taking. He jumped off the bed.

"Lester, you're going to wear yourself out," Alafair warned.

Lester ignored her. "He's fell in with some bad company of late, too, this pathetic, worthless, do-nothing son of Buck Collins. Name of Ellery. The dad owns half the town and schemes to own the other half. Knows everybody's business. I think he owns somebody, maybe two or three somebodies, at city hall, the courthouse."

Alafair was becoming alarmed at Lester's rant. His ashen cheeks sported hectic red spots, and his voice sounded husky and frantic. "Now, don't get all excited, Lester. This can't do you any good at all."

"Naw, that dope is doing its business. Let me say my piece before it puts me out. I was scared that after I cut him off from the business money, Kenneth would borrow from Ellery—or worse, from old Buck. That Buck is a nasty creature. Got no conscience at all, Alafair. A killer. He preys on the weak, or folks in trouble. He's like a snake. When a body is down he strikes fast, before the victim can think. Yes, I was scared Kenneth would go to that poisoned well after I cut off the spigot. I give Kenneth a tongue lashing to beat all. Said I never was so disappointed in anybody in my life. He promised to get shet of his unsavory friends. And now Ruth Ann says that Ellery left town last month, went back east." He hesitated a moment to catch his breath, such as it was, then continued. "I was relieved to hear Ellery is gone. I think it'll be all right now."

Alafair didn't know if she was expected to comment, but it didn't matter. Lester fell asleep at the end of his sentence.

Alafair sat at the dining room table by herself in the quiet house, snapping and stringing beans for supper. Lu was upstairs, changing bed linens, and Ruth Ann was with Lester. Olivia had taken Grace and Ron to her house until suppertime. Martha had gone with them, but told her mother that she only intended to stay for a few minutes before she walked back to the Yeager house to help with the meal preparations.

Alafair usually appreciated whatever solitude she could get, but at the moment, she wasn't enjoying the fact that she couldn't stop thinking about Lester's unexpected tirade. What on earth made him confide such a thing in her? What did he think she could do about it?

He probably didn't expect her to do anything, she thought. The problem had more than likely been preying on his mind, and he just needed to get it off his chest. And who else could he tell? Not Ruth Ann. He had spent half a lifetime protecting Ruth Ann from unpleasant realities, though Alafair was quite sure Ruth Ann was capable of dealing with whatever she had to. Lu? Now, there was an interesting thought. Probably not, though. No matter how much Lester might trust their shadowy housekeeper, she wasn't family, and this kind of information could only be safely shared with family.

She couldn't help but fume a little as she considered what that wool-brained Kenneth was putting his family through. She had just thought him inconsiderate. Now her opinion of him had slid quite a bit south of that.

She gave her head a tight shake, trying to derail the unpleasant train of thought.

"Wish I had something else to occupy me," she murmured aloud.

As the words hung in the air, Alafair heard the front door slam and Streeter McCoy's voice call Martha's name. Before she could react, Martha's blurred form appeared momentarily as she dashed across the foyer and ran upstairs. Alafair's forehead wrinkled. Martha was not a woman given to dramatics, and in any other circumstance, Alafair would have been alarmed enough by this display to run after her. Over the last week she had become aware enough of Martha's situation, though, that her concern was tempered with slightly amused pity.

She dropped a half-strung green bean back into the bowl and eyed the parlor entrance until McCoy slouched into view and stood gazing forlornly up the staircase with his hand on the newel.

"Streeter," she called, and he tore his eyes away from the stairwell to look at her. When he realized she had been watching, he looked chagrined.

"Mrs. Tucker."

"What's going on?"

"I happened to meet Martha on her way back from her cousin's and she let me walk with her for a ways. We got to talking. I guess the conversation took a turn she didn't like."

Alafair's eyebrows peaked. How had he "happened" to meet her walking back from Olivia's place? His office and hotel were downtown. Neither the Crawford house nor the Yeager house was on any logical route of his.

She stood up and wiped her hands on her apron before walking back into the parlor and making herself comfortable on the settee. Ike the cat, curled up at the other end, briefly opened one eye to check her out before resuming his nap. She picked up a partially stitched quilt panel from the sewing basket she had left on the side table earlier.

"Come on in here and talk to me for a spell."

He threw one more hopeful glance up the stairs before he hung his hat on the rack by the door and trod into the parlor. He sat down in a tufted armchair across the tea table from her.

Alafair didn't speak for a minute. She added a stitch or two to her quilt panel, allowing McCoy to catch his breath and regain his equilibrium. He drew his handkerchief from his breast pocket and absently mopped his forehead, carefully refolded and replaced it, and flopped back into the chair. Alafair gave him a brief glance, trying hard to spare his dignity and not smile.

Finally, it was McCoy himself who engaged. "I just don't understand, Mrs. Tucker."

"What is it you don't understand, Streeter?"

He propped his elbow on the arm of the chair and leaned his chin on his hand. "Why, women, ma'am. And it surprises me some to admit it. I thought I had a better handle on the fair sex than it seems I actually do."

"I think there's one woman in particular that stumps you."

He straightened a little and laughed, suddenly looking much more like himself. "Mrs. Tucker, you've got the truth of it, there. If there's any advice you could give me concerning that particular woman, I'd be eternally grateful."

"I don't know what you think I could tell you, Streeter. Besides, if you want to know what Martha is thinking, you'd better ask her."

"That's the rub, ma'am. I've been asking until I'm blue in the face. It seems she doesn't want me to go, yet she doesn't want me to stay, either. She just wants to be friends, she says."

"You don't want to be 'just friends'?"

"Oh, Mrs. Tucker, I've asked her to marry me half-a-dozen times."

Alafair felt her cheeks flush and quickly looked down at her sewing, trying not to burst into tears of joy.

"But she's turned me down every time," McCoy was saying. "And now, if I even get near the subject...well, you've just seen the result."

Alafair's heart sank. "Well, then, I guess she's given you her answer. You can't make her love you."

"But the way she... I mean, I swear she feels... I don't presume to know what your daughter feels, ma'am, but I think she does love me. Am I wrong, Mrs. Tucker? Am I just fooling myself?"

His voice had taken on a plaintive quality. Alafair kept her eyes on her stitching. "I think maybe she cares for you, Streeter."

He made an unintelligible noise that suggested joy, but when he spoke, he sounded calm and in control of himself. "Then can you tell me why she won't marry me?"

Alafair looked up. McCoy was sitting right on the edge of his seat. "It's not that simple, Streeter. Martha tells me that she doesn't want to marry at all. And then you come along, and she's fallen in love with you whether she likes it or not. She doesn't know what to do."

McCoy thought about this for a moment. "Any idea what she has against marriage, Mrs. Tucker?"

"Now, you're telling me that y'all haven't talked about this?"

"Like I said, I've tried to talk about it. If she'd tell me what the difficulty is, maybe between us we could do something about it."

Alafair took a minute to consider how far she could go if she offered McCoy her opinion. The idea of meddling didn't bother her, if it would help Martha, but she wouldn't like to say anything that Martha might consider a betrayal of her trust. She couldn't remember actually promising her daughter not to talk to McCoy about the problem, so she plunged ahead.

"I can only tell you what she's mentioned to me, son. Whether or not it helps you understand her, well, I can't guarantee that. She did tell me that she don't want to give up her job at the bank, and Mr. Bushyhead has made it right clear to her that he thinks a married woman has no business working except in her own home."

McCoy's perplexed expression changed to one of understanding. "I see. Well, I never thought of that, and I feel like a perfect fool. I kind of expected she was maybe afraid of...marriage." He flushed red.

But Alafair wasn't bothered by the implication. "I don't think so, Streeter."

He emitted an uncomfortable laugh. "No, you're right. I just couldn't think of a more likely reason. But, knowing Martha, it makes sense. I just assumed every woman wanted her own home to run, and a family."

Now Alafair did smile. "Where'd you get an idea like that, sugar?"

McCoy reddened a bit at her teasing tone. "From my mother, I guess, and my sisters. All the girls I know seem to be happy to marry, and I expected..."

"Not all girls are alike, any more than all fellows are. Where I grew up, you didn't have no choice. If you were a girl, you either took your chances and married up with the best man you could get to ask you, or you stayed home all your life and took care of your ma and pa until they died. Then you hoped one of your relatives would take pity on their spinster aunt or sister and take you in as an unpaid nursemaid to their babies and sick folks. If you were like me or my sister Miz Yeager, you'd get lucky and find yourself a good man who'd treat you with respect and leave you alone to do your business your own way. If you weren't, well, you were pretty much stuck.

"Now, Martha, she has choices. Besides, she's proud and I think the idea of having to obey her husband rankles her some. She'd rather be her own boss."

"Mrs. Tucker, I've never known a smart woman to obey her husband if it didn't suit her."

The comment made Alafair chuckle. "You're a smart man."

"Why, I'd never try to lord it over Martha, and if she wants to have a job, that's up to her, even if it isn't with Mr. Bushyhead."

"Don't be telling me, Streeter. Talk it over with Martha. Just don't tell her you and me put our heads together over it, because I guarantee she'd take exception to that."

"Mrs. Tucker, I can't thank you enough for telling me all this." He stood up. "I was feeling pretty stumped. I'll leave now, and talk to Martha again later, when she's cooled down some. If you'd please let her know that I'm sorry and that I'll telephone her this evening to make plans for tomorrow morning, I'd be obliged."

"I'll be glad to."

He walked across the parlor, then paused at the entryway and turned. "I sure appreciate it that you're on my side, Mrs. Tucker."

"Now, Streeter, I like you. You seem like a fine man, and if my girl sees fit to marry someday, I think she could do a lot worse than you. But don't be fooled. I'm on Martha's side, and nobody else's."

McCoy's lip twitched in amusement. He retrieved his hat from the coat tree in the foyer and gave Alafair a little bow before he put it on. "Just as it should be, ma'am."

After he left, Alafair went back to her appliqué, feeling vaguely troubled by the renewed hope in McCoy's voice and stance. To tell the truth, she wasn't at all sure that Martha's reluctance to hear McCoy's suit was entirely due to her desire for a career and independence. Alafair had seen no evidence, but she had a feeling that there was some other reason that Martha hadn't told her. What it was, she couldn't imagine. Perhaps Martha didn't know herself, or was simply unable to put it into words. In any event, she feared that Streeter McCoy still had a way to go in his quest for Martha's hand.

Her darling Martha, her eldest, the apple of her eye. Complicated, thoughtful, responsible to a fault. Her best friend. Yes, if she were forced at gunpoint, she might say that even though she'd die a thousand deaths for any of her children, Martha was her favorite.

She looked over at the cat, who was watching her expectantly from the other end of the couch.

"What do you think, Ike?"

He sat up, stretched, and yawned hugely.

"You're a big help. Go make yourself useful. Catch a mouse."

He sniffed his disdain and curled up to resume his beauty sleep.

Wednesday, September 15, 1915

McCoy called for them after breakfast. The rain was holding off for the moment, the sun trying to shine through the intermittent breaks in the cloud cover. Ruth Ann's house was only a few blocks from the square, and almost as soon as they began walking, they could hear the sound of ragtime music in the air and smell the odors of chili and onions and popcorn. When they reached the square, the crush and smell and noise of thousands of people milling around energized Martha and Olivia, and Grace nearly pulled her mother over in her anxiety to rush into the crowd. But Ruth Ann seemed anxious, and Alafair was feeling claustrophobic within a minute of entering the melee.

"It's beautiful! It's beautiful!" Grace crowed.

"What on earth is that wild music?" Alafair raised her voice to be heard over the din of barkers' spiels, laughing fairgoers, and the tinny piano music coming from one of the long carnival tents that lined one side of the courthouse square.

"That's ragtime music, Ma," Martha said into her mother's ear.

McCoy leaned in to Alafair's other ear. "I believe that tune is called 'When I Was a Tulip and You Were a Red, Red Rose.'"

"What a noise!"

After McCoy insisted on buying them all bags of peanuts from a vendor, they resumed their walk down West Randolph on the north side of the square, past Parker's Bookstore and Pfaeffle's Jewelry Store, Owl Drug, and the Jackson Studio. All the storefronts were shaded by red-and-white striped awnings to protect shoppers from the sun and reduce the glare on the shop windows. The fact that every store was covered by the same type of awning gave the entire square a festive and inviting look, Alafair thought. If she mentioned how nice the awnings were to Shaw's uncle, the mayor of Boynton, perhaps the council would consider subsidizing something of the sort for the shop owners on the main street of her little town.

They continued down Randolph, pausing to comment on the darling hats on display in the window of Clutter Millinery before they passed Klein's Department Store. Martha and Grace were reliving their shopping adventure of the day before when the group turned south at the big white bank building on the corner of Randolph onto Grand.

Streetcar, automobile, and horse traffic had been banned from the square for the duration of the celebration, so they only had to contend with the crush of foot traffic as they crossed to Maine and turned west.

"I can't see, Mama!" Alafair lifted Grace into her arms to keep her from being smothered by the press of people.

Olivia swept the air as she gestured toward the buildings lining the street. "You know, this entire south side of the square, and a bunch of the buildings on South Grand burned to the ground when I was little. Not a thing here is more than fifteen years old."

"I was afraid the whole town was going to go up," Ruth Ann said, raising her voice to be heard over the din.

Across Maine the white brick Federal Building sat back to back with the beautiful red brick "Cherokee Gothic" Garfield County Courthouse, with its white stone trim and six gables, all surrounded by elegant white globe lights. The courthouse square was huge, two blocks long and a block wide, and every open inch of the parklike grounds was covered with tents, booths, pavilions, and carnival rides.

The girls grabbed Alafair and Ruth Ann by the arm, propelling them through the crowd and across the street, down the long line of carnival attractions. McCoy trotted hot on their heels in an attempt to keep up with the excited young women.

Grace was about to twist her head off in her desperate attempt to see everything. "Bears, Martha! Look at the bears in the cage!" she exclaimed. "There's a man eating fire, Aunt Ruth Ann!"

"Lord have mercy, I can't watch!"

Olivia pointed at a hugely tall young woman sitting on a platform under a sign which declared her Giganta—The Tallest Girl Alive. "Oh, my goodness, that poor girl, everybody staring at her."

"Why, she looks happy enough," Alafair decided.

"Look yonder, Ma, there's the Ferris wheel. Let's take a ride. We could see the whole festival from the top."

"You girls are going to be exhausted before you get halfway around the square. Mercy, I'd think y'all were five years old instead of grown women. This fair will be here for three days. We don't have to see it all within the next hour."

"You don't want to ride the Ferris wheel?" Martha asked, disappointed.

"Why, I'll be glad to take you for a spin," McCoy offered.

Grace was game. "I want to ride the fair's wheel."

"You three go on ahead and give Grace a ride, if you want. Me and Ruth Ann will do some sightseeing. Just don't come complaining if Grace starts screeching at the top or throws up on your dresses."

Offended by Alafair's lack of faith, Grace told her in no uncertain terms that she would neither screech nor throw up.

"I'm sure she'll be fine, Ma. Are you sure y'all don't want to come?"

"Would you like me to escort you ladies, Mrs. Tucker?" McCoy offered gallantly.

"Oh, mercy, no. I feel like doing a little meandering, here."

Ruth Ann agreed. "Maybe I'll buy me another bag of peanuts and walk around and watch all these folks for a spell."

"Well, don't get lost, Ma," Martha said. "The parade starts in an hour, and I'd like for us to see it together."

"We'll meet y'all right back here in front of the Tallest Girl Alive at three-quarters past ten. That should give us time to find a good spot to see the parade."

Alafair and Ruth Ann bought another bag of peanuts to share and walked around the square, discarding shells and watching the fair-goers. One entire side of the courthouse lawn along Independence was taken up with a dozen or so tepees, housing for the Cheyenne from Woodward, who had contracted with the city of Enid to lend color to the festivities and lead the opening parade. Several long-haired, young Cheyenne men, dressed in full tribal regalia, stood together in the midst of their temporary village, painting their ponies and weaving feathers and other talismans into the manes, laughing and talking together as they readied themselves for the parade. A score of Indian women and children, some in native garb and some not, stood together in a companionable group, watching with amusement as their men decorated their horses and themselves. A gang of little boys, some Indian, a couple colored, but most white, ran around the lawn hollering and whooping in a warrior-like fashion. Three or four of the boys were playing some game of dare, and the women stopped to observe as they finished their peanuts. The boys huddled together and giggled for a moment, then one screwed up enough courage to dash up to one of the tepees and slap the side a couple of times, then retreat posthaste into the crowd. One after another, little boys periodically launched themselves out of their huddle and tore forward to pound on the lodge and dash away.

Alafair and Ruth Ann watched the kids for five minutes, wondering idly what the purpose of this activity was, when suddenly a giant Cheyenne in an eye-popping war bonnet, a face full of war paint, and a tomahawk in his hand, burst out of the tepee with a hair-raising whoop and chased the screaming youngsters for a couple of yards.

Ruth Ann laughed. "Those boys disappeared into thin air faster than spit on a griddle!"

The Cheyenne turned around to go back to his lodge, but paused when he locked eyes with the laughing women. His fearsome face split into a white-toothed grin, and he gave them a conspiratorial wink before he lifted the door flap and disappeared inside.

Still chuckling, they resumed their walk around the square, taking in the sights. Alafair found herself wishing that her younger kids, Charlie, Blanche, and Sophronia, were here to enjoy this. And Shaw, too. He'd get as big a kick out of the fair as the kids would. Because of the time of year it occurred, they had never taken the time to visit Enid for the Cherokee Strip celebration. Alafair made a mental note to talk to Shaw about it. Perhaps now that they had so many grown kids and sons-in-law, they might be able to make special arrangements next year to come up just for the occasion. She never thought much about leisure, since she had so little of it. She found she rather liked it, by the teaspoonful, at least.

The press of the crowd did annoy her, though, and she found herself suggesting to her sister that they walk straight down Grand, rather than turning the corner and continuing on around the perimeter of the square. She felt her shoulders relax as she walked away from the noise and into the quiet, leafy neighborhood, past big, white Victorians, red or golden brick, and native stone Craftsmans. Sometimes they would see someone sitting on her front porch in a chair or rocking in a porch swing. Ruth Ann always knew the person, and they would call a friendly greeting to one another.

The sisters had been engaging in innocuous small talk until Alafair took advantage of their solitude to ask a question.

"What's the story on this Buck Collins fellow, Ruth Ann?"

Alafair took a couple of steps before she realized that Ruth Ann had stopped. She looked around, surprised, and Ruth Ann fell back in beside her as they resumed their walk. "Buck Collins? Why do you ask about him?" Ruth Ann said, without looking at her. Her cheeks were flushed.

"Lester has a pretty low opinion of him."

Ruth Ann seemed quite herself again, but walked a little further before she answered. "There's been bad blood between Lester and Buck for years."

"Really?"

"Before either of them came to Oklahoma." Ruth Ann glanced at her sister. "You know, I knew Buck even before I knew Lester."

Alafair was surprised. "You don't say?"

"Yes. It was in Wichita. You remember that summer I went to stay with Aunt Cena?"

"In '92. Yes, I recall that. That's where you met Lester."

"I met Buck first. He worked in Uncle Homer's hardware store. He had come out from Baltimore on the train, thinking to see the West and make his fortune. He came out to Uncle Homer and Aunt Cena's house for Sunday dinner once or twice. He took a shine to me, and I thought for a spell that he was courting me. But he wasn't. He was already married to Mazie at the time. She was still back in Maryland. He brought her and the kids out to the Strip after the run. Besides, one day, Lester Yeager walked into the store, fresh off the train from Ohio, with a handbill in his hand for the Cherokee Strip land run, and as far as I was concerned, that was that."

"I remember how upset Mama was that you wanted to marry some penniless wastrel you'd just met two weeks before."

"Wasn't that a dustup?"

"You couldn't be talked out of it, though."

"It worked out fine, didn't it?"

Alafair grinned. "I'd say so."

"Look how pretty the asters are in the bed under that window, Alafair!"

"What a color! They're as bright as a new copper penny! So you think that's why Lester doesn't like Collins? Jealousy?"

"Oh, Lester knows he doesn't have a reason in the world to be jealous. Lester can't stand a crook, which Buck is. A crook and a bully. Lester thinks he was a sooner, too."

"You're joshing! You think he jumped the gun?"

"Lester's convinced of it. Lester made the run fair and square on that long-legged red of his. He galloped eighteen miles, straight as a plumb line, and was practically the first person to reach the Enid town site. Said he never saw hide nor hair of Buck. But when he went to that plot right downtown that he wanted, it was already staked, so he hotfooted it off to his second choice and planted his stake. When he got to the land office to file, he asked who got that first plot, and lo and behold, it was Buck Collins! Lester got him a mighty good claim anyway, right where the warehouse is now, by the tracks. But he's dead sure that Buck snuck in early somehow and stole his claim out from under him."

"I'll swan! I never heard that Lester lost the claim he wanted."

"He's not eager to mention it."

"You think Buck beat Lester out of his claim just for meanness?"

"I don't know. Maybe he did. I didn't think so at the time, but Buck has proved himself to be a spiteful creature, I'm afraid. A few years after that, the two of them got into it over some fool thing at a town council meeting and ended up in a fist-fight right on the boardwalk outside city hall, for heaven's sake! Nobody tried to stop them until the town marshal showed up.

I think the council members were taking bets! Ever since then, they've barely had a civil word to say to one another. They've managed to live together in the same town, though, and even done business.

"Over the years, Buck just grew twisted, somehow. Lester may hate him, but he's right about Buck being dangerous. He's done some mighty nasty things to folks, and I fear that he's not one to let go of a grudge. He owns half a dozen enterprises in Garfield County, most of them having to do with land, and most of them acquired by cheating somebody else out of them. Rumor is he's got himself some hired persuaders, in case a business associate needs help to become more enthusiastic about one of Buck's projects. There have even been a couple of unsolved murders laid at his door."

"Why hasn't he been arrested?"

"He's mighty smart, I reckon. Sheriff Hume has never been able to prove anything against him."

"Well, then, you're lucky you never got involved with him!"

"Yes, thank the Lord for Lester. Oh, look yonder! What a pretty bunch of tomato vines in that garden!"

◇◇◇

They had about decided that they had wandered long enough and it was time to meet the girls and McCoy in front of the Tallest Girl Alive when Ruth Ann noted that they had reached the corner of Cherokee and Grand, and were walking toward the sprawling headquarters of the Yeager Transfer and Storage Company.

"Would you like for me to show you the new addition, Alafair?"

Alafair had not been inside the warehouse for several years, not since it had been expanded so. "Yes, I would! Just a quick walk through, though."

Ruth Ann grabbed her hand and practically skipped down the street, excited at the prospect of showing off Lester's pride and joy. "Come on, Alafair! I expect the girls won't miss us for another ten minutes."

◇◇◇

"Sure is quiet in here," Alafair observed.

"It's because of the Jubilee," Ruth Ann told her. "In fact, there's going to be a Yeager float in the parade. It'll be manned by a goodly number of Lester's employees. He had considered closing for the duration. A lot of other businesses are."

Alafair couldn't see a single person hovering about the usually bustling warehouse. However, one of the three garage doors stood open, with a big van parked inside, nose out to the street, so somebody was there.

They walked into the warehouse through the open garage, into the dark, cool, cavernous interior. At first, Alafair thought the place was deserted, but a light was coming from the windows of the manager's office, overlooking the loading dock.

"I see that Mike Ed is here, at least," Ruth Ann said. "He's probably taking advantage of the lull to catch up on some paperwork."

Alafair had met Mike Ed Beams several times over the years. He had worked for Lester since he was a youngster, eventually becoming the general manager. He was in his early thirties, now, married with young children, and fiercely dedicated to Lester and the Yeager Transfer and Storage Company. The women only had time for a quick look-see before they were due to meet the kids, so they didn't take the time to mount the stairs to greet Mike Ed.

The huge warehouse stretched out into the shadows as far as Alafair could see. They took a right at the garage door, toward the interior. Tall windows stretching two stories high along the outside walls were open to admit the light and air. Only the one van was parked close to the loading dock, but Alafair could see spaces for three more. Most of the rest of the interior was packed with crates and boxes, neatly aligned in rows and on shelves, awaiting transport or pickup.

The place smelled of tires and exhaust, sawdust and cement, and a dozen other exotic and, to Alafair, unidentifiable smells. The building was at least three times longer than she remembered, and she was duly impressed by the fruits of Lester's industry and skill. Ruth Ann guided her through the gloomy interior, proudly pointing out all the sights along the way, to the big refrigeration unit at the far back of the building. There wasn't much to see—just two thick wood and iron doors with little windows at eye-height. Alafair had to stand on her tiptoes to look into the ice room, but the lights were off, and all she could see was blackness. She didn't attempt to look into the cold storage lockers next to it. The loud machine hum was bothersome to her, but not nearly as much as the cold. The two refrigeration units looked to be solidly sealed off from the rest of the warehouse, but she had noticed the change in the climate when she was still twenty feet away. Standing up close to look through the little window was like stepping back into winter, and it didn't take two minutes for her to become chilled. She stepped back with a shudder and shook her head.

"What an amazing invention, artificial refrigeration, Ruth Ann. Whatever will they think of next?"

Time was growing short before the start of the parade, and they decided they'd better get on with it. As she turned to leave, Alafair stepped on something sharp lying close to the wall by the cold storage door. She absently scraped her shoe on the cement floor in order to dislodge whatever it was, but only succeeded in driving it further into her sole. Annoyed, she lifted her foot to inspect the object, and was surprised to see a small gold ball stuck to the bottom of her shoe.

Ruth Ann cocked her head in curiosity. "What's the matter, Alafair?"

Alafair pulled the offending item out and brought it up to her face, the better to inspect it in the dim light, and saw that she was holding a rather expensive collar stud that some unfortunate man had managed to lose. "Why, it looks like a gold collar stud!"

"Let me see. So it is. Looks like something that Kenneth would wear. He loves to get all gussied up."

"You suppose this is his?"

Ruth Ann shook her head. "I don't think so. Kenneth doesn't come into this part of the warehouse if he can help it, especially since Lester put in the refrigeration units. He detests anything cold. Said he got enough of being cold to last a lifetime when he was growing up in Michigan." She laughed as though she thought this a charming peccadillo.

"What on earth was a banker or lawyer or other fat and wealthy gentleman doing back here by the cold storage lockers that would jerk his collar stud loose?" Alafair wondered idly. She slipped the gold stud into her skirt pocket and promptly forgot it as the two women hastened to get back to town in time for the parade.

McCoy met the ladies in front of the Tallest Girl Alive and escorted them down the block. The girls had already found themselves a place to view the parade, directly opposite the speakers' dais, and they were all sitting on newspapers draped over the damp curb, eating popcorn, when Alafair and Ruth Ann walked up. Grace practically threw her popcorn bag at Martha in her haste to rush over and tell her mother every detail of her ride on the Ferris wheel. The sisters sat down on either side of Martha and Olivia while McCoy positioned himself on the sidewalk behind them. Alafair settled Grace into her lap, listening to her piping chatter with one ear while planning what remedy to give all these youngsters later, when they finally developed their inevitable stomachaches from too much carnival food.

"You've found a good spot," Alafair noted to Olivia, once Grace had talked herself out and regained an interest in her popcorn. The speakers' platform that they had watched being constructed was now draped all around in somewhat rain-bedraggled red, white, and blue bunting. Chairs for the local dignitaries had been arranged in a row behind the podium, which sported a large, red and white Oklahoma flag. Several well-dressed men were at this moment mounting the stairs and milling around the platform. Halfway up the block, where Broadway bisected Independence Avenue, Alafair could just make out the color guard waiting for the signal to begin the parade.

"Yes, we figured we'd better get ourselves settled pretty quick if we wanted to be able to hear the governor's speech."

Alafair straightened and eyed the men on the platform. "Governor Williams is here? Which one is he?"

Olivia pointed out a man with a cleft chin who was wearing a black suit. "Nice looking, isn't he?

"He looks just like the picture I saw of him in the paper last January, after he got inaugurated."

The governor and a man whom Alafair didn't recognize were moving toward the podium, and the other men were settling themselves in the chairs at the back. She leaned back toward Olivia. "Do you know any of those other fellows?"

Olivia craned her neck a little to see around the men at the podium. "Well, that one in the first chair is a city councilman. I've seen him at Daddy's house, but I don't know his name. That bald man there is Mr. Debs."

"Eugene Debs, who ran for president last time?"

"That's him. He's giving a speech tomorrow."

"I declare!" Alafair regarded the man for a moment. Eugene V. Debs was easily the most famous person she had ever seen. It took her a moment to realize that Olivia was still speaking to her.

"Over there is Dr. Zollars, from Phillips University. That one there is the mayor, then Sheriff Hume, and next to him is Chief of Police John Burns."

"Who's that with the governor?"

"That's Buck Collins. He's one of them who made the run in '93. His son Ellery used to be a friend of Kenneth's. He's going to do the introductions, I reckon."

Alafair straightened and unconsciously squeezed Grace tightly enough that she squeaked. The very man who caused Lester such distress! She leaned around Olivia and caught Ruth Ann's eye before raising her eyebrows and gesturing with her head. Ruth Ann responded with a shrug and a nod of her head.

Alafair studied the man carefully. He was talking quietly with Governor Williams, absently fingering his gold cufflinks, a perfectly pleasant expression on his face.

Alafair leaned back toward Olivia. "Your daddy mentioned Mr. Collins to me yesterday. He sure didn't have anything good to say about him."

Olivia shrugged. She didn't appear to be surprised that her father had shared his opinion of Buck Collins with her aunt. "No, Daddy and him don't care for one another, is a mild way to say it. A lot of bad water has run under that bridge. Mr. Collins and Daddy have had a few run-ins over the years." She paused and gave the man on the podium a thoughtful glance. "There's some talk that he's a criminal."

"What is he doing up there at the podium if he's a criminal?"

Olivia gave her an ironic look. "Money and power talk loud, Aunt Alafair. Besides, he's one of the founders, you know. You can see that he's wearing one of those 'I Made the Run' buttons. Besides, he's rich as Rockefeller, and a high mucky-muck around here. Daddy says several town officials are in his pocket. He thinks that those who are ill-used by Collins are too scared to press charges or testify either."

"I declare!"

Martha, sitting on her other side, plucked her mother's sleeve. "Look yonder, Mama. I think they're about to start!"

Collins stepped up to the podium and the crowd quieted. He had to practically yell in order to be heard by the throngs of people, but he managed to do it in a surprisingly dignified way. Alafair was interested to note that he had a hint of an Irish accent that was not unlike her stepfather-in-law's. Collins welcomed everyone to the Founders' Day Commemoration in honor of the twenty-second anniversary of the Cherokee Strip Land Run of September 16, 1893. He briefly outlined the major events that were scheduled over the next three days, and invited all to visit the exhibit of agricultural products and children's artwork on display in the basement of the Collins Building on the corner of Randolph and Grand.

Alafair scrutinized Collins as he introduced Governor Williams. If she had met him on the street, she would have thought Collins the finest-looking gentleman she had ever seen. She certainly would never have picked him out for a thug and a murderer. But if he was as bad as Ruth Ann and Olivia seemed to think, it was no wonder Lester was worried at the idea that Kenneth may be involved with him in some way.

After the governor's brief opening speech, the parade, led by a showy troop of mounted Cheyenne Indians, in the full regalia of their tribe, began the march from West Broadway. Following the Indians came the band from the town of Arnett, and then the lines of old settlers, each wearing a badge which read "I Made the Run." The Brunswick band came next, just ahead of the Grand Army of the Republic, which made quite an impression on the crowd. The march of the schoolchildren was almost a whole parade by itself. Over two thousand pupils from Enid High School, St. Joseph Institute, and all the grade schools marched under the banner of their respective classes. The Boy Scouts followed, and floats representing Phillips University, headed by the university band, and the University Hospital. Practically every business in town had contributed a float, from the Union Motion Picture Operators to the Kennedy Mercantile Company to Enid Electric and Gas.

The Yeager Transfer and Storage float was decked out with a moving van and a cutaway storage unit, filled with crates, employees, and machinery. The bright red hook and ladder from the city fire department was covered with pretty decorations, and firemen in their helmets and blue uniforms hung off the sides of the truck, waving at the crowds.

The people were several rows deep and standing out in the street close to the marchers. Olivia and Ruth Ann both grew

hoarse from calling out to people they knew in the parade.. Grace set a new record for the use of her favorite word, and it was all Alafair could do to keep her from dashing out to join whatever group or float was passing by at the moment. Alafair didn't blame her. She was entirely impressed by the pageant herself.

Anxious to get back to Lester, Ruth Ann left before the parade was over, for it was so long that nearly two hours passed before the last horse made its high-stepping entrance onto the square. It was a beautiful horse, all tricked out with a Mexican silver saddle, but by that time, Alafair's senses were so overwhelmed that she barely noticed. The sky had clouded up again, and it was beginning to sprinkle, and she had had about enough excitement for one day. The girls and McCoy had wandered down the block to socialize with some of Olivia's friends, leaving Alafair with an overstimulated, exhausted, and cranky Grace. "I want candy!" the child was wailing. "I want a fried pie. I want to go!"

"I think you really want a nap," Alafair told her, to which suggestion Grace responded by wailing even louder.

Alafair picked her up and elbowed through the throngs toward Martha, who turned to meet her.

"I'm taking Grace back to the house," Alafair told her. "She needs a nap, and I want to see if I can help Ruth Ann with Lester."

Martha nodded. "Streeter is going to his office, and Olivia has invited me to come over to her house. I thought I would, unless you think I can be of some help back at Aunt Ruth Ann's."

"What about little Ron?"

"Olivia seems to think he'll be fine with Lu for an hour or two more. She said he's taking a little cereal with goat's milk, now."

"All right then, honey, you go on. I expect Olivia could use some distracting, as well."

Alafair walked back to the Yeager house, glad to get out of that milling, noisy crowd, even if she did have to drag a whiney child all the way. At least that was one sound that she was capable of tuning out, thanks to long years of practice.

She managed to get Grace upstairs by promising to tell her a story, and the girl had calmed down by the time her mother tucked her into the little pink daybed. "I liked the parade, Mama."

"I know you did, punkin. So did I. I sure am tired though. I bet you are, too."

Grace ignored the hint. "I don't think it's cold in here."

"No, it's pretty warm. I'll open a window."

"That man's pretty silly."

"What man is that, cookie?"

Grace turned over on her side and clutched her dolly to her chest. "That man I saw in the sky. He had wings on his neck."

Alafair's hands hesitated on the window sash. She looked back over her shoulder at the girl in the daybed. "Wings on his neck? Like an angel?"

A brief look of disdain passed over Grace's face. "No, not big wings like an angel, Mama. Little wings, on his neck." She demonstrated by sticking her hands out akimbo on either side of her head and wagging her fingers.

"What did he say, Mr. Wing-Neck?" Alafair asked.

Grace laughed at the appellation. "Mr. Wing-Neck said he's very cold."

"Did he say where he is that it's so cold, sugar?"

Grace snuggled down on the pink sheet. "He's nowhere, Ma. He's in the sky."

It really wasn't cold in the room, but a chill went through Alafair just the same. "That was just a dream, honey," she said. But Grace was already asleep.

Olivia's house was only two blocks from her mother's, straight down Elm Avenue to just past Kenwood. The Crawford house was much smaller than the Yeager manse, but it was still larger than the house that Martha had grown up in, with its large airy parlor, two big bedrooms with actual built-in closets, and a study for Kenneth. Not to mention a kitchen and bathroom with indoor plumbing.

Martha had been to Olivia's wedding a couple of years ago, but had never seen her house. Olivia treated her to a tour before seating her at the kitchen table, which was the proper place for a relative. While she bustled about making coffee, retrieving dishes and silverware and half a leftover white cake from the pantry, Olivia filled her cousin in on her husband's latest business undertaking.

"After Daddy got sick, Kenneth took money from the shipping business and bought himself a quarter-section of land out south of Garber, along with the mineral rights. He's sure that there's a big pool of oil just waiting to be found somewhere around Enid, and he took a notion that his field is the place. Enid's gotten to be a big oil and gas distribution center in the past few years, and they're already building a pipeline and a refinery. The Sinclair Company sunk some wells outside of Garber. That gave Kenneth the idea he could make a big strike, and all our troubles would be over.

"So when a doodlebugger came through last year, Kenneth got him to run his oil-finding machine over the ground out there. The man told Kenneth that his doodlebug machine made it possible for him to see right through the ground like it was water, and that he's sitting on a big oil deposit. He paid the man twenty-five dollars for this hogswollop! I didn't like any of it. I told Kenneth that maybe there's oil on his land and maybe there isn't, but that swindler sure didn't know which it was. But Kenneth believed him like he was Mathew, Mark, Luke, and John all rolled into one, and has mortgaged us to the hilt to hire a crew and put in a well.

"Daddy was upset that Kenneth hadn't even talked to him before he went off on this ridiculous jag. Well, there wasn't much we could do about it after the money was spent, but at least Daddy fixed it with Mr. Lawyer so Kenneth can't use the Yeager Transfer and Storage Company funds for anything but the business any more. Mike Ed keeps a close eye on the books for Daddy, so I know Kenneth hasn't drunk from that well again."

She cut a couple of pieces of the white cake and poured some coffee before she joined Martha at the table, took a bite of cake, and continued.

"I didn't like to mention it to him, but if he was so all-fired determined to put in some wells, he'll have all the money he wants when Daddy dies. What worries me is that he's gone ahead and hired a crew and partnered up with a wild-looking fellow called Pee Wee Nickolls, who drives those twisters like a teamster drives mules. They've been drilling for a couple of months, but it looks like it's going to take forever, if they're lucky enough to strike oil at all.

"They keep running out of money and having to stop for several days until they can scare up more funds. This Nickolls is crazy as a bedbug. Doesn't care about anything but his well. He's worked the oil fields all his grown-up life. He's a shooter—a nitro man. He blasts out the oil sands in the wells with nitroglycerin. I've heard from more than one that he's the best there is, but that's hard to believe from looking at him. He only has a thumb and forefinger on his right hand, a patch on his right eye, and burn scars."

Martha laughed at her description. "Well, I've known a couple of shooters in my time, and most of them are missing some kind of body part. Have you met this fellow yourself?"

"Oh, yes, several times. A young fellow. He's polite enough and all."

"But is he any good at finding oil?"

A golden brown strand of hair had come loose from Olivia's coif, and she tucked it behind her ear. "Kenneth tells me he's one of the best, but I don't know how he'd know. I hope he is, because Kenneth has gone in with Nickolls fifty-fifty. He couldn't do it alone. He doesn't have the money or the know-how. And I don't know where they're getting the money to keep the operation going, now. Kenneth won't tell me anything. I keep a weather eye on our finances, and nothing has gone missing. I'm afraid he's getting it from Buck Collins, who has probably asked him to do a couple of 'favors' in return."

"The Buck Collins who spoke before the parade this morning? Streeter said he's the one who built the Collins Building over on the northeast corner of the square."

"That's him. For the last year or so, Kenneth has been keeping company with Ellery Collins, Buck's youngest son. That's why I'm thinking Kenneth may be involved with the old man. I'm sure he's met him through Ellery."

"Well, what kind of favors do you think Kenneth is doing for such a man?"

"I'd think smuggling spirits. It would be quite a money-making proposition in a dry state like Oklahoma. Kenneth is in the shipping business, after all. It'd be a handy racket on the side for him."

"You know he's doing this?"

"I don't know for sure. But before it got outlawed altogether in the United States this year, Kenneth and Ellery and a bunch of boys used to get together one or two nights a week at Buck's big house and play cards and drink absinthe. I kind of liked Ellery. He's sort of sad and funny at the same time. Him and his dad don't get along, I hear. But it was Ellery who put Kenneth on to the absinthe. Ellery made regular trips up to Kansas to bring it in, just half-a-dozen bottles at a time, or a case, for his private use, he said. Everybody knew it, but Sheriff Hume never managed to catch him at it.

"I asked Kenneth straight out if there was more to it than that, if he was selling it, too. Told him I wouldn't appreciate being the wife of a criminal. He acted all insulted and denied it up and down. I'm hoping that since the whole U.S. government has banned it now, it's too difficult to stay in the absinthe business."

Martha was shocked. "Liquor is one thing, but that absinthe will make you insane!"

"Well, it doesn't make everybody insane. Kenneth sure likes it and went to some disturbing lengths to get it when he could. I think there're a lot of people that are of the same mind about it. And if it isn't absinthe, there's plenty of other illegal spirits that dishonest folks will pay money for, though. I know my Kenneth. He wants to be a good husband and father, wants to provide for us, but I fear he's not long on scruples."

Martha hesitated a moment before she responded. "I hope you won't be insulted when I say I never thought Kenneth was really suited to the shipping business. But I surely never thought he was crooked! What makes you think so?"

Olivia shrugged. "I'm not insulted. Kenneth never thought he was particularly suited to the shipping business either. Since Daddy got so bad he had to give up going in to the office, Mike Ed Beams has been keeping me up on things. A couple of times during the last month, the teamsters have told him there were some crates in the warehouse that weren't on the shipping manifests. But by the time Mike Ed got down there to see what was what, the extra crates had disappeared, and nobody seems to know anything about them."

She put down her fork, upset by her own story. "In fact, I'm pretty scared, Cousin Martha. I can't think of any other way Kenneth could keep getting money except from doing bad things for Collins. And if he has his claws into Kenneth, then I'm afraid we're up a creek. Even if that oil well comes in big and Kenneth pays him back every nickel he borrowed, Buck Collins will find some way to take the well from him. And if Kenneth used them as collateral, Collins could take our house and probably our share of the warehouse."

Martha grasped Olivia's arm across the table. "Oh, Olivia, I'm so sorry. I had no idea it was so bad. Have you talked to your parents about this?"

"No. Mama wouldn't have any idea what to do, and I don't know what Daddy could do, now. Besides, I don't want to send him to his rest with this worry on his soul."

"What about a lawyer, Olivia? Surely you could at least get some legal advice."

Olivia shrugged. "I've thought about it, though I haven't done it yet. My father's lawyer, Russ Lawyer, is a good man, and he hates Buck Collins like poison. But can I go behind my husband's back? The truth is I have no proof that Kenneth is in debt to Buck Collins. Even if I did, I don't know if any lawyer would even talk to me about my husband's business without his permission."

This statement gave Martha an immediate stabbing pain behind her eyes. She closed them and rubbed her forehead with one hand. "Certainly none will," she agreed carefully, eyes still shut, "unless you ask."

Olivia considered this. "You're right. I ought at least to try. But I'd feel more certain about it if I had some proof, some papers or something."

"Do you have any idea where Kenneth might keep such a thing?"

"Well, not in the house where I might find it, surely. Maybe in the safe at the warehouse, but I've never looked to see."

"You should look around the house and in his office at the warehouse while he's gone. See if you can find something that'll tell you what he's been up to. At least you'd know what you're facing."

"Why, I'll do it! Thank you, Martha. I don't know if it'll do any good, but at least I'll feel like I'm not just sitting around waiting for the sky to fall in on me." Invigorated by hope, she picked up her fork and ate another bite of cake.

Lester's face was pinched and he didn't seem comfortable, but his eyes were closed and his breathing regular. Alafair sat by his bed long enough to assure herself that he really was sleeping, then gathered herself up and crept out of the room. Grace was not in bed, where she had left her. Since they had gotten to Enid, Grace was not sleeping normally, and Alafair determined that she was going to have to keep a closer watch on her naps. She peeked in the other bedrooms down the hall and found Ruth Ann, clad only in her shift, sound asleep in one of them, but no Grace. She went downstairs feeling—not alarmed, exactly—but pressed to locate an active little girl loose in a strange house.

As she passed through the parlor, she heard childish laughter coming from the kitchen and altered her course with a sigh of relief.

She found Grace sitting on several pillows at the kitchen table, dipping a cookie into a ceramic mug of milk, chattering away at a middle-aged Asian man who was sitting across the table from her. Lu was at the counter, peeling vegetables with her back to the door. Little Ron was kicking and gurgling in a bassinet in the corner.

When Alafair opened the kitchen door, Lu turned around and the man stood. Grace gestured at her mother with her cookie. "Look, Ma, I got a Chinese cookie! I can count in Chinese, listen—*yi, er, san*. Ma, what's *Chinese*?"

"I'll tell you later, sweet pea." She looked at Lu. "She hasn't been sleeping her nap like she does at home. I'm sorry if she's bothering you."

"No bother, no bother," Lu assured her. "Good little girl, like my granddaughter." She pointed at the standing man with the tip of her paring knife. "Miz Tucker, this my son, Arnold Han. He drive truck, make delivery. Drive up today from Oklahoma City with supplies for fair, come visit his Ma."

Arnold was standing quietly with the fingertips of one hand perched on the tabletop and the other by his side. He was much bigger than his mother, but still less than average-sized. He was dressed in a trim dark uniform with a small logo over the breast pocket that said "Birk Trucking Company." His black hair was long on top and slicked straight back from his face, and he regarded her calmly out of eyes so black that she couldn't discern his pupils from his irises. They nodded at one another. "How do you do, Miz Tucker," he said.

As far as Alafair could tell, he had no Chinese accent whatsoever. "Just fine, Arnold," she replied. "Nice to meet a man who visits his mother regular."

A whisper of amusement passed over his face. "I do my best, ma'am, but I'm afraid I can't get up here enough to suit Ma."

"I expect no son does. Sit down, Arnold. I don't stand on ceremony in my sister's house." She turned back to Lu. "I've just come from Mr. Yeager's bedside, Lu. I gave him a dose of medicine about half an hour ago, and he's got to sleep. I expect he'll be out

for a couple of hours. I'll take Grace out of your hair, now, and let you get on with supper. I'd be glad to take Ron, too, if you've a mind. Let you visit with your son without so many distractions." She glanced at Arnold, who had not taken her up on her invitation to sit and was still standing by the table, with his arms crossed over his chest. Patiently waiting for her to leave.

Lu shook her head. "I no mind Ron. Very good baby. Miz Yeager, she go upstairs to rest a long time ago. I check Mr. Yeager directly."

"Yes, I saw my sister napping when I came down. Come on, Grace, let's go see if we can make ourselves useful around here."

Having determined some minutes before that the adults' conversation was going to culminate in her being removed from the kitchen, Grace was busily stuffing little milk-soaked almond cookies in her mouth. Alafair grabbed up a napkin and wiped off the trail of milk and crumbs that adorned her chin and the front of her smock. "I declare, girl, I'm sure these folks are mighty impressed with your dainty manners."

As she hustled Grace out of the kitchen, she just caught sight of Arnold finally sitting back down at the table. It took them a couple of minutes to get back up to the second floor, since Grace was a bit chary of the stairs but too independent to allow her mother to help her. So Alafair followed slowly behind as Grace hoisted herself up the staircase one step at a time on her feet and hands. Coming down was an even lengthier proposition, but Alafair didn't care. She was glad that Grace was just wary enough to be careful. When some of her other kids were three years old—Charlie and Alice came immediately to mind—they would have gone roaring up and down the stairs and pitched headlong to their deaths in a minute without constant supervision.

Alafair was worried about waking her emotionally exhausted sister, but when they finally got to the second floor landing, she could see through the open bedroom door that Ruth Ann was sitting up on the edge of the bed. She stood and scrubbed her

sleep-creased face with both hands as Alafair and Grace walked into the room.

"Lester's asleep," Alafair opened, and Ruth Ann nodded.

"Yes, I just checked on him. Did you like the parade, Grace?"

Grace scrambled up onto the bed and proceeded to tell her aunt all about it as Alafair moved unhurriedly around the room, retrieving a dress that had been flung over the back of a chair, stockings from the end of the bed, shoes from under the dressing table, and helping Ruth Ann put herself back together.

Ruth Ann was sitting at the dressing table and Alafair was brushing and arranging her sister's long, chestnut-colored hair by the time Grace was relating the tale of the almond cookies.

"My, my, baby," Ruth Ann exclaimed. "Sounds like you've had quite a day!"

"Oh, she has," Alafair answered for her. "And she didn't have much of a nap, either. I expect I'll have one cranky little gal on my hands come this evening."

Grace was highly affronted by this remark. "I'm sweet as pie, Ma."

"Crabapple pie, maybe," Alafair teased, as she rolled Ruth Ann's hair into a long coil at her neck. "Come here and hold this box of hairpins for me."

Grace leaped to the job and Alafair turned back to her sister, who was sitting with her eyes closed, enjoying the feel of hands gently ministering to her.

"Do you remember how Mama used to sit the three of us girls down in front of the fire at night and brush our hair like this?" Alafair asked.

Ruth Ann smiled. "I loved that. She'd go on at it for hours. When she'd get done, I'd be so relaxed I'd practically have to be carried to bed. She'd twist our hair up in rags so it'd be curly in the morning."

"I'd get so impatient I'd like to jump out of my skin. I couldn't hold still long enough for her to get them rags the way she wanted them. Maybe that's why I never can do a thing with my hair to this day."

"I sure will be glad when Mama gets here."

Alafair nodded. In times of trouble, even middle-aged women sometimes longed for their mothers. "Are you feeling better after your lie-down, Ruth Ann?"

Ruth Ann opened her eyes and regarded Alafair's reflection in the mirror. "A little bit. I wish Kenneth would come home, though."

"Yes, Lester said that was preying on your mind."

"Oh, Kenneth takes these long business trips regular, and it's not unusual that he comes home a day later or a day earlier than he reckoned. But he always wires Olivia once or twice while he's away, and he hasn't done it at all this time."

Alafair's hand paused in mid-stroke. Ruth Ann's worry, coming so close on the heels of Lester's rant about their son-in-law, gave her a jolt of alarm. She found herself remembering her dream of Kenneth, and Grace's strange remarks. Her concern must have shown on her face, because Ruth Ann said, "What's wrong?"

Alafair fiercely tamped down her dread and poked a hairpin into Ruth Ann's hairdo. "I just don't like to see you worrying about Kenneth, on top of everything. I'm sure his business has taken him a little longer than he expected, and he's in such a rush to get it done and get home that he just hasn't taken the time to find a telephone or a Western Union office."

Ruth Ann considered this theory and apparently liked it, because the tension in her face eased. "Yes, I'm sure you're right. That sounds just like what he would do."

Alafair put down the brush and placed her hands on Ruth Ann's shoulders while they regarded her hairdressing artistry in the mirror. "How does Aunt Ruth Ann look, Grace?"

"Beautiful," Grace stated, and the women laughed.

"Now, Sister, I think a bit of exercise would do you good," Alafair said. "Martha is over to Olivia's and Lu has little Ron downstairs. Lester is having a good sleep. I think me and Grace are going to tend to your garden in the back. The rain has perked it up considerable, but I noticed this morning that it could use a good weed. Everything is well in hand for a while, so I'm going to hand you your hat and scoot you out the door for an hour or so. There's still a passel of things for you to see at the Founders' celebration."

"Oh, I don't know, Alafair."

"It'll refresh you, and you'll be better able to comfort and support Lester. I figured you'd like to take a stroll on your own and be relieved of the need to visit for a bit, but if you have a yen for company, me and Grace would be proud to come with you."

"No need for that. You're right, I wouldn't mind some time to myself. So I guess I'll let you boss me yet again, just like I always did when we were kids."

Alafair snorted, mostly amused but a little embarrassed by her sister's comment. "Well, I ought to apologize for being such a tyrant back then, I expect. But having you younger sisters and brothers to order about sure turned out to be good practice for my mothering career."

They walked together out of the bedroom and to the stairs, where they patiently went down beside Grace as she picked her way toward the bottom one step at a time. Ike trotted past on his way downstairs, intent on his own business.

Martha stretched one arm over the back of her chair and eyed her cousin thoughtfully. Since Olivia had brought up the subject of husbands, she decided to take advantage of the opportunity to garner another opinion on the subject of marriage. "Are you sorry you married him?"

Olivia didn't seem surprised or offended, but she did skirt the question. "I do care for him, Martha. And he does try. But I can see plain as day where he goes wrong. He hates the shipping business. I wish he'd just forget about working at the warehouse and do something he likes. I can run the business, with Mr. Beams' help. Yet Kenneth would rather eat dirt than to take advice from his wife." She gave a rueful smile. "Well, marriage isn't easy, as my mother tells me ten times a day. I figure he'll grow up one of these days, and then we'll be happy enough with each other. I'd be a bunch happier right now if he'd quit trying to be a big shot, though."

"So would you do it again, if you had the chance?"

"I might wait a few years," she admitted. "But of course I wouldn't give all the gold in Fort Knox for little Ron."

An introspective silence fell as the two women pondered their fates. The rain had stopped and Olivia had opened all the windows on the north and east sides, to let in the breeze and air out the house. A light wind was rustling the trees and bushes in the yard, and Olivia could hear the distant sounds of the Founders' celebration taking place a few blocks away. The clouds were breaking up. A swath of sunlight suddenly poured through the open back door and lit a path across the kitchen floor.

"I found where Kenneth hid his latest bottle of absinthe," Olivia said.

Martha blinked at this unexpected statement. "You don't say?"

"Up in the top of the closet in his study, behind some boxes of papers. It's been opened. About two-thirds full."

"Is that so? I'm surprised you haven't poured it out. He could get arrested if the wrong person catches him with it."

"Oh, I've poured many a bottle down the drain over the last two years. He just brings in another and finds someplace else to stash it. Funny, he has to know I'm the one who finds the bottles and gets rid of them, but we've never said one word about it to each other."

"You mean to say that in all this time you've never told him you want him to quit it?"

Olivia snorted. "Of course I have. When we were first married. But he just laughed at me for worrying and said it was none of my business."

"That's annoying."

"Thing is, Martha, when I found this last bottle, I went to pour it down the sink, like I did with the others, but I'll be jiggered if I didn't just stand there and look at it in my hand for the longest time. Finally, I put it back where I found it. I'll get rid of it, too, one of these days. But, you know, I begin to wonder what the attraction is."

Martha studied her cousin for a minute while she considered what to say to this revelation.

Olivia stared back at her, her brown eyes calm. She reached up and adjusted her glasses before she continued. "You ever been curious to find out what spirits taste like?"

Martha opened her mouth to reply, but Olivia cut her off. "Are you shocked?"

The idea made Martha laugh. "If I figure right, Olivia, you're telling me that you're aiming to take a taste of the stuff before you toss it out, and you're looking for an accomplice."

"Well, yes, if you want to come right out with it. Have you ever tasted liquor before?"

"I can't say as I have. I've seen it, though, and seen plenty of people in a bad way because of it. Have you ever had any?"

"Never. Are you interested in taking a step or two down the dark path with me?"

"Mama would keel over dead."

"So would my mama, but I don't intend that either of them ever find out about it."

"Won't they smell it on our breath?"

"Well, Martha, I'm not proposing that we get falling down drunk. Just one sip, that's all, then down the drain she goes." She demonstrated with a swooshing motion.

"I have to admit I've had the odd curious thought, Cousin. And we are both over twenty-one, after all. Of course, it is still illegal. If the law busts in on us right about now, I reckon we'll be shamed forever and have to leave the state."

"After our stretch in prison, that is. In the little cabinet over the sink, there're some special glasses Kenneth got for drinking the stuff before it was outlawed. They have little bulbs at the bottom. You can't mistake them. Why don't you get down a couple of those for us? I'll fetch the bottle and be right back."

Olivia stood and disappeared into the study at the back. Martha knew her mother would disapprove mightily, but she felt no guilt whatsoever. Just a little bit naughty and a slight thrill at the adventure.

Olivia returned with a slender, opaque bottle and set it on the table next to the two glasses that Martha had retrieved from the cabinet. She filled a tin pitcher with water from the faucet at her kitchen sink and dropped a couple of handfuls of ice chips into it from the top of the icebox. She then put the pitcher on the table, took a large slotted silver spoon from a drawer, and completed her preparations by setting the sugar bowl in the midst of it all. Finally the two women sat down at the table and pondered the pretty bottle and glasses thoughtfully. They both looked up and locked eyes across the table at the same time, and burst into laughter.

"Well, here we go," Olivia said. "I've seen Kenneth and his friends do this enough times, so I reckon I'm doing it right." She uncorked the bottle and filled the bulbous reservoirs at the bottom of the glasses with the emerald green liquor.

"How pretty!" Martha exclaimed.

"Just watch this."

Olivia balanced the slotted spoon over the mouth of one of the glasses and deposited a sugar cube into the bowl of the spoon. She took the pitcher and slowly tipped it over one of the glasses, allowing iced water to drip over the sugar cube and through the slots one drop at a time.

As it hit the clear green liquid, each drop of the sweetened water burst into a pearly, opaque bloom, which swirled and danced in patterns through the drink like windblown clouds.

"Oh, my goodness," Martha managed.

"Kenneth called that changing color the 'louche.' I figure it's part of the appeal."

Olivia patiently filled both glasses nearly to the brim before she corked the bottle. Then each woman lifted her glass and examined its seductive contents for a long moment.

Martha finally broke the silence. "Well, here's hoping…"

"*Chin-chin*, as Lu likes to say."

They clinked their glasses and took a tentative sip. Martha rolled the slightly viscous drink around on her tongue for a moment, testing the flavor as carefully as the most discerning wine enthusiast. "A little bitter," she observed.

"Tastes herby. A bit like licorice."

"Goes right up my nose."

"It's kind of nice," Olivia admitted.

Martha took another sip, larger than the first one, and swished it around in her mouth before swallowing. "I declare, it's making my tongue numb!"

"Mine too. I feel warm in my throat."

"I'm getting a warm feeling in my chest. Are you feeling insane yet?"

"Can't say as I am. But maybe I just don't know it. Do you suppose insane folks know they're insane?"

Martha's next sip was more like a mouthful, and she didn't bother to study the taste much before she swallowed it. "I doubt it. That's one of the problems with being insane."

Olivia slouched back in her chair. "I don't feel much different. Just warmer."

"It probably takes a while to get to your head."

"It made my tongue numb right quick," Olivia pointed out.

"Maybe drunks don't know they're drunk."

"Do I seem drunk to you?"

"No."

"You don't to me, either."

The conversation suddenly struck Martha as exceedingly odd. She pushed her glass away and stood up. "I think we'd better pour this out right now."

Olivia blinked at her. "You don't like it?"

"Yes, Cousin, I like it a lot. That's what's scaring the liver out of me."

Martha's alarm was infectious, and Olivia succumbed immediately. She leaped to her feet, grabbed Martha's glass along with her own, and dashed what was left of their drinks into the sink, followed shortly by the remains of the bottle.

Olivia sat back down at the table once the offending liquid was safely down the drain. "Surely you can't fall prey to it so quick," she said. "Surely we were just enjoying the curiosity of it all."

"I don't intend to give myself another opportunity to find out," Martha assured her.

When Martha got back to her aunt's house, Alafair was tending the children, Lu was with Lester, and Ruth Ann had taken advantage of the break to get out of the house for a little while. Martha didn't feel particularly affected by her few swallows of the demon drink, but she was wary enough of Alafair's extraordinary perception that she was relieved not to have to do more than say hello when she first got back.

Not that I have to explain myself to my mother, she thought.

Olivia had gone to the warehouse to talk to Mike Ed Beams again, which took Martha aback. Alafair would never have spent four or five hours at a time apart from a four-month-old. But Olivia apparently had no such scruples, which was a new and intriguing concept for Martha. She unburdened Alafair of Grace and little Ron, allowing her mother to go back to Lester and the housekeeper to finish supper. She then spent the rest of the afternoon changing diapers, getting snacks, listening to stories, watching Grace dig a hole in the back garden while she restrained a very interested cat, all the while pondering her cousin's problem.

Supper was another enormous affair. Martha had no intention of discussing Olivia's concerns in front of her aunt, so she kept her counsel and joined in the discussion about the fair, the weather, and Uncle Lester's condition.

Lu served up bean soup, an unusual spiced beef dish, mashed potatoes, scalloped onions, and some sort of strange vegetable called "parsnips," which she had dredged in flour and fried. They had finished with an apple cornmeal pudding with a sweet, rich, cinnamony sauce, and hot tea with a sprig of peppermint in it.

They repaired to the parlor after supper, but after such a meal no one was in the mood for conversation and eventually retired to their rooms. Martha climbed to the top of the house and sat on the bed in her attic room for half an hour or so, until she was reasonably sure that her aunt was abed and Grace was taken care of. Then she slipped down the stairs to the second floor, tapped on her mother's door, and entered without waiting for an invitation.

Grace was asleep in the big bed, and Alafair was sitting at the dresser in her nightgown, brushing her hair. Martha closed the door behind herself, and Alafair turned around on the stool to give her a curious look.

"What's up, sugar?"

"Can I talk to you for a minute, Mama?"

"Of course, darlin'." Alafair stood up and gestured to the two chairs nestled into the alcove formed by the small bay window. After they sat down, Martha began the conversation as innocuously as she could.

"That was some supper."

Alafair smiled, willing to make small talk if that was Martha's desire. "It certainly was. How do you figure these city folks can manage not to ruin their constitutions? They sit around all day and then eat like the Sultan of Araby at night. I don't know how a body's supposed to sleep with her stomach packed like a sausage. I expect to have wild dreams all night."

"Doesn't seem to have bothered Grace any."

"No, she went out like somebody clonked her on the head."

"How'd you get her to take off her new shoes?"

"I didn't."

"Do you mean to tell me that you've been letting her wear her shoes to bed?" Martha was shocked to her core.

"I just didn't feel like fighting about it," Alafair admitted. "I did scrub off the bottoms with soap and water, so as not to ruin Ruth Ann's nice sheets."

"You sure do let her get away with a lot more than you did me."

Alafair heard the slightest hint of resentment in Martha's tone, and she laughed. "I had a lot more energy when you older ones were little, but y'all have managed to suck most of it out of me by now."

"So it's our fault?"

"That's how I'm telling it."

Martha smiled and shook her head, then broached the subject she had come in to discuss. "Ma, I'm pretty worried about Olivia. She told me some things about Kenneth this afternoon that didn't sit well at all. She's afraid that he's gotten himself into some mischief. She said he diverted some funds from the Transfer and Storage to buy a piece of land south of Garber to drop a test well." She filled her mother in on Olivia's fear that Kenneth had resorted to borrowing money from the evil Collins. "If she's right," she finished, "it sounds to me like Uncle Lester is all that's standing between them and financial ruin. When he finally passes on, Olivia and Kenneth will inherit the business, and Olivia thinks this Collins will figure out a way to get it away from them, as well as the land and the oil well."

As she listened to Martha's story, Alafair grew concerned. "Yesterday afternoon, Uncle Lester was champing at the bit to tell me more or less the same tale."

"Uncle Lester knows? I don't think Olivia is aware her dad suspects that Kenneth may be mixed up with Collins. She said she didn't want to worry him with it."

"Well, he does know, but he thinks that he nipped Kenneth's folly in the bud before he got around to approaching the Collins family for money. He bent Kenneth's ear about it good a while ago, let him know that he was on to his shenanigans. I imagine that's why Kenneth is bending his back to the plow so hard, lately—trying to get back in his father-in-law's good graces. Lester told me that Kenneth promised he'd divest himself of his friend Ellery Collins, and as far as he knew, he did. Ellery left town to go back east last month, which Lester took to indicate that him and Kenneth are quits."

"That's what Olivia thought, Ma! It looks like Olivia and Uncle Lester have been trying to protect each other from the sad truth. If they'd confided in each other from the beginning, they'd probably both feel a lot better. You think it'd be all right if I told Olivia what Uncle Lester said to you?"

"I don't know why not, things being as they are."

"How much do you suspect Aunt Ruth Ann knows about Kenneth's foolish ways?"

"Probably nothing, if the way she talks about Kenneth means anything. Ruth Ann is generally more than happy to be protected from unhappy facts."

"Oh, I could strangle that Kenneth for putting Olivia and Uncle Lester through this. I hope he's seen the light for good and all. I'm like to give him the benefit of my opinion when he finally gets home."

Alafair's gaze wandered off and for a few minutes she rocked in her rocking chair and stared at a gloomy corner across the room. Finally she stopped rocking and looked over at Martha. "Honey, has Olivia mentioned whether or not Kenneth has contacted her during this trip?"

"No, she mentioned particularly that he hasn't."

"Does she seem worried about him at all?"

"No, doesn't seem to be. He's not overdue by that much. What're you thinking, Ma?"

Alafair shook her head. "Well, I'm thinking that Kenneth might not be coming home."

Martha couldn't restrain a gasp. "You think he's scampered? Why on earth…?"

Alafair spoke over her. "Now, don't you be breathing a word of this to Olivia or Ruth Ann. It's just a hunch. A quiver in my innards. I fear Kenneth may have run afoul of Collins, or some other scoundrel, in spite of Lester's warning, and has either run from his troubles or met with foul play."

"You must have some reason for thinking so, Mama."

An ironic look passed over Alafair's face. "Not anything I want to be generally known, at least right now. Tell me, does

Olivia know where Kenneth was supposed to be going on this trip, who exactly he was supposed to be calling on?"

Martha was a practical young woman, not at all given to belief in psychic powers. But she had seen enough evidence throughout her life to believe in her mother's intuitive skills utterly. "She mentioned that he was going to Guymon, and a couple of other places I can't remember right now. I expect she or Mike Ed or Uncle Lester knows who all he was supposed to call on. There's probably a list somewhere, an itinerary."

"Ask her about it. If Kenneth doesn't show up tomorrow morning, suggest to her that she wire the places he was supposed to visit, see if he actually made it."

"I'll do it. And then what will we do if he didn't?"

"Call out the law, of course." She resumed her rocking and staring for a few minutes while Martha tried to come to grips with the situation.

"Well," Martha finally ventured, "Olivia said she thinks Kenneth isn't that interested in her daddy's business, and really hates the icehouse and refrigerators. So he probably wouldn't care that much if they had to sell it. But she thinks he loves that wildcat well. And I can't see him doing anything that could lose him Olivia."

Alafair sat bolt upright, suddenly feeling pretty icy herself. "Ruth Ann told me that Kenneth hates to be cold," she remembered. "In fact, she said that was one reason he came down here from Michigan, to get away from the horrible cold winters."

"What are you thinking, Mama?"

"See if Olivia can find out if Kenneth made it to Guymon, honey, and then I'll know what to tell you."

Thursday, September 16, 1915

Martha kept up a brisk pace down Maine, elbowing her way through the carnival crowds as she walked across the square on her way from the Western Union office to Aunt Ruth Ann's, so distracted by her thoughts that she didn't realize that she was being accompanied until she heard someone calling her name.

And how that was, she couldn't imagine, because the noise from the motorcycle tailing her from the street was loud enough to wake Rip Van Winkle. She stopped walking and turned, and Streeter McCoy pulled up beside her and grinned from the seat of his brand-new Harley-Davidson Model 11-F three-speed twin.

"Good morning, Martha," he said, raising his voice to be heard over the engine idle. "My, you seem to be engrossed by something."

She blinked at him, coming into the present. "Oh. Streeter. I forgot about your motorcycle race this morning. I reckon that's what all the racket was. Rattled my teeth all the way over to Olivia's house. How'd you do?"

"Came in third." He shrugged, but didn't look unhappy about it. "I'm entered in another race at one o'clock, if you'd like to take the opportunity to cheer me on."

Martha eyed him before she replied. His sandy hair was hidden under a leather helmet. The unfastened chinstrap dangled loose, and a pair of goggles perched on top of his head. His face was gray with dust, except for the white, raccoon-like mask that circled his eyes where the goggles had protected them. He wore a grimy leather jacket and tan jodhpurs which were tucked into a pair of tall brown cowhide boots that laced all the way up the front. His hands gripped the handlebars and one booted foot was balanced on the ground. He was still grinning at her. "You're a sight," she observed. "Where's the sidecar you usually have when you drive around Boynton?"

"It's parked in the hotel stable until after the races. But I can hook it up fast if you'd like to take a ride."

"Sorry, Streeter, but I'm busy with family right now. I need to get home. The situation with my aunt's family just keeps getting more and more complicated."

McCoy's grin faded at her obvious distress, and he dismounted the cycle, dropped the kick bar, and stepped up on the curb next to her. "What's the matter, Martha? Is there anything I can do to help?"

She looked up at him in silence for a moment, while she considered whether or not she wanted to involve him in this tangle. She was entirely torn. She had accompanied her mother to Enid specifically to get away from him, after all. But she did admire his sense, and the idea of being able to express her fears to a friend was appealing. Especially this friend.

She heaved a sigh and made her decision. "Oh, all right, Streeter. Actually, it may be a good thing that you turned up. I think my cousin may be in a fix, and I want to help her. But even worse, I'm afraid my mother is going to haul off and get herself into some pickle again. She has a habit of sniffing around where she isn't welcome and running afoul of folks who want to do her harm. There's no way to stop her once she gets to going, but maybe between the two of us, we can keep her out of trouble."

"I'd be happy to do whatever I can. What seems to be the problem?"

"You know that Olivia's husband Kenneth is supposed to be on a business trip to Guymon?"

"Yes."

"He said he'd be back before the Founders' Jubilee started, but he hasn't turned up yet. Olivia wasn't particularly worried, since he's often a day or two off on his return from these trips, one way or the other. Well, my mother got a bee in her bonnet that something has happened to Kenneth..."

"What..." he attempted, but she cut him off with a look and continued.

"Ma suggested that I go over to Olivia's today and get her to wire around to the places Kenneth had told her he was going to call on, and make sure that he had actually done it. Well, I humored her, because it's hard to get Mama off a trail once she's got a scent in her nostrils. I went with Olivia to Western Union just now, and she sent a wire to Kenneth's contact in Guymon. And lo and behold, not only did he never show up, he never even made an appointment to show up in the first place. So she got panicky and telephoned all the other stops he had listed, and turns out he never made it to any of them. So now she's out of her mind with worry, and this is just going to upset Aunt Ruth Ann and Uncle Lester no end. I'm on my way back to tell Mama that her hunch has stirred up a hornet's nest good and proper. I told Olivia to call the police, but other than that, I don't know what we can do to help her." She shook her head. "To tell the truth, Olivia is more mad than worried. She thinks Kenneth is probably up to no good—bringing liquor in from Kansas or some such."

"Why are you worried about what your mother might do?"

Martha chewed her lip for a second before she answered. "She didn't say it right out loud, but I think she's decided that Kenneth is dead."

McCoy blinked at her. "How'd she decide that?"

"Who knows how Mama decides anything? She makes these connections...I don't know. But she told me that if we couldn't scare Kenneth up, she's going to go down to my uncle's warehouse and ask the manager, Mr. Beams, to let her look inside the cold storage lockers."

"What in the Sam Hill for?"

"I'm guessing she thinks Kenneth is in one of them."

McCoy's eyes widened and he laughed, which gave Martha an odd stab of resentment even though she rather agreed that the whole idea was ludicrous. "No matter what you think of it, she's going to do it, and I'd just as soon she'd not go haring off by herself." Martha spoke a little louder than she intended.

McCoy knew he'd made an error, though he wasn't entirely sure what it was. He hastened to correct his attitude. "My goodness! This does sound worrisome. You're right to go to the police. They can get in touch with the law out in the No-Man's Land, ask for them to keep an eye out. I have a land office in Guymon. Just a part-time agent, covers most of Texas County. If I can have a list of places Kenneth has been known to go out there, I'll send my man a telegram right away, have him ask around, see what he can turn up."

He stepped back into the street and remounted his motorcycle. "Go on back to your aunt's house, and I'll come by after I get this done and we'll decide what to do next."

"Now, wait a minute." Martha was plainly irritated at his attitude. "There's no call for you to rush in like the cavalry and save us just yet."

He paused with his foot on the starter, taken aback that she should see it that way.

She gauged the look on his face and relented just a little. "What I mean, Streeter, is that I'd appreciate it if you'd wire your agent in Guymon. Why don't you go ahead to the Western Union office and send that telegram, then run your race like you intended? Are you going to be in your office later today?"

"I hadn't planned on it. I gave Mr. Miller the day off. I expected to go back to the hotel after the races and get cleaned up."

"Well, that's good. If you'll call on me later at Aunt Ruth Ann's I'll let you know what's happening. If Ma really does decide to go to the warehouse, I'll suggest to her that it might be useful if you went along."

"All right, then."

Martha nodded and took an awkward leave of him. Streeter sat on his bike for a long time, with the crowd flowing around him like water as he watched her walk away. He felt a slight irritation of his own. He could never figure out the right thing to say to her to save his life.

Mike Ed Beams had worked for the Yeager Transfer and Storage Company for exactly twenty years, since it had operated out of a hastily constructed wooden building about a fifth the size of the one in which it was now housed. He had worked his way up from mover to teamster to clerk to manager. And now, since Lester Yeager's illness, he was to all intents and purposes running the business all by himself. Kenneth Crawford may have been part owner of the business, but as far as Mike Ed was concerned, that was just on paper. Kenneth didn't have the sense God gave a goose, and Mike Ed felt under no obligation to pay attention to him, at least not while Lester Yeager was still alive. As for what he was going to do after Lester passed, he didn't really know. He liked his job, and he was good at it. He didn't want to quit, but working for Kenneth would be intolerable. His best hope was that Kenneth would hold true to form and be too impatient to attend to the daily nuts and bolts of running the business, and either leave it to his wife, Olivia, or to Mike Ed himself.

Mike Ed had never worked for a woman before, but he had known Olivia since she was a little girl, and he admired her grasp of business. Taking orders from her was certainly a better option than working for Kenneth.

He was sitting in his office on the warehouse floor, going over shipping orders and pondering this very problem, when someone knocked on his door and startled him out of his reverie.

He had only met Mrs. Yeager's relatives a couple of times in passing over the years, but he had heard that her kin were in town. So when he looked at the women through the glass in his office door, he immediately recognized the older one as Mrs. Yeager's sister, Mrs. Tucker. She was colored differently, but otherwise, the woman's face resembled Mrs. Yeager's quite a bit. Mrs. Yeager had another dark-haired sister who lived in Arizona, Mike Ed knew, but there was no mistaking which one this was. The eldest of the Gunn sisters had a direct gaze that could bore a hole right through you. The younger woman was obviously Mrs. Tucker's daughter, but he didn't know the well-dressed man who accompanied them.

Mike Ed opened the door and ushered his visitors into the office. The two women took the seats before his desk, all the while exchanging pleasantries and bemoaning poor Lester's condition. The man shook his hand and quietly sat himself in a chair in a corner, which told Mike Ed who was in charge of this expedition. When they were well settled and all introductions properly made, Mrs. Tucker launched right into the reason for their visit without waiting for an invitation.

"Mr. Beams, am I right in thinking that you have a master key to the rented cold storage lockers back there in the back of the warehouse?"

"Yes, ma'am, I do. Did Miz Yeager send you to fetch something for her?"

Alafair hesitated and glanced at Martha. For an instant, she considered saying yes, since this was such a logical assumption. But that would only get her into one locker, and she wanted to inspect all six of the ones big enough to hide a body.

Martha relieved Alafair of the decision to lie. "No, sir, Mr. Beams," she said. "As you've probably realized by now, my cousin's husband, Kenneth, is overdue to return from his latest business trip."

"Please call me Mike Ed, ma'am. And, yes, I know about Kenneth. It's not unusual for him to be late from these trips." He wondered what this had to do with anything.

"Olivia wired the companies on his itinerary list and he never called on a single one," Martha told him.

"Oh?"

"Were you by any chance aware that Olivia thinks that Kenneth owes money to Buck Collins?"

Mike Ed drew a sharp breath in spite of himself. "I hate to hear that."

Alafair took up the tale. "My sister and I had a little walk-through of the facilities here on Wednesday, while we were at the fair. It was real quiet, and nobody was on the warehouse floor, so we didn't figure to be interrupting anything at the time. When we got over by the lockers, I found a gold collar stud on the floor, exactly like the ones that my sister tells me Kenneth likes to wear. Now, both my sister and my niece say that Kenneth hates the cold worse than anything. So if that stud belongs to him, how did it end up there? And since it turns out that no one knows where Kenneth is, I propose to have a look in those lockers."

Mike Ed was aghast that this perfectly conventional-looking woman would come up with such a notion. "If you're suggesting what I think you're suggesting, Miz Tucker, I've got to say that it's mighty unlikely. There are people in and out of those lockers all the time. And if you fear that something evil has happened to Kenneth Crawford, why not just go to the police?"

"I don't want to put words to what I fear. I agree with you that it's mighty unlikely. My evidence is pretty thin, and I don't believe that the police would take me very seriously at all. I don't want to be upsetting my niece or sister with my suspicions, either. If I could have figured out a way for us to check inside the lockers without anybody knowing, we would have. But aside from busting in to the place after dark, we couldn't come up with anything. Lester thinks mighty highly of you, Mike Ed, so I feel safe in telling you my suspicions. You know what Kenneth is like, and you know Buck Collins. All I want to do is have a quick gander inside the lockers that are big enough for a side of beef."

Mike Ed shot an incredulous glance toward McCoy, but if he was expecting an expression of male solidarity against this female illogic, he was disappointed. McCoy perched his elbows on the arms of the chair and gave Mike Ed a pleasant and totally unrevealing smile. Mike Ed slouched forward with his elbows on his desk and eyeballed the woman across from him with extreme skepticism. "Or a body?"

"Like I said, I don't want to put words to my fears. I hate to be bothering you, but it should only take five minutes to have a peek, and then my fears would be laid to rest."

Mike Ed flopped back in the chair. "Well, Miz Tucker, this is the most dad-blamed wild notion I've heard in a long time, pardon me for saying so. If I didn't have such high regard for the Yeagers and their kin, I'd be inclined to send you packing. But just to set your mind at ease, I'll take you back there and you can examine the citizens of Enid's slabs of meat to your heart's content."

Alafair nodded and stood, not at all surprised that this strange errand had gone just the way she wanted it to. "Five minutes, Mike Ed. I'll not keep you longer than that."

Martha and McCoy trailed behind the manager and Alafair as they trekked across the warehouse floor, weaving between trucks and bales and boxes of goods on their way to the refrigerated rooms on the far end of the building. All the while Martha was wondering how Alafair managed with such regularity to get people to do whatever unlikely thing she asked of them. If Martha herself had been as straightforward with Mike Ed Beams, would he have indulged her like he had her mother? Somehow Martha didn't think so. Alafair had a talent for carrying people away on the tide of her certainty.

Or maybe it was just that folks were loath to say no to someone who reminded them so forcefully of their own mothers.

She gave Streeter a sidelong glance to judge his reaction, but he was sauntering along as calmly as if he were escorting his best girl on a stroll in the park. Her mouth quirked.

Mike Ed obviously wasn't taking Alafair's fear seriously. As they walked along, Alafair was quizzing him about his wife and children, and he seemed more than happy to fill her in on the brilliance of his two little boys.

He unlocked the heavy outer door to the first cold room with one of the large keys that dangled from the iron key ring he had retrieved from his desk. "Now, it's mighty cold in here, ladies," he warned. "I reckon we'd better step lively." He stood back and allowed them to precede him into the dim interior, then stepped in after them and pulled the chain of the single lightbulb that hung at the end of a long woven cord suspended from the high ceiling. Six walk-in lockers lined one wall. The other lockers along the other three walls ranged from the size of an icebox to a mailbox.

Martha gasped at the shock of the cold, which was a mistake. The frigid air seared her throat and lungs. She wrapped her arms around herself and shuddered. McCoy offered his suit coat without a word, and she draped it over her shoulders.

Alafair exclaimed at the temperature, but Mike Ed didn't seem bothered. "Now, ladies, this first big locker belongs to Miz James. Her son Marquis is a newspaperman down in New Orleans. Every year Miz James buys a whole cow from one of the ranchers around here, and the butcher cuts it up for her into handy pieces." The locker was only about as large as a standard armoire, lined with shelves that were packed with brown paper-wrapped bundles of meat. Mike Ed said nothing, but his expression was just a shade condescending when Alafair backed out. He closed and locked the door.

He opened the second door. "This one is rented by Mr. Edwards, who likes to hunt anything in season. He's got ducks and rabbits and sides of venison in here that he dresses himself. I expect he hasn't bought a piece of meat in years." This locker was deeper and wider than the first. Paper-wrapped pieces of meat lined shelves on one side, but several long deer haunches hung from wicked-looking hooks in the ceiling.

After the women satisfied themselves as to the contents, Mike Ed continued his narrative as he slid his master key into the third lock. "Now this locker belongs to Mr. and Mrs. Yeager themselves. They've got a couple of nice sides of beef as well as pork and every kind of poultry. Miz Tucker, you might want to take your sister along a nice hen for supper."

"Thank you, Mike Ed. I believe supper is up to my sister's housekeeper these days."

"I must say, Mr. Beams," McCoy interjected, "I'm impressed. Perhaps before I leave town, I might talk to you about renting one of these smaller lockers myself."

Martha shot him a puzzled glance. When he was in Enid, McCoy lived at a hotel.

Mike Ed was just glad to know that the man talked. "Well, I'd be proud to tell you about it, Mr. McCoy. In fact, this fourth locker here may be available before long. It's leased out to old Mr. Livingston, but he's been out of town for a few weeks looking for some land to buy closer to the City. Now this is one of the bigger ones..."

He swung the door open.

Kenneth's body was sitting on the floor, propped against the shelves that lined the back wall, facing the door with eyes wide open. He was leaning slightly askew, his arms out at an odd angle. His celluloid collar was missing the front studs and had popped open. It stuck out on either side of his neck, like wings.

Both the women shrieked, and even Mike Ed couldn't suppress a startled yip. He slammed the locker door, and McCoy seized Martha and Alafair by their arms and hustled them from the room.

The four of them stood for one horrified second outside the cold room door in a knot.

"I'll be go to hell," Mike Ed finally managed. "I'll be go to hell!"

Martha could hardly catch her breath, and Streeter looked ashen, she noticed. Alafair herself may have instigated this activity, but she appeared to be as taken aback as the rest of them.

Mike Ed swung his wide-eyed gaze toward Alafair. "How did you know?"

She shook her head. "I didn't. It was just an idea. Oh, poor Olivia!"

"We'd better call the police," McCoy said. "Right now."

Enid's Chief of Police John Burns appeared to be studying the body of Kenneth Crawford as it lay awkwardly on the warehouse floor, but he wasn't really aware of what he was looking at. Instead, he was wondering how it was that Buck Collins was here.

Somehow, Collins had found out that a body had been discovered in a rented meat locker before the deceased's family had even been notified, and had managed to get himself down here at practically the same time as the law. Collins had separated himself from the crowd of policemen as well as from the horrified civilians who had made the discovery. He was alone but for Hanlon, his constant shadow, bodyguard, and sometime chauffeur, who stood two or three respectful paces behind his boss.

Burns shook his head. Collins either had the best spy network in the state, or he was a mind reader.

"I don't see any wounds," Burns said to nobody in particular. He looked up, his brown eyes fastening on Buck Collins' elegant figure. Collins met his gaze, cool and seemingly as perplexed as the chief himself.

◇◇◇

From her position in the shadows, Alafair peered out from between McCoy and Martha and sized up the man talking to the chief. So this was the notorious Buck Collins, up close. Collins was taller than most, and far too thin, but he seemed to take up a lot of space, just the same. His gray-streaked hair, the color of polished oak, was parted neatly on the side and shining with pomade. He was dressed in a dark silk suit and a snowy tailored white shirt. The tastefully patterned tie sported a pearl tie pin. Collins grasped a bowler hat in one hand, and his wrist in the opposite hand, his stance relaxed as he regarded the chief.

"How do you expect Kenneth Crawford ended up dead in a meat locker, Buck?" Burns' tone was mild.

Alafair couldn't read Collins' expression when the chief questioned him. He didn't seem distressed.

"I have no idea, John," he said. His Irish accent sounded more pronounced now than it had when he spoke before the parade.

"His folks tell me that Crawford may have been in to you for some money."

Collins shrugged.

"So it's true?"

"A lot of people are in to me for money. I'm not inclined to kill my clients before they pay me back."

"So you're just as puzzled as the rest of us as to how this happened."

"I am. Why on earth would I kill Crawford, and then put his body in a meat locker, of all things, where he was bound to be found sooner or later? I'm not stupid, Chief."

"Nobody accused you of that, Buck. So, being so smart, you got any theories?"

Collins shrugged again. "In the course of business a man can make a number of enemies, and young Mr. Crawford was rash in his dealings, I understand."

"Not unlike yourself," Burns observed.

A meager smile crossed Collins' face. "Perhaps. Though less successful about it, it seems."

Burns looked over at Mike Ed and raised an eyebrow. "Who all can get hold of the key to this here locker?"

Alafair could hear the slight sigh that escaped Mike Ed before he answered. "There are two master keys, Chief, one of which I keep in my desk in the office yonder. That desk ain't locked, nor is my office, during business hours. There are times when nobody is in there. I reckon it would be easy enough to sneak in and filch the key for a spell without me knowing it."

"You said there are two keys. Who has the other one?"

"Lester Yeager. Of course, he's presently on his death bed. I don't know where he keeps his key, or whom he might have given it to."

Burns nodded and withdrew a small pad and pencil from his breast pocket. There was a moment of silence as he jotted down a few words.

"Buck, what are you doing here?" he said at length. "I don't recall sending anybody to fetch you. This fellow's widow hasn't even been notified yet."

"Coincidence, Chief. Just damn lucky coincidence. Pardon my unfortunate language, ladies." Collins made a smooth little bow in the women's direction before turning back to Burns. "I've been at the agriculture exhibit in the Collins Building most of the day. Mr. Hanlon here was driving me down Grand on my way home, when I spotted you and your cohorts getting out of your police cars and entering the warehouse with some urgency. I confess I was curious, and I also wondered if I could be of any assistance, so I asked Mr. Hanlon to stop. The policeman you have posted at the door was reluctant to let me in at first, but imagine my surprise when Patrolman Wilmot informed me that a body had been found in a meat locker and perhaps I'd better come in."

Alafair noted with interest that Burns slid a narrow glance at one of the policemen standing by the wall. Wilmot, she presumed. His actions had not endeared him to the chief. If Burns was angry, though, he took some pains not to show it.

He turned back toward Collins. "I understand that Crawford and your boy Ellery were friends."

"Ellery has been in Baltimore for the past several weeks. Crawford was last seen alive a couple of weeks ago, I believe."

"Believe we'll check that out, Buck."

"As you wish, John."

Burns nodded toward the door. "Yonder comes Dr. Lamerton. Wilmot, escort these people up to the office." He gestured toward Alafair's group. "Y'all just wait up there and I'll come up directly. I have some questions I want to ask you. Buck, you can go. I'll be around to your house later this afternoon."

"I'm at your service, Chief."

"Good. Now, let's all stand aside and let the Doc do his business."

Alafair took Martha's hand and led the way as Patrolman Wilmot shepherded the four of them up the short flight of stairs leading to Mike Ed's office. She glanced over her shoulder to see Collins and his driver walking toward the exit. Chief Burns, hands on hips, was watching them go. He snorted.

He didn't speak very loudly, but Alafair just caught the word he mumbled to himself before he turned to greet the doctor.

It was "coincidence."

Alafair crept into Lester's room, intending to leave him undisturbed if he was sleeping. She had volunteered to tell him about Kenneth's shocking end, but she was unwilling to wake him to do it. Such unpleasant news could wait until he awoke on his own.

Her delicacy was unneeded, though. Lester was wide awake, propped up on pillows to a half-reclining position. Lu was sitting in the chair beside the bed, embroidering a pillowcase and determinedly not looking at her patient. Both of them turned toward the door when Alafair entered, and Lu stood up. As usual, they nodded at one another as the housekeeper slipped quietly out of the room. Alafair took her place beside Lester's bed.

"I reckon you've got some bad news to tell me," Lester said.

At first, Alafair took his statement to mean that Lu had spilled the beans, which surprised her a little. Alafair had seen her hovering about behind the dining room door when Chief Burns broke the news to Olivia earlier, but she had pegged Lu as a woman with a great deal of discretion. And this was news best delivered by a family member.

"Did Lu tell you?"

"Lu won't tell me a thing. I heard the caterwauling all the way up here. I may be dying, but I ain't deaf, you know."

"Ah. Well, it's true, Lester. I've got a piece of news to share that's like to grieve you pretty bad, and I'm real sorry to disturb your last days with it, but it can't be helped. I'm afraid Kenneth is dead. Seems he's been dead for a spell. His body was found today, froze in one of the meat lockers down to the warehouse."

She paused to let this sink in, and to determine by his reaction how much more to tell him about it. In her experience, some people wanted all the sad details right away, and some couldn't stand to hear another word beyond "dead."

They gazed at one another for a long moment. Lester appeared to have turned to stone, he was so still.

When he did speak, his voice was little more than a creak. "How's Olivia?"

Alafair shook her head. "Pretty broke up. The preacher over to your church is here, and his wife. Doctor Lamerton offered to give her a sleeping draught, but she wasn't interested. She's calmed down a bunch, though, and her and Mr. Burns are wringing all the information they can get out of each other."

"And Ruth Ann?"

"Still like to bust out weeping, but she's plenty strong when she needs to be, Lester. She'll do whatever she can to support Olivia."

He nodded, and reassured that his loved ones were bearing up, he asked, "How did Kenneth come to be dead in a meat locker, do they know?"

"The doctor didn't find any wounds. I reckon he'll know more after the autopsy."

"So Kenneth never did go to Guymon?"

"Looks like not. And Olivia didn't know to look for him until he was overdue back."

"How'd he get found?"

She hesitated before she answered. "It was just an accident that he got found, Lester. Somebody was bound to open that locker door eventually."

Lester fell silent. He seemed to have shrunk down to nothing since she told him, and she impulsively reached out and squeezed his birdlike hand.

"Can I get you anything?"

"I sure would appreciate to see Ruth Ann if she can manage it, Alafair."

"I'm so sorry, Lester."

"Poor Kenneth," he murmured. "Poor foolish Kenneth."

When Alafair went back downstairs, she found Ruth Ann and Olivia were next to one another on the settee, holding hands and talking to Dr. Lamerton. Martha was in the dining room with a mewling Ron on her shoulder, patting his back and walking around the big table in slow circles with Grace at her heels. As Alafair sat down in one of the parlor chairs, she and Martha exchanged a glance.

Olivia was composed as she listened intently to the doctor. "So you still can't tell for sure how Kenneth died," she was saying.

Lamerton shook his head. "No, ma'am. I'll not be doing the autopsy until tomorrow, and it will be several weeks after that before we know the full results of any chemical tests we may do. But I can tell you right now that there are no apparent signs of trauma. He wasn't shot, stabbed, or beaten."

"You don't believe it was murder?" Alafair asked.

"I wouldn't be willing to say one way or the other, at this point."

"Well, he sure didn't lock himself in that cold storage room," Burns said.

Alafair shot a look at the man seated in the wingback chair opposite her. Chief of Police Burns was a man of about Alafair's own age with a tan, rugged mien and a no-nonsense expression. As he listened to the doctor, he clutched his round-brimmed, tall-crowned Stetson in one hand and absently patted it against the other hand.

Lamerton, who had at least twenty years on anyone else in the room, addressed Burns patiently. "That's for sure, Chief. However, he may very well have died from his own actions before he was assisted into the position in which we found him. His pupils were unnaturally constricted, which may indicate narcotic poisoning." He turned back toward Olivia. "Mrs. Crawford, have you ever known your husband to use opium, or anything like it?"

Ruth Ann was indignant at the accusation. "Certainly not!"

But everyone else was watching Olivia as her face reddened and her gaze slid away from the doctor's. Lamerton sat back in his chair and nodded.

Burns stood up. "Miz Crawford, perhaps you would be more comfortable if the doctor and I discussed this with you in private."

Olivia stood as well, and the doctor did likewise. "Let's go to my father's study, gentlemen. Mama, y'all wait here, and I'll be back in a bit."

"But, honey, what…"

Alafair leaned over and grasped her sister's hand. "It's all right, Ruth Ann. Let these fellows do their work, now."

Ruth Ann didn't look at all pleased as her daughter led the men away to Lester's study at the back of the house, but she kept quiet. Martha came into the parlor, sat down in Olivia's vacated seat and arranged Ron on her lap, while Grace crawled up into Alafair's.

"What could Doctor Lamerton possibly have to say to Olivia that she wouldn't want her mother to hear?" Ruth Ann insisted.

"I'm guessing that Olivia fears the doctor will tell her something about the way Kenneth died that will diminish your opinion of him, Sister, and she doesn't want that to happen."

Ruth Ann was distressed. "You can't believe that Kenneth would do anything as awful as use opium."

Alafair glanced at Martha before she ventured a cautious reply. "Even good folks can have a weakness they keep from them they love. Or maybe just a single slip can lead to tragedy. It could be that Kenneth was persuaded by an unscrupulous acquaintance to try some dope—just once, mind you—and being unused to it, he succumbed. And then this acquaintance got scared and tried to get rid of the body quick."

"That Ellery Collins!"

"Now, I'm not making any accusations. I'm just making up stories. Let's wait to find out what really happened before we get all het up."

"Or maybe poor Kenneth was poisoned!"

"That could be, too."

"Well, that's way more likely!" Despite Alafair's cautions, Ruth Ann was indeed getting all het up.

"Ma, what's 'dope'?" Grace asked.

"Dope is a stupid thing," Alafair told her without missing a beat.

Little Ron began to cry, and Martha lifted him back up onto her shoulder. "I think he needs his mama."

"She'll be out in a minute. There's some bottles and nipples in the pantry, right in front. See if he'll take a little water," Ruth Ann told her.

"Go help Martha," Alafair said to Grace, who slid off her lap and trotted after her sister through the dining room and into the kitchen.

"Oh, that Collins boy!" Ruth Ann returned to her rant as soon as the girls left the room. "I knew he wasn't a fit companion for

Kenneth. I'd bet money that he's behind this one way or another. Look how he left town all of a sudden..."

"I hear he left a while before Kenneth disappeared," Alafair interrupted her. "Try to calm yourself, Ruth Ann. Let's just try to take this awful journey one step at a time. Rushing headlong is just like to lead us down the wrong path."

Ruth Ann wasn't inclined to follow that advice, but before she could comment, a pale Olivia emerged from the hallway, trailed by Burns and the doctor, who took their leave of the women with promises to return in the morning.

"Chief Burns says he's put his best men to figuring out what happened, and he'll come early tomorrow and try to have a word with anyone who calls on us," Olivia said, then made a brave attempt to escape questioning. "I hear little Ron fussing." She took a step toward the kitchen, but didn't get far.

"He'll keep a minute," Ruth Ann informed her in no uncertain terms. "What was so all-fired secret that those men wanted to talk to you about?"

Alafair noted that Olivia's shoulders sagged as she gave in to the inevitable. "Doctor Lamerton didn't say much more than you heard, Ma. He just wanted to tell me that there's a possibility that Kenneth's death was an accident. Could be he went to the meat locker for some reason and lost consciousness, then either died of narcotic poisoning or froze."

Alafair couldn't help herself. "Why would he go into an empty meat locker if he hated the cold so? Can drugs make you do something you never would do ordinarily?"

Olivia shook her head. "I don't know. Maybe some evil wag found him dead and thought it would be funny. Of course, it's way more likely that Kenneth was murdered."

"But who would want to murder Kenneth?" Ruth Ann said.

"Oh, Mama, I don't know. But Kenneth wasn't quite the paragon you make him out to be, I'm afraid. He had been doing some pretty risky speculating in the last few months, and if he got himself in with some bad folks, I wouldn't be surprised."

"I think it was Ellery Collins led him astray."

"Could be, Mama, or maybe even old Buck Collins himself."

Ruth Ann stiffened. "Buck!"

"Or maybe somebody we don't know a thing about. I don't know. I can't think about it anymore. I have to get to little Ron."

Olivia swept out of the room, and Ruth Ann leaped to her feet and headed for the foyer.

"Where are you going?" Alafair asked, surprised.

Ruth Ann answered on the run. "I'm telephoning Russ Lawyer to get over here as fast as he can."

Out of the corner of her eye, Alafair saw Lu come down the back stairs from Lester's room, quietly pass through the hall, and disappear into the kitchen. Taking advantage of everyone's preoccupation, Alafair slipped out of the room and made her own way to the kitchen. When she walked through the door, the tiny housekeeper looked up at her from her seat at the kitchen table. She may have been surprised to see an interloper. Alafair couldn't really tell.

Lu stood up.

"I don't mean to disturb you, Miz Lu, but I was wondering if I could talk to you for a spell?"

"Please no 'Miz.' Just Lu, please."

This was the tenth time over the last fifteen years that Lu had asked her not to use an honorific, but since the woman looked to be at least as old as Noah's wife, it was hard for Alafair to do. She felt she should be polite to her elders, after all, even if they were Chinese. She nodded. "May I sit down, Lu?"

"I get you something, Miz Tucker?"

Alafair settled herself in a chair across the table from Lu. "What is that you're drinking? Is that hot tea? That would be nice."

Without comment, Lu set a small china cup before her and filled it with tea from the teapot sitting on a trivet in the center of the table. The tea was a very pale greenish color, like nothing Alafair had ever seen before, and she picked up the cup and sniffed it with interest. It smelled like flowers. She took a sip and made an appreciative noise. It tasted like flowers, too.

"How I help you, Miz?"

Alafair set the cup down. "Well, Lu, what with all this bad business, Mr. Crawford dying, and all, I expect the house will be full of callers for the next few days. I don't expect my sister will be up to helping you with the cooking and such, so I thought I'd ask if you could use another pair of hands. Seems you'll have a lot to do, considering you're nursing Mr. Yeager, as well. I've done plenty of cooking in my time, and nursing as well. I've asked my brother-in-law if he'd object to my helping to care for him, and he said that if Ruth Ann and you didn't mind, he wouldn't either. I'd feel a lot more useful if I had a task."

Lu eyed her for a silent second. She wasn't used to being asked. If Mrs. Yeager felt like cooking or nursing, she did it without consulting her housekeeper. "No, Miz Tucker, I manage, no trouble."

Alafair nodded and stood up. "I understand. I don't much like folks banging around my kitchen, either." She stood to go, but before she reached the door, Lu called her name.

"Miz Tucker, how you know about Mr. Crawford in cold room?"

Alafair started to say something about a coincidence, or a hunch, but something about the exotic little woman looking at her so oddly made her reconsider. "It was a dream."

Lu neither moved nor changed expression for a long moment and Alafair expected the conversation was over. Eventually, Lu nodded, apparently coming to some sort of decision. "You know chocolate pie?"

Alafair smiled at this. "Do I know how to make chocolate pie? Yes, I know the recipe. I only make it on special occasions. It's one of Ruth Ann's favorites, if I remember right."

"Yes, Miz Yeager talk sometimes about how you make chocolate pie. I never learn to make. Maybe you teach me. We make her a pie."

"My sister would like that."

Friday, September 17, 1915

Pee Wee Nickolls was not at all happy about having to take time from his work to call upon the grieving widow of his late oil field partner, Kenneth Crawford. The rainy weather had finally cleared up, and it was a perfect day to bring out a charge of nitro and do some blasting. But he supposed it had to be done, under the circumstances, especially since the widow was now his business partner whether he liked it or not.

Pee Wee wasn't particularly surprised that Crawford had come to a bad end, not when he thought about the company the man kept. He hadn't respected Crawford all that much. He was rash and not overly scrupulous, certainly not the kind of man that Pee Wee relished partnering with.

Pee Wee had been on a job in a field over in Osage County when Crawford approached him about going in on an exploratory site in the Cherokee Strip.

"I've heard you're a good oil man," Crawford had told him. "I need a partner who knows what he's doing, and I'll sell you fifty percent interest in the land and mineral rights."

Pee Wee had always thought of himself as a good judge of folks, and at first he rejected the offer out of hand. But Crawford was nothing if not persistent, and as he kept repeating and even sweetening the deal, Pee Wee had found his resolve weakening. Not that his opinion of Crawford improved. But he was damn tired of being a shooter, no matter that his skill and reputation, not to mention the gigantic hazard premium he received on every job, had given him a bigger bank account than he ever in his life imagined.

After all, what else did he have to spend the money on? Ever since he had left Tennessee when he was a shirttail lad of twelve, after his ma died, he had lived in tents and bunkhouses on oil fields throughout Oklahoma and Texas and Louisiana. He had started out as a novice—a "boweevil," in oil field parlance—doing any odd job he was given, eventually becoming a roustabout, then a driller. In fact, there wasn't an oil field job in existence that he hadn't done, and he'd even done some that don't exist.

By the time Kenneth Crawford started pestering him back in Osage County, Pee Wee was getting close to twenty-five years old. He had been a shooter for several years, having learned the craft of blasting oil sands and well obstructions with nitroglycerin from a man in Louisiana who looked to be about fifty, but was probably not much older than Pee Wee was now. At first, Pee Wee had been fascinated by the science of it all, by the care and delicacy it took to create and handle and use the stuff, as well as the precision of sending the torpedo down the well to blast it open. And he had been young, after all, and enjoyed blowing the hell out of things. He hadn't even been too bothered when an ill-considered move with a "dud" torpedo had cost him a couple of fingers and the sight in one eye. He had felt that his scars were his badge of honor, and the ordinary twisters looked at him with respect.

But when Crawford had showed up, Pee Wee was ready for a change. He had been around oil fields for half his life, and had developed almost a sixth sense about the black gold. He could eyeball a piece of land and know instantly if it was a likely prospect. He couldn't explain his talent himself. He just knew that when it came to oil, he could almost smell it.

So, when Crawford wouldn't leave him alone, Pee Wee let himself be persuaded to look at the site. What was the loss, after all? He could always get another job if it didn't pan out. Besides, there was an outside chance that the field in Garfield County was a likely prospect, and Pee Wee Nickolls could run his own show at last.

Crawford had driven him from the train station in Garber out to the property two days later, and the instant he had seen it, he knew that his fortune was about to be made. He sunk every penny he had into the project.

Since then, he had been single-minded. He had thrown up a couple of small buildings on the property, hired as big a crew as he could afford, rented equipment from over in Tulsa, and started drilling his wildcat well in the spot his special sense told him was the most likely to strike.

He never left the field if he didn't have to, and Pee Wee reckoned that this was one occasion when he had to.

The square was still blocked off for the Founders' fete, so Pee Wee had to take an annoyingly roundabout route to reach the Yeager house, where the family was holding Kenneth's visitation. He shifted his truck down into second as he rounded the corner onto Washington and cast a glance at his passenger, a big kid from Waukomis by the name of Zip Kolocek, who as usual was gawking about as though he had never been to a town before. Ol' Zip was about seventeen, Pee Wee figured, and had been eager to learn the oil business when he came to Pee Wee looking for a job. So Pee Wee had his own boweevil, now, to run and tote for him and the crew.

Zip was especially interested in learning about the blasting. Pee Wee liked the big, good-natured youngster, and had tried to put him off it, but Zip was not to be dissuaded. So, in between the boy's runs to town for beans and bacon and coffee, Pee Wee was teaching him about nitro in the most careful manner he knew. In recent weeks, he had been showing Zip how to pack the nitro for transport from the magazine, which was a storage shed that he had erected in a remote corner of the property, far enough from the well and outbuildings that any accident wouldn't destroy everything they'd worked for, at least.

In fact, he and Zip were supposed to be there now, preparing the square five-quart cans of the stuff for transport in the "soup wagon"—a large Ford truck that had been fitted with specially modified shocks and a complicated sling-and-padding arrangement in the bed. The well was finally deep enough that damp, packed oil sands, mixed with the slurry mud they used to cool the drill bit, kept plugging the hole. The crew was having to stop too often to clean the drill. It was time to shoot a torpedo down the hole and clean it out with a blast.

The upcoming blast was all Pee Wee had on his mind right now, and it was hard for him to get into the proper spirit to make a sympathy call, especially for someone who he didn't admire very much.

He found a place to park among the numerous vehicles of all descriptions, motorized and horse-drawn, arrayed along the curb in front of the Yeager house, and turned off the engine. Well, think of the widow, he admonished himself. He didn't know Mrs. Crawford all that well, but their few meetings had led him to form a higher opinion of her than of her husband. She was young, but it was likely that she would be a more sensible and informed partner than Kenneth had been. After all the excitement about Crawford's bizarre death died down he would offer to buy Mrs. Crawford's share from her, but he could only offer a middling price, and pay it out over time, to boot. If she was as smart as he suspected, she'd hold on as long as she could for the well to come in. And if she had to sell, she would be wise to find someone who could pay her a better price. As long as she didn't sell her half out to somebody impossible, like that Ellery Collins whom Crawford had been hanging around with, Pee Wee could live with it.

He sighed and looked over at Zip, intending to say something like, "well, let's get this over with," but he hesitated when he saw that the kid was staring at the house, his big blue eyes filled with tears. Pee Wee stifled a fond smile, suddenly feeling rather ashamed of himself. Tenderhearted Zip had hardly known Crawford. He gave the boy's shoulder a rough shake.

"Let's go pay our respects," he said.

The front door was standing open, and Pee Wee would have knocked, but he didn't get the chance. As they approached, the screen was opened by a middle-sized woman in a plum-colored dress, with dark hair that was caught up in a slightly askew twist. Her sharp dark eyes inspected them from crown to toe as he and Zip crossed the porch.

Both men snatched off their hats and pressed them to their chests.

She held the screen open with one hand and reached out to beckon them with the other. "Come in," she said to them. "I'm Miz Crawford's aunt, Miz Tucker. I'll take your hats."

They stepped inside and surrendered their hats, murmuring their thanks. A sooty-gray, long-haired, squash-faced giant of a cat was stretched out on the floor beside the hat rack, inspecting the new arrivals.

"I'm Pee Wee Nickolls, Crawford's partner in the test well."

Alafair smiled. "I reckoned you must be. Olivia has told us about you."

Pee Wee smiled and unconsciously touched the patch over his bad eye with the remaining fingers of his damaged hand. "I expect I'm easy to spot. This here is my assistant, Zip Kolocek."

"I'm awful sorry about what happened," Zip said. His eyes flooded again, and Alafair's sharp gaze softened immediately. She unconsciously put her hand on Zip's chest. The cat got up and wove around the boy's feet before taking himself off into the parlor.

"Thank you, son. Miz Crawford will be touched that y'all called. Olivia and her mother are in there. Y'all go on through."

The house was full of people, coming and going, sitting and standing around the big parlor in little whispering groups. Olivia and Ruth Ann were in the middle of the room, enthroned in the wing side chairs. No coffin, Pee Wee was pleased to note. Kenneth was more than likely still at the undertaker's. Mike Ed Beams and his wife were already there, along with Chief of Police Burns, who was sitting in the corner with a plate on his lap, eyeing the visitors as they arrived and left. A small Asian woman was quietly tending the buffet that had been set out on the dining table, and a big, sandy-haired man whom Pee Wee didn't know sat, silent and unobtrusive, in a hard-backed chair behind the women.

The widow was puffy-faced and watery-eyed behind her glasses, but she was calm and dignified as she greeted her visitors and accepted sympathy. In truth, she looked quite lovely in her somber navy shirtwaist, her dark blond hair tied up at her nape with a blue ribbon. Pee Wee adjusted the uncomfortable collar on his unaccustomed dress shirt and straightened his jacket before he moved to do his duty.

Olivia looked over at the two men as they walked toward her and gave them a tremulous smile.

"Mr. Nickolls," she said, holding out her hand.

"Miz Crawford. I'm plumb sorry as a body can be."

"Thank you. It's kind of you to come. I don't believe I know your friend."

He grabbed Zip's arm and pushed him to the fore. "Zip Kolocek. He's the new boweevil for us out at the field."

"Oh, yes, I've heard of you, Zip. Kenneth told me that Mr. Nickolls had hired a young man who was learning to be a shooter. Your name is hard to forget."

"Oh, Miz Crawford." Zip's lower lip trembled and a tear escaped and rolled down his round cheek.

Zip's inarticulate distress caused Ruth Ann to burst into tears, but Olivia seized the boy's hand.

"Your sympathy means the world to me, Zip. Thank you so much for coming. My mother's housekeeper has laid out quite a spread, and we sure would appreciate it if you'd help us eat it before it goes to waste. Go on and help yourself."

Still choked up, Zip nodded and did as he was told. Pee Wee moved to follow him, but Olivia gestured for him to linger. He leaned toward her, curious.

"I really am glad you called, Mr. Nickolls," she said. "Saves me having to send someone out to the field to fetch you. Our lawyer, Russ Lawyer, is coming here in a couple of hours to acquaint us with the state of Kenneth's legal affairs. Mr. Lawyer seems to think there are things in Kenneth's papers that it would be better for us to know sooner rather than later. I gather that you are involved, which only makes sense, since y'all were in business together."

Pee Wee straightened and pooched his bottom lip out thoughtfully. "Well, shoot a bug! I guess I'd be glad to know what's going to happen with Kenneth's half. When we made up the partnership papers, we fixed it so that if he should pass on, you'd inherit his share, ma'am. I expect that's one thing the lawyer aims to tell you."

"Yes, I expected as much. May I ask, Mr. Nickolls, what arrangements were made for your half if anything should happen to you?"

"Call me Pee Wee, ma'am. Well, if I was to get knocked on the head, it was fixed so that your husband would take over my part in the well free and clear."

Olivia glanced over her shoulder at McCoy before she responded. "Don't you have a wife or a brother or some other relative to pass your interest on to, Mr. Nickolls?"

"Call me Pee Wee. No, ma'am. Made sense to do it that way. I got no family. I reckon that considering what happened, that means that if I meet my doom anytime soon, you'll own the whole shootin' match, now."

"I'll be more than happy to revise the contract, let you name another heir, any time you wish, Mr. Nickolls."

He blinked. "There's plenty of time to get into that, Miz Crawford. No need to be worrying about business now, so soon after your bereavement."

"Thank you for being so considerate. But let's see what Mr. Lawyer has to say about Kenneth's affairs before we go to setting up any timetables."

Something about her tone gave Pee Wee a pang in his gut. What was she getting at? Did she suspect that there would be something in Kenneth's papers that would warrant concern? Or did she just know her husband? He turned away, troubled.

He was too preoccupied to notice that the sandy-haired man had left his chair behind the women and was now in the foyer, head to head with Mrs. Tucker, whispering.

From her station in the foyer, Alafair watched curiously as Pee Wee Nickolls and Zip Kolocek talked to Olivia. She could tell by the way McCoy leaned forward a bit in his chair that Olivia and Pee Wee were having an interesting conversation. She wasn't surprised. Pee Wee looked like the kind of person with whom you'd have an interesting conversation.

Pee Wee fit his nickname, she thought. He was a small man, but he looked robust and well put together, and had a direct and straightforward gaze. His missing eye and fingers gave him a dangerous look, but Alafair suspected that his scars indicated a man who had had a bit of bad luck, more than anything else. Olivia had called him "crazy." Alafair didn't see it.

After the family planning conference of the day before, Alafair had discreetly drawn McCoy aside and asked him to keep her informed, since she would perforce not be able to hear what was going on from her station by the front door. She knew that whatever McCoy felt about spying for her, he would be anxious to keep on Martha's mother's good side and acquiesce. She didn't feel particularly guilty about manipulating him. She used whatever tools were at her disposal.

Martha was upstairs with the children, which didn't please her much, but someone had to do it, and Lu was busy enough feeding the visitors and tending to Lester at the same time.

When Pee Wee took a preoccupied leave from Olivia and wandered toward the buffet table to join his young companion, Alafair looked toward McCoy. He was looking back.

He stood and walked across the parlor, and they stepped back away from the entrance.

"What did Nickolls have to say?" she asked.

"Him and Mrs. Crawford spoke about the provisions of the partnership agreement he had with Kenneth. Seems they arranged it so that if Kenneth died, Olivia gets his interest in the field. But, had Pee Wee died first, his shares would have gone to Kenneth."

Alafair's eyebrows flew up. "So if something happens to Nickolls right about now, Olivia inherits the whole field."

"Yes, but she offered to make whatever changes Nickolls wants in that part of the agreement. He told her not to worry about it right now. It does seem he hasn't thought about the implications."

"Hasn't had time to, more likely. Besides he don't look like the type who's concerned with much outside his well."

◇◇◇

Alafair knew before they appeared that more visitors were about to arrive, because Ike sauntered back into the foyer with his tail at attention, ready to render assistance as a greeter.

Alafair spoke to him, but he offered no comment, so she walked to the screen just as the most amazing open-front limousine she had ever seen glided to a stop in front of the house.

"Well, what do you…" she said to the cat, but swallowed the rest of the sentence when she saw that every hair on his body was standing on end. He unceremoniously slunk away down the hall.

She turned back to the door and watched with interest as a liveried driver dismounted and walked around to the side of the automobile to open the door for the natty, narrow-faced man who got out. Collins took a second to adjust the piercing white cuffs peeking out from the sleeves of his gray suit before he strode up the walk and mounted the stairs. He was followed closely by his chauffeur, the same man he had had with him yesterday; Mr. Hanlon, Alafair remembered. Collins paused on the porch to allow Hanlon to open the screen for him before he entered the house alone.

Alafair stepped in front of him, and for an instant, they stood there, eye to eye.

"I'm here to see Mrs. Crawford," Collins said. He didn't seem to recognize her. She saw no reason to remind him that she had been at the warehouse and heard the conversation between him and Chief Burns.

"I'm Miz Tucker, Miz Crawford's aunt," Alafair told him, though he hadn't asked.

"Please tell her that Buck Collins is here to offer condolences."

Until now, she had simply been telling callers to go on through, but given the circumstances, Alafair thought that preparing Olivia for this particular caller might be the kind thing to do. "I certainly will, Mr. Collins. If you'll wait here, I'll be right back."

She left Collins standing in the foyer and hurried into the parlor to warn Olivia, but she could tell by her wide-eyed stare and stiff posture that her niece had already caught sight of the unwelcome visitor. The room had fallen completely silent, and Chief Burns stood up from his corner seat and moved to Olivia's side.

Alafair leaned over Olivia's chair to murmur into her ear. "You want me to send him packing?"

Ruth Ann attempted an outraged comment, but Chief Burns spoke over her. "It might be useful to hear what he has to say, Mrs. Crawford."

"Can you stand to speak to him, sweetheart?" Ruth Ann asked.

Olivia had been listening to her elders' comments while keeping a wary eye on the man in the foyer. Just like watching a snake, Alafair thought, which is exactly how Lester had described him—a snake, who moves fast and strikes fast. Alafair feared that this visit didn't have anything to do with Collins' sympathy for the widow's loss.

"Mr. Collins, I have been told what you said at the warehouse yesterday, after my poor husband was found. Why are you here?"

"I am here, Mrs. Crawford, to assure you that I had nothing to do with Kenneth's unfortunate death. His death profits me nothing. And I do want to express my deepest sympathy on the loss of your husband. I'm sure it was quite a shock, finding him that way. My son Ellery will be sorry to hear of it. He considered Kenneth a friend. Has the coroner decided what killed him, yet?"

Olivia eyed Collins with distaste and didn't reply.

When no response was forthcoming, a hint of amusement flitted across his face, and he glanced at the police chief. He reached into his breast pocket and withdrew a business card, which he handed to Olivia. "I won't intrude any longer, ma'am. However, I did want to inform you that your husband and I did have some outstanding business matters which we will need to attend to forthwith. As soon as you're feeling up to it, I'd appreciate it if you'd call on me. Or if you'd prefer, telephone and I will be glad to come to you."

"How dare you…" Ruth Ann attempted, but Olivia hushed her mother with an upraised hand.

"I gather that my husband owed you some money, Mr. Collins. Is that the 'business' you are referring to?"

"I don't think this is the appropriate time to address the matter, Mrs. Crawford. I'm sure next week will be soon enough."

Olivia's pale and shaky demeanor had totally disappeared, and she sat bolt upright, clutching her handkerchief in her lap, staring narrowly at Collins as he spoke. "If this will affect my husband's estate, I'd just as soon know what it is and not wait to get started on my lawsuit, sir."

The young widow's spirited counteroffensive took Collins by surprise, and his eyes widened with appreciation. "Why, Mrs. Crawford, you're quick to assume the worst."

"I think you've set a precedent in that regard, Mr. Collins."

"I'm sure the matter can quickly be worked out to everyone's satisfaction."

"I think you'd better tell me right now what 'the matter' is."

Chief Burns finally broke his silence. "I'd like to hear that answer, myself, Collins."

"All right, if you insist." Collins turned back to Olivia. "Your husband was in debt to me for eleven thousand dollars." He was interrupted by gasps and murmurs from the people in the room. He heard one particularly colorful oath and noted without looking that Pee Wee Nickolls was present. "The loan will come due at the end of the year. As his widow and heir, the debt falls to you, Mrs. Crawford. I'm sorry about what has happened, and I have no desire to cause you any more distress. I'd like to discuss the situation with you. Kenneth put up for collateral his interest in both Yeager Transfer and Storage and the property and mineral rights of the well south of Garber. If you sell either your share of the warehouse or the property, you can make enough money to cover the debt, but I have no wish to deprive you of your assets. In fact, I think this can be worked out to your benefit. I'd like to propose that we go into partnership together…"

"Yeager Transfer and Storage is my father's life and legacy to me, and I'm not willing to see you get your claws into it, Mr. Collins."

"And I'd ruther have a mangy rat for a partner."

Collins cast Pee Wee a glance before he continued. "As you wish, Mrs. Crawford. But I think you'll find all the papers are in order and quite legal, and the likelihood is that we'll end up partners in the end, anyway. And I assure you that having me as a partner will be of tremendous financial benefit to you. I did wish to postpone this conversation for another time, if you'll remember, but even though you insisted, I'm sorry to have brought this to your attention at such an occasion. I was hoping we could address this in a cordial manner."

His gaze shifted to Ruth Ann, and they stared at one another for a moment, until she reddened and looked away. Collins turned back to Olivia. "I have no intention of hurting you, Olivia. My quarrel was never with you."

"I'll have my lawyer call on you tomorrow."

"Very well, ma'am. Might just as well get it over with." He gave a little bow. "Good afternoon, Mrs. Crawford, Mrs. Yeager. Give my regards to Lester. Chief."

Alafair followed Collins through the foyer and opened the front screen to usher him out. He gave her a preoccupied glance as he passed and walked toward his car. Hanlon was leaning against the fender with his ankles crossed, cradling Ruth Ann's pug-nosed cat and absently stroking its belly as it lolled contentedly in his arms. Hanlon straightened as Collins approached and gently put the cat down on the sidewalk. The cat disappeared like smoke before Hanlon opened the car door for his boss.

The bedroom was hardly big enough to contain all the people who were arrayed around Lester's bed. After Collins had left, all the church and club ladies and business acquaintances were hustled out as fast as it could politely be done. Besides family, only Pee Wee Nickolls, Mike Ed Beams, Streeter McCoy, and Chief Burns remained. They had spent the previous several hours with their heads together in the parlor, trying to figure out what this all meant.

Russell Lawyer had appeared in the afternoon, briefcase in hand, still breathless from his day of scuttling hither and yon, gathering papers and contracts, meeting with bankers, and most importantly, Buck Collins' lawyers.

There had been a long discussion, but in the end all agreed that it was really necessary for Lester to be included in on this information session. No one knew the warehouse situation better than Lester, and besides, while he continued to reside on this earth, he was still the head of the Yeager family.

So, Zip Kolocek volunteered to watch the kids, and the rest of the party trooped upstairs to Lester's room. Ruth Ann had dosed him with just enough laudanum to take the edge off the pain while leaving his mind clear. He had been apprised of the situation, and he sat propped against his pillows, eyeing the group thoughtfully.

"What did Collins' pack of lawyers have to say, Russ?"

Lester's voice was strong. He looked better than he had since she had been here, Alafair thought. Being engaged in the business of living was powerful medicine.

"I examined all the agreements between Kenneth and Collins, and as you might guess, everything looked perfectly in order. Seems Kenneth has been borrowing from Collins for a long time, ever since he bought the Garber property. Kenneth was even borrowing to make the payroll for the drillers. You asked me to see if Collins' son Ellery had anything to do with the loans, but I didn't see evidence of it."

Ruth Ann sniffed into her handkerchief. "Mercy! Kenneth has been murdered, and he ain't even in the ground yet. Can't this wait until after his funeral, at least?"

Russell Lawyer turned toward Ruth Ann and shook his head, not unkindly. "I think not, Ruth Ann. Collins is going to take advantage of the situation, if he can. We'd better try to cut him off at the pass. If we can." He turned in his seat to address Olivia, on his other side. "I'd advise you to let me contact Judge Langley and explain the situation. Nothing can happen to your property until it goes through probate, which will take a long time, since Kenneth died intestate."

"Collins still might try to pressure Olivia to agree to sign over her property before the ruling," Lester said, "even if he couldn't take legal possession right away."

"But why?" Olivia asked. She sounded plaintive. "Why be in such a hurry? All he has to do is be patient. If everything is as neat and legal as you say it is, Russ, then he'll get his money sooner or later. And it's not like he needs it."

A moment of silence ensued as everyone considered this.

"Maybe..." Alafair ventured absently. There was a rustling noise as all turned to look at her. Her eyes widened and she swallowed her words. She hadn't realized that she had actually spoken aloud.

"Do you have an idea, Miz Tucker?" Chief Burns prompted.

"Well, it just looks suspicious, don't it? Like maybe he's trying to get Olivia all flustered and do something fast while she's grieving and not thinking straight. Maybe it's not the money that he wants. Maybe he wants to make sure he gets the property."

"But which property? The warehouse or the oil field?" Martha asked.

Russ Lawyer shrugged. "Why not both?"

Olivia sighed. "Well, once again, I'm wondering why he's in such an all-fired hurry. And, why he'd want the businesses instead of cash money."

Pee Wee Nickolls leaned forward in his chair. "I don't expect he cares a fig about our piddly wildcat well. He's got oil wells from here to Beulah Land. Even if we come in like gangbusters tomorrow, it'd just be a drop in his oil bucket."

"Nickolls, did you have any idea that Crawford was getting money from Buck Collins to run your operation?"

Pee Wee blinked at Chief Burns. "No, sir, I did not. I never did ask Kenneth any questions about where the money come from. I figured he had plenty of money of his own. Now that all this has come out, though, I sure been thinking about things. For the last couple of months, that big lug of Collins', that Hanlon, has come by the well a few times…"

"Buck's bodyguard?" the chief interrupted.

"Yes, sir. Somehow him and Zip got to be friends. Didn't surprise me none. Zip's always picking up strays when he goes to town. Zip showed him around at least once, that I know of. He said Hanlon was interested in maybe working roustabout on some well after his parole was up. I never gave it a second thought, until now."

"Guess I'd better talk to Zip," Burns said.

Pee Wee was quick to defend the boy. "Well, if Collins set Hanlon to spy on us, Zip sure never knew about it."

"It's not the money Collins is worried about, then." Lester steered the conversation back on track. "There's something else that's got Buck's ears pricked up. He thinks Kenneth has something he wants. I'd bet on it." Shifting his ravaged body was obviously not something he wished to undertake, since only his eyes swiveled to look at Mike Ed, across the room. "Mike Ed, get some of the men and go over the place from top to bottom, see if there's something stored in some corner that ain't supposed to be there. Open the crates, see that what's supposed to be in 'em is in 'em."

"Won't the owners object?"

"I expect they don't need to know. Just be sure to nail everything back up good."

"Lester!" Ruth Ann was shocked.

"What's going to happen, honey? Burns going to throw me in jail?" Lester looked back at Mike Ed. "Use men you trust," he warned. "And don't forget to look through the icehouse, the trucks, every unlikely place you can think of. Go over the books, too."

"I'll hunt through Kenneth's things at home," Olivia offered, "and I'll search his desk at work, too."

"Just in case, Pee Wee, give the field and well the once-over."

"That'll take me a while, Mr. Yeager," Pee Wee warned, "what with the outbuildings and all, and if we're worrying about Collins having spies among us, I got to say that the youngster Zip Kolocek is about the only one of the twisters I'd trust a hoot."

"I won't be leaving town for a day or two," McCoy said to Pee Wee. "I'll volunteer to help you out, if you think you can use me."

"I can help check your inventory lists against your equipment, if that would be useful," Martha offered. "Or look at your books, if you'd trust me, Mr. Nickolls. I work at a bank and deal with numbers all the time."

Lu fixed a plate of sandwiches for the family and their company, and everyone ate in a haphazard way as they refined their plans in the parlor. After they had gone over every possible course of action for the tenth time, people began to drift away one by one. Lester had been drugged to the nines to help him sleep. Ruth Ann went upstairs shortly after supper to drop onto the cot in the corner of the master bedroom. Grace was long abed. Olivia and the baby had moved into one of the guest bedrooms for the moment. Martha and McCoy helped her haul Ron's bassinet up the stairs.

"Be sure and close the bedroom door," Alafair called after them. "Don't let the cat in there with that sleeping baby."

When Mike Ed Beams finally took his leave, Alafair walked him out and they said their goodbyes on the front porch. It was a fair night, filled with music on the air from the street dance that was ending the Jubilee festivities.

Alafair turned to go back in the house and saw Pee Wee Nickolls and Zip sitting in a couple of Adirondack chairs at the end of the long porch. It was completely dark, now, and if it hadn't been for the dim light coming from the front window, Alafair wouldn't have seen them at all. She waved them down as they started to stand when she approached.

"Don't get up, boys. I expect you'll be wanting to get on the road pretty soon. Might as well catch your breath, first." She sat down in the porch swing, at right angles to Zip.

"Yes, ma'am," Pee Wee affirmed. "I expect we ought to get going right quick. It's a long trip back to Garber by car in the dark, especially since I've got to take the dangedest roundabout route out of town, what with this to-do going on. Me and Zip was just talking about it. I'd like to do a blast-out on that well tomorrow morning before your folks show up to search the place. Reckon we'll be getting up pretty early to get the job done."

"Well, I hope you blow a gusher. Just be careful and don't blow off any more body parts, Pee Wee. Looks like you found out the hard way that nitro is dangerous stuff."

The comment made Pee Wee smile. She had found an interesting way to ask what had happened to him while leaving him plenty of room to politely ignore her curiosity if he didn't want to tell her. He wasn't particularly sensitive about his injuries, and he appreciated a straightforward approach instead of the all-too-frequent furtive attempts people made not to look directly at them. He touched his eye patch. "Yes, ma'am, I sure did. This here is a stupid mistake I made when I was a foolish wisp of a lad learning how to shoot. It was in Louisiana. We was using one of them old-fashioned torpedoes that you set off with a go-devil…" He hesitated at the look of interested incomprehension on her face. "That's a weight that you drop down the well on the wire when you get the torpedo in place, ma'am. It hits the firing cap on top and sets it off. I reckon they call it that 'cause it can make you go to the devil right quick. Well, sometimes the torpedo is a dud and the charge don't fire. Then, if the boss is a cheapskate, which he usually is, he has you haul the dud out rather than leave it in there and send down a second torpedo on top of it. Usually nothing happens. But sometimes it does. I was looking down the well like an eejit when I was hauling up one particular dud that decided to go off after all when it was about halfway up."

A pained look crossed Alafair's face. "Mercy!"

Pee Wee shrugged. "I was lucky I just lost a couple of fingers and the sight in one eye. My looks could have been downright spoiled. Besides, since then nobody is more careful with the nitro than me. Sometimes the Lord has to give you a good knock in the head to teach you to pay attention."

"Well, you surely take your misfortune in stride." Alafair made no attempt to keep the admiration out of her voice.

Pee Wee leaned back in his chair and his one visible eye crinkled as he relaxed and warmed to his subject. "Nitroglycerin is mighty handy stuff for clearing an obstructed well, ma'am, but I'm sure you know it's devilish tricky to work with. It's like a temperamental gal—no matter how careful you handle her, you never know what's going to set her off. And it's never the same thing twice, neither. Depends on the temperature, the age of the stuff, all sorts of things. Sometimes you can toss it around like a baseball and nothing happens. Then you put a foot wrong and that's the end of you. No kidding. Once down in Texas, a friend of mine stepped in a few drops that had dripped from a leaky can onto the floor of the magazine shed. Blowed his foot right off."

"What on earth makes you want to work with such an awful mixture?"

"Oh, it's safe enough if you mix it with alcohol or some such. It's just when you draw off the pure stuff for a blast that you've got to be on your toes. Besides, a shooter makes a load of dough what with all the hazard pay."

"All the money in the world ain't no good if you're blown up," Alafair pointed out.

Pee Wee nodded his agreement. "Well, that's true. And forget about anybody selling you life insurance."

"Yet you still do it?"

"Truth is, I can't stand the suspense to watch somebody else do it. I don't relish the thought of picking bits of one of my drillers out of my hair. At least I know what I'm doing."

This conversation had taken a turn that was too grisly for Alafair. She looked at Zip. "Did Chief Burns talk to you about Mr. Hanlon?"

"Yes, ma'am. I told him I couldn't hardly believe Mr. Hanlon was a spy! He's such a nice fellow. I met him last spring at the railroad station, when I was in Enid to pick up a load of pipe for Pee Wee. He was waiting to drive Miz Collins home after she come in on the train from the City. We got to talking and I told him how I liked working at the field. He don't like being a driver. He's looking for some different kind of work he can do after he don't have to work for Mr. Collins anymore. So I told him to come on out to the well any time and I'd show him around. He did, too. I think he liked it. He came to visit with me a couple times. Brought me a half a fried chicken once, from Mr. Collins' kitchen."

"Why does Mr. Hanlon have to work for Mr. Collins? He ought to just quit if he doesn't like it."

"He's probably an ex-con from Leavenworth on parole under Collins' guarantee," Pee Wee told her. "One bad word from Collins and he's back up the river in a flash. I heard Collins gets some of his muscle that way."

"Mr. Hanlon is looking to start a new life," Zip said. "He's tired of rough ways."

Pee Wee didn't comment, but Alafair saw him shake his head at Zip's credulity.

"I hear from Grace that you're a crackerjack babysitter, son. I could see y'all out the bedroom window, running around together like monkeys in the backyard with Ron in your arms and Grace on your heels, laughing to beat the band. You have younger brothers and sisters, I'm guessing."

"Oh, no, ma'am." Zip's disembodied voice answered her out of the dark. "Reckon I hung a toe when I was born, 'cause there weren't no more after me. It's just me and my ma, now. She lives with my grandma down in Waukomis since Pa died."

"You've got a way with the little ones."

"I love babies." He sounded enthusiastic. "I'd like to have a passel of 'em someday. Babies and dogs. I like all kinds of animals."

"That's the truth." Pee Wee sounded amused. "We'd be running a regular menagerie out there to the field if I didn't keep a tight rein on him. As it is, he picked up the ugliest dog I ever seen somewhere and downright refused to drown it."

Zip was hurt. "Why, he's a good watchdog."

"I reckon. He don't even have to bark at trespassers. Anybody who takes a gander at him runs off screaming."

"Aw, Pee Wee!"

Alafair steered the conversation back on track. "Olivia said you even changed Ron's diaper, Zip."

"Well, I got no quarrel with baby shit. The little fellow didn't mean nothing by it."

Zip delivered this comment so innocently that Alafair nearly choked on the laugh that threatened to explode from her. She glanced at Pee Wee. She could just see his face in the dim light from the window. He was looking off into the dark, trying not to make eye contact and biting his lip in a valiant effort not to guffaw. He stood, and a shadow leaped from his chair to the porch. In the dark Alafair had not been able to see Ike in Pee Wee's lap.

"Come on, pea brain," he said. "I think it's time for us to hit the trail." He hauled Zip up by one arm and plopped the boy's hat on his head. "Good night, Miz Tucker. Please don't hold the boy's lack of refinement against him. Hope we'll see you again before you leave for home."

"Good night, boys," she managed. She waited until they walked down the steps, found their truck, gave it a crank to start it, and drove away, then allowed herself to laugh until she cried.

◇◇◇

"What's so funny, Ma?"

Alafair hadn't heard Martha and McCoy come outside. They walked over toward her end of the porch as she wiped her eyes and tried to get hold of herself. "Oh, just something that Zip said. That young'un is funnier than a bucketful of kittens without even meaning to be."

"He's about as worldly, too, I think," McCoy said. "I saw him with the kids earlier. He and Grace are just about on the same level."

"I reckon. Are you going back to the hotel, Streeter?"

"Yes, ma'am, I expect I ought."

"What time are y'all going out to the oil field tomorrow?"

"There's a train leaves for Garber in the morning at about eight. Zip will pick Martha and me up at the station out there and drive us to the field."

"Pee Wee told me he plans to shoot out the well first thing in the morning."

McCoy nodded. "Yes, we figured that if we got there around nine that'd give him time to get his blast done and his crew back to work before we show up."

"I wish he'd wait until we've come and gone," Martha said. "I don't see how his blast is more important than trying to figure out what happened to Kenneth."

"That's how these oil men are, Martha," McCoy said. "Death isn't a good enough reason to interfere with drilling."

Martha wasn't convinced. "If the blast opens a gusher, he's sure not going to be thinking of helping us much."

"Pretty unlikely," he assured her. "I don't think his well is deep enough yet."

Alafair interjected herself into the conversation. "Would y'all mind if I came with you?"

Martha and McCoy spoke at the same time.

"Why, Ma?" Martha said, sounding alarmed.

"Why, certainly, Mrs. Tucker," McCoy said, sounding perfectly delighted.

In the dark, Alafair could just see their heads turn as they looked at one another. "Good, then," she said, before any more discussion ensued. "Listen, kids. You can hear the music coming from downtown. Tonight's the last night of the Founders' Jubilee, ain't it?"

Martha looked back at her mother. "Yes, according to the paper, the street dance should be starting right about now."

Alafair sat back in the swing. "Y'all ought to walk down there and have a look before you call it a day. It's not all that late. Besides, the next few days ain't shaping up to be very pleasant. You young folks might as well have a little pleasure while you can."

Martha said, "Would you like to, Streeter?"

He stood there for a fraction of a second with his mouth open in surprise before he answered. "Well, sure. Would you like to come with us, Mrs. Tucker?"

"I don't think so, Streeter." She sounded just the littlest bit amused. "I'm taking myself up to bed."

Martha took McCoy's hand as they walked down the stairs. "We won't be gone long, Mama," she called, as they headed for the street.

McCoy was gratified at how easily, and even eagerly, Martha had acquiesced when her mother suggested that they take this last opportunity to enjoy the festival. He hoped it was because she relished the idea of spending some time in his company, but he was more realistically inclined to think that she wanted a break from the gloomy circumstances and the press of her relatives.

In any event, he had no intention of questioning his good fortune as he walked Martha down Washington toward Grand. She looked achingly lovely, he thought, as she strolled next to him, her arm casually strung through the crook of his. The dark waves of her hair didn't quite want to stay tucked into the roll at the back of her neck. Her cheeks were a bit flushed, whether from the exercise or from emotion, he wouldn't speculate. They didn't talk for more than a block, as she kept her thoughts to herself and he wondered how he could begin the conversation in the most innocuous fashion possible.

He finally took the plunge. "Nice night, but damp. Feels like it might rain some more."

"Doesn't seem to be keeping people away from the festivities. It sure has cooled things off, though. That's nice."

"This has been a corker of a couple of days."

She slid him an ironic glance. "I'd agree with that statement. In fact I can't remember so many life-changing events happening to one bunch of people in one five-day span since God created the world."

"Not even the flood?"

"That took longer than five days."

"How about the Resurrection, then?"

A brief smile touched her lips and was gone. "All right. I'll give you the Resurrection."

"How are your aunt and cousin doing? Do you think they'll be all right?"

Martha shrugged. "Olivia is doing real good, considering. This whole thing was a horrible shock to her, but she's a real strong girl, and I think she's up to the challenge of building a new life for herself and little Ron. Aunt Ruth Ann is mighty sad and shocked. It'll really help her to have Grandma and Grandpa here, when they finally come."

"When do you suspect you'll be heading home?"

"I don't know, now. Before this business with Kenneth, I imagine we'd be getting ready to leave right now. I can tell Mama's mighty eager to get home. She misses Daddy and the kids. But she always wants to be as much help as she can. Tell you the truth, she's handled this trip a lot better than I expected her to. I figured she'd just barge right in and take over Aunt Ruth Ann's life, but she's stood back and let things alone a lot more than I'd have ever guessed."

"Really? It seems to me that your mother is pretty much the one who got right in there and made things happen."

"Well, that's Ma. But what surprised me was that she took time to go to the fair and to go shopping with me, and wonder of wonders, let me buy something for her! She's been reading that book I loaned her, and actually took at least one nap that I know of. I've been feeling like the trip has been good for her, but now Kenneth has gone and got himself killed, and I'm worried about what Mama will do."

"What could she possibly do about that, honey?"

Martha shot him a look. "She'll go to find out what happened to Kenneth or die trying. And that's what just frets me no end. Do you remember that ugly business out at our place last year after my Uncle Bill McBride got shot?"

"Oh, yes! Your mother went after the killer tooth and nail, didn't she?"

"Well, he was after Mary, and yes, she did. And nearly got herself killed in the bargain. And that's not the only time she's put herself in danger, either. Now she's got that gleam in her eye again, and I'm scared to death for her."

By this time, they were walking through the fairgoing crowds. The Cheyenne tepees had been taken down, and the square had been transformed into a giant ballroom. Crushes of people were waltzing, two-stepping, and clogging across the courthouse lawn and in the streets to the accompaniment of a brass band. Multitudes of electric lights gave the square a surreal brightness.

"That's a pretty song they're playing," Martha noted. "I don't believe I know that one."

"That sounds like "Todd's Sweet Rural Shade." My old Irish granny liked that one."

Martha smiled. "You sure know your songs."

McCoy took Martha by the hand and turned toward her. As naturally as walking, they melted into the river of dancers and began to waltz down Randolph.

He sang along to the music.

"Oh, come my fair and lovely maid,
Will you consent to love?"

She puffed, whether amused or irritated, he couldn't tell, but he expected he'd best not push it.

"We'll help your mother, Martha." He spoke softly into her ear. "You and me, we'll do whatever needs to be done to keep your ma safe. Just don't borrow worry, darling. Could be that Mrs. Tucker learned her lesson better than you think."

Martha's breath warmed his neck as she sighed. "I hope so. She's always surprising me. I thought I knew her pretty well, Streeter, but she said some things to me over this week that nearly made me swallow my teeth, things I never thought my mother thought about or even knew about."

"I had an experience like that with my dad, once. Seems we never know our parents as well as we think we do. I admire your mother a lot, the way she's so competent. Her life can't be a bowl of cherries, what with all you kids."

Martha had nothing to say to this. They were moving down Grand, now, and for a few minutes they simply allowed themselves to be carried along by the music.

Martha stopped dancing. "I don't want to be like my mother."

McCoy paused on the sidewalk and looked down at her, waiting, his expression mildly curious and concerned.

A puzzled look crossed her face as she gazed up at him. She seemed to be more taken aback by this statement than he was.

Finally she spoke. "I love my mother like crazy, Streeter. But she has no life of her own at all. Every single thing she does is for somebody else—mostly for us kids, or Daddy. And it seems to me that everybody just expects it of her. She doesn't care a flip about what's happening in the world. Not the war in Europe or votes for women or anything. She never reads, or goes anywhere but to church or to visit relatives, or takes any time for herself. She's like an ox in yoke."

"She seems happy," McCoy said.

"I know. None of it bothers her in the least. I'd go out of my mind to have to live like that. I want to do something interesting with myself. I want to make a mark in the world."

"Why, honey, you are your mother's mark on the world, you and your brothers and sisters. That seems to me like a mark as deep as the Grand Canyon."

She laughed. "Oh, I know it. I don't mean to belittle my mother, not at all. She doesn't have to get rich or create a work of art. She is rich in the only way that matters to her, and her whole life is a work of art. She's found her calling, all right. It's just not my calling. Not all women are alike, Streeter, same as men."

McCoy's golden eyes had brightened somewhere in the middle of this speech. Alafair had said almost the same thing to him. "Is this why you hesitate to consider my proposal?" he asked, when she paused.

She looked away from him, troubled, and didn't answer.

McCoy considered telling her about his conversation with her mother on this very topic, but Alafair had warned him that Martha might not take it well, so he approached from another direction. "Martha, I don't have any expectations that you'd have to act one way or another if we were to marry. I like to think I'm a modern man, with modern ideas. I'm looking for a partner in my life, not a servant."

"I like having a job," she said, without looking at him. "I like working."

"Well, shoot fire, Martha, go on and work. You don't need my permission. In fact, if Mr. Bushyhead is such a knucklehead that he'd let go of the most important person at the First National Bank of Boynton, then come and help me run McCoy Title Company. Be my partner in business as well as life."

She didn't answer, and she still didn't look at him, but her cheeks flushed and a slow smile grew on her lips, and for the first time since he had so forcefully and inconveniently fallen in love with this impossible woman, he felt a bloom of real hope.

"Speaking of Mama...," she said.

His brain was so a-roil that her words didn't mean anything to him at first. "What?"

She nodded toward the street. "Look there, Streeter, I just caught sight of Mama. I thought she said she was going to bed."

McCoy looked to where Martha had nodded, across the intersection they had just crossed, back on Grand. All he could see were people, intent on each other, dancing in front of the shops on the sidewalk, bathed in artificial light from strings of bulbs festooned between poles around the square. "I don't see her."

She pointed. "Over there, in front of Klein's. Wait 'til those people get out of the way."

A woman in a big hat passed, and suddenly he saw what Martha was pointing at, and guffawed. "Why, honey," he managed. "That's you!"

Before he even spoke, Martha realized what she had seen and turned several shades of red. Her own reflection was staring back at her from the dark display window of Klein's Department Store. The irony of it struck her like a blow and laughter spewed out of her. "Mercy! I'm feeling a bit disturbed, Streeter," she said, after she caught her breath. "Buy me an ice cream. I need to ponder this a while before I go back to the house."

Saturday, September 18, 1915

Pee Wee Nickolls stood next to his truck on the long, sloping rise that overlooked the oil field and peered at the automobile coming toward them down the road from Enid. All the previous summer, an automobile traveling down that road would have announced its approach for miles with a giant column of red dust. But the gentle rains of the last couple of days had laid down the dirt without turning the highway into mud, greatly improving the driving conditions.

Pee Wee absently removed a pouch of tobacco from his pocket and rolled himself a cigarette as he squinted against the bright sun into the distance, then struck a match against his thigh and fired up his smoke.

The automobile pulled off the road in front of him. The man in the nice suit, McCoy, stepped out from beside Zip and helped the two dark-haired women to get out of the backseat. Pee Wee had been expecting McCoy and Martha. But he had not expected Alafair.

Pee Wee took a final deep drag and ground the cigarette under his heel before he approached his visitors. He tipped his hat to the ladies and shook hands with McCoy.

Both Zip and Pee Wee were dressed in their oil field attire of a flannel shirt and corduroy trousers tucked into high-topped boots, or in Zip's case, leggings and heavy shoes. They looked quite a bit different than they had when they called on Olivia yesterday, Alafair noted. "How'd your blast go this morning, Mr. Nickolls?"

"Well, ma'am, we haven't done it yet." He slammed his hat back on his head to punctuate his irritation. "When we got back from Enid late last night, we found out that somebody had made hisself at home and broke into every building, hut, and doghouse on the property. Looks like a tornado went through. Of course, all the hands were in Enid at the dance and the watchman was sleeping like the dead and didn't hear a thing—or so he says. The guard dog was gone, and we figured he was shot, but he showed up this morning, all wobbly. Poisoned, I expect. We've been setting things to right ever since we got back, trying to figure out what got took."

"Oh, my, did you call the law?" Martha said.

"I sent a man back to Breckinridge to wire Sheriff Hume, but he ain't showed yet." His good eye narrowed. "Seems *y'all* were right about Collins looking for something."

"Now, wait a minute," McCoy cautioned. "Best not go off half-cocked. We're just guessing about Collins. Have you found anything missing?"

"Yes, I'm sorry to say. There were two five-quart cans of nitroglycerin in the magazine when we left yesterday. I'd prepared one for the blast, and it was ready to transport up here to the well. We found that canister had been opened and the explosive drained off."

A moment of ominous silence followed as everyone pondered the implications.

Finally McCoy ventured a comment. "That points to somebody other than Collins, I think. I doubt if he'd be hunting for a canister of nitro."

"He might be hunting for a way to shut us down." Pee Wee had obviously been thinking hard about the situation. "If an explosion put us out of production, he'd have a free hand to go to looking around. Or maybe scare Miz Crawford into signing her share over to him. There was enough nitro gone out of that can to leave nothing of this well but a smoking hole."

"If that was why the nitro was taken, why didn't the thieves go ahead and blow up the well when they had the chance?" McCoy asked.

Pee Wee shrugged. "We drove in pretty late. Maybe we interrupted them before they could do the deed."

Alafair didn't say it, but another possibility had occurred to her that didn't make her happy in the least. If something happened to Pee Wee, his interest in the well would go to Olivia. All the handier for someone intent on getting his hands on the entire operation. She resolved to share this unsavory thought with the sheriff as soon as he showed up.

"Well, I reckon we'd best get on with it," Pee Wee said. "They's a bunch more to eyeball, Mr. McCoy, and not much time to do it. If y'all ladies will go with Zip, he'll take y'all down to the office and let you get to going at the books. Zip, show Miss Tucker where I keep the books and set her at my desk."

"Yessir, Pee Wee."

The party turned as one and eyed Alafair, unsure of what to do with her. Her eyebrows peaked.

"Don't y'all worry about me." She leaned back on the fender of Zip's truck. "Martha or Zip can put me to some useful task, or else I'll just stay out of the way."

◇◇◇

There was nothing that Alafair could do to help Martha with the books and ledgers that Pee Wee had neatly arranged on a shelf behind the rickety table he had christened his desk. The equally rickety, bare-board shack that served as the oil field business office had already been inventoried and restored after the break-in, so Alafair was deprived even of the opportunity to clean up. Martha shooed them away with a suggestion that Zip show her mother around the field for an hour or so, and perhaps they could discover some other mess to set right.

Alafair was reluctant to take Zip away from some more useful occupation, but the youth was so eager to show off the drilling operation that she gave in—gladly. There was no telling what one could see when one kept her eyes and her mind open.

As soon as they walked out of the office, they were greeted by a dog that appeared out of nowhere. He was a medium-sized, black-and-white mongrel who looked healthy and well cared for, but he was perhaps the ugliest dog Alafair had ever seen. He was some kind of bull terrier mix who appeared to have had more than his share of misfortune. The left side of his head was caved in, and he was missing his left ear and much of the fur on the left side of his body. His bottom jaw was lopsided, and his tongue lolled out one side, and when he walked, his back half seemed to want to go in a slightly different direction than his front half.

Zip was delighted to see him, though, and the dog was delighted right back at Zip.

"My heavens!" Alafair exclaimed, in spite of herself. "I expect this is the critter Pee Wee mentioned last night."

"Yes, ma'am. Miz Tucker, this here is Muddy, our watchdog." The animal reared himself up on his hind legs and propped his front paws on Zip's chest, affording the boy an easy angle for an ear rub. "My, I'm glad to see him up and about. Why, last night, we couldn't find him at all. I was afraid the burglars had done him in, but he showed up this morning, sick as...well, a dog. He just crawled under the shed and wouldn't come out, 'til now. Pee Wee reckoned the thieves slipped him some bad grub to put him out of commission while they ransacked the place."

Muddy lowered himself to the ground and trotted over to Alafair, interested in checking out the stranger. He didn't seem to be much of a threat. Alafair thought herself more likely to be drooled upon than bitten. She held out her hand for Muddy to sniff. He evidently approved of her, because he sidled up comfortably and trotted along beside her as Zip led the way back up the path to the road overlooking the field, where the truck was still parked.

"This dog don't look very vicious, for a guard dog," she observed.

"Oh, he is, Miz Tucker. Why, ol' Muddy can take your leg right off if he's a mind to. He knows you're a friend, is all. Ol' Muddy has got the magic eye when it comes to telling friend from foe. That's why the thieves had to get him out of the way last night. He'd of ripped them limb from limb, wouldn't you, Muddy?"

Alafair wondered idly why the burglars hadn't just shot the dog rather than feed him something to put him to sleep or make him sick. That seemed like an awfully delicate and time-consuming course of action for outlaws. "I guess you call him 'Muddy' because he's ugly as a mud fence."

"Yes, ma'am. That's Pee Wee's name for him. I didn't want to, 'cause he can't help it that he's all bashed up. I wanted to call him Junior, but Pee Wee liked Muddy, and it just sort of stuck."

"What happened to him?"

"Don't rightly know. He just showed up at the rig one day, looking like he does now, except all skinny and mangy. I expect he got run over by a wagon when he was a puppy, or some such. He's a good old dog, though. Been a good watchdog and a pretty good rat-catcher, too."

The dog was walking so close to her that his ungainly trot kept knocking her off her stride. He was intent on his task, though, which Alafair expected was to escort her to wherever she was going. She smiled at the top of his distorted head. He was ugly, but he was a gentleman.

When they reached the top of the rise, Zip stopped and turned to face the well. His arm swept the horizon from left to right. "You can see the whole site from here."

About a mile to the east, a forest of derricks marked the location of the Sinclair field. To the north, they could see the entire Crawford field, with its one solitary wooden derrick in the middle of the flat, prairie grass-covered plain, outlined against a pale sky. Since Pee Wee had not been able to carry out his blasting operation that morning and clear out the obstructed well, the drilling operation was suspended. At the moment, the twisters were drawing lengths of pipe and a damaged drill bit out of the hole. Next to the derrick, Alafair could see the engine house and part of the generator inside. Three or four roustabouts were working the machinery, one at the generator, a couple at the drill, and one off to the side doing some task involving a bucket. A large pool of what looked like mud stood some yards from the rig, along with piles of pipes and a stack of lumber, and a few small, rough outbuildings. Aside from the Sinclair derricks in the distance, the only other features for miles were the well-graded road from Enid to Garber, and the utility road on the property, if two parallel ruts running straight from the northern horizon could be called a road.

"Quite an operation," Alafair said to Zip. "It's much bigger than I expected! From the way Olivia told it, I half expected it was just you and Mr. Nickolls."

Zip grinned, as proud as if it were all his own doing. "No, ma'am. Pee Wee, he don't do nothing halfway. He expects that if you're going to do a thing, you ought to do it right. We got but one well right now, but it's a good'un."

"Looks like an expensive proposition," Alafair observed.

"I don't know nothing about the finances, ma'am. That was Mr. Crawford's lookout. Pee Wee, he just takes what money is give him and does what needs doing."

"I wonder what Mr. Nickolls expects to do for money now?"

"I don't know, Miz Tucker. I've been pondering on that myself. Pee Wee ain't said nothing to me about it. He just keeps going on like he always done, like he don't expect nothing to change."

Alafair considered this as Zip continued his tour of the field. Just what did Pee Wee expect would happen now? Would Olivia be able—or willing—to continue financing him? And even if she wanted to, her money might be tied up in probate for months or even years. And what about Lester's will? Did he have the strength or the time to make changes now that Kenneth was no more, or was Olivia's financial fate going to be in the hands of her uncle George Gunn after Lester passed?

She was so involved with her thoughts that she was unaware of the vehicle that came to a stop a few yards up the hill until Zip spoke.

"Yonder's the sheriff," he said.

She turned to see an extremely tall, gangly, ruddy-faced man of about fifty unfold himself from an open Ford roadster with the words "Garfield County Sheriff's Department" printed over a big yellow star on the door. He was dressed in a fedora hat and a dark, wrinkled, three-piece suit with a badge on the breast of the coat. A floppy brown mustache graced his upper lip, which reminded Alafair so forcefully of Shaw that she smiled, instantly disposed to like the man even before she met him. He was unarmed.

Zip turned and walked toward him, and Alafair trailed behind. The sheriff stayed where he was, next to his automobile, and let them come to him. He folded his extra-long arms across his chest and eyed them with an expression that looked like annoyance, but his mouth twitched when he glanced down at Muddy, then back up at Zip. "Y'all the ones who called me?"

Zip snatched off his hat. "I wired you from over to Breckinridge, Sheriff. I'm Zip Kolocek. I'm the boweevil for Mr. Nickolls, who runs this outfit. This here is Miz Tucker. She's aunt to Miz Crawford. Miz Crawford owns the field, now, I reckon." Zip turned toward Alafair. "Miz Tucker, meet Sheriff Hume."

"Glad to meet you, Mr. Hume." Alafair extended her hand, and Hume took it. His hand was bony and calloused and squeezed hers briefly.

"Ma'am." One of Hume's eyes narrowed as he assessed her, before addressing himself to Zip. "I hear y'all been burgled."

"Yes, sir. I'll take you to Pee Wee. He can explain things better than me."

Zip led the way and Alafair fell in beside the sheriff as they walked down the hill toward the well.

"Don't believe we've met, Miz Tucker," Hume said. "You from around here?"

"No, me and my family have a farm over in Muskogee County, outside of Boynton. Olivia Crawford's mother, Ruth Ann Yeager, is my sister. Me and my daughters just come up a couple of days ago to take our leave of Lester when all this bad business happened." She didn't bother explaining who Lester was or what the "bad business" consisted of. The Garfield County sheriff was based in Enid, the county seat. He would know all her leading citizens and Chief Burns would have fully apprised him about Kenneth's suspicious death.

Hume grunted, which she took to mean that he understood the situation.

"Everybody seems to be of the opinion that Mr. Collins has something to do with the goings on of late," Alafair ventured.

Hume grunted again.

"That's why we're here, me and my daughter and her friend, to help Mr. Nickolls search for some reason Mr. Collins might be interested in this field. My daughter knows all about books and numbers and such and offered to study the records in the office there. Then lo and behold, when we get out here this morning from Enid, we find that somebody had torn everything up looking for something."

She had hoped that volunteering information would encourage Sheriff Hume to reciprocate and tell her something she didn't know, but Hume was not inclined to indulge her. He shot her a sidelong glance and kept silent.

Alafair fell back a step or two when Pee Wee approached, and stood listening unabashedly as he told the sheriff what had happened. Hume's eyebrows knit when Pee Wee told him about the missing nitroglycerin.

"Well, I don't like to hear that. And as far as you can tell, there ain't anything else missing?"

"As far as we can tell to now, Sheriff."

"So, you got any ideas about who done this?"

"Well, seems my late partner, Kenneth Crawford, was in to Buck Collins for a bunch of dough, and the Widow Crawford has an idea that there was more to it than that."

"Like what?"

Pee Wee shrugged. "Like maybe Crawford had something that Buck wants pretty bad. After what happened out here, I'm thinking she may have a point."

Hume flicked another glance at Alafair before he turned back to Pee Wee. "You got any proof to add to your opinion about Collins?"

Pee Wee shrugged. "Not a shred."

"You leave everything like you found it?"

"Well, no, we got everything back into order right smart."

Hume sighed his disapproval, but Pee Wee was unmoved. "We've got a business to run, Sheriff. I've still got men walking the property, looking for tracks, anything of the like."

"Find any?"

"I ain't heard of it yet if they have."

"And none of the crew heard or saw anything last night while all this demolition was going on?" Hume sounded skeptical.

"It was Friday night, Sheriff, and the last night of the Founders' Jubilee. Most of the boys hitched themselves up a wagon or two and rode in to Enid. Didn't get back 'til the slim hours, and a couple of 'em ain't back yet."

"So nobody was at the field at all last night?"

"There's always somebody here. Usually me. But I had to go to Enid because of Crawford getting himself dead, so old Bull Heath volunteered to stay on the property. He went to bed near to eight o'clock, though, and didn't hear anything. We got us a dog that'll bark to beat the band at anything suspicious, but whoever wrecked the place tossed him a piece of bad meat, I reckon, 'cause he was mighty sick this morning."

Hume glanced down at the dog, who was still glued to Alafair's side. "He looks to be all right now." A twitch of his cheek betrayed the fact that he thought that 'looks all right' was a relative notion in Muddy's case.

"He either didn't eat enough to hurt him, or the villain just meant to keep him out of the way for a spell rather than kill him."

"Maybe it was somebody Muddy knows." Alafair blinked in surprise when Hume turned that sharp, speculative gaze on her again. She regretted that the comment had slipped out. She had not meant to draw attention to herself, lest the sheriff wonder why she was eavesdropping on their conversation and tell her to go.

Hume turned his attention back to Pee Wee without saying anything to her. "I'll be wanting to talk to this Bull Heath, and the rest of the crew, as well."

Pee Wee nodded. "Zip, go find Bull and fetch him yonder to the bunks. We'll meet you there directly."

"Sure enough, Pee Wee." Zip took off toward the derrick at a trot, and after a moment of indecision, Muddy abandoned Alafair and followed him. At a pretty good pace, she thought, considering that his front half and his back half were moving at different speeds.

◇◇◇

They arrived back in Enid on the afternoon train. They had left Lester's Oldsmobile parked at the station that morning and McCoy drove them back to Ruth Ann's house. It was a shorter trip across town today than it was yesterday, since the square was finally open to traffic again. The grandstand was almost down and most of the tents and rides were already gone, and the streets were full of horses, pedestrians, and automobiles once again. McCoy had to stop once on Randolph to let a streetcar go by.

As soon as they arrived at the Yeager house, each went his or her own way. After Alafair found Grace playing with Olivia and Ron on the porch at the side of the house, she went upstairs to relieve Ruth Ann at Lester's bedside. McCoy pulled the Yeagers' car into the small wooden garage at the back of the property, retrieved his motorcycle, and left to go back to his office for a couple of hours.

Martha took charge of her sister and sat down next to Olivia in a cushioned wicker chair on the porch, facing the garden. Little Ron was balancing on his mother's lap, chuckling at the bear and dolly play that Grace was putting on for him, unaware and unconcerned that he had recently become fatherless. Olivia, on the other hand, looked pale and sleep deprived, with dark circles under her eyes that weren't entirely camouflaged by her spectacles.

"How are you doing?" Martha asked her.

Olivia smiled and shrugged without taking her eyes off of Ron. "Oh, all right. I've kept too busy to think much. Mr. Henninger called 'round a while ago to tell me that Kenneth will be laid out tomorrow morning in one of the viewing rooms at his new funeral parlor. I expect I'll be going over there first thing in the morning to see how he looks." She glanced at Martha. "I'm dreading it."

"So y'all aren't having him here at the house?" Martha's comment was delivered mildly, but she was shocked. She'd never heard of such a thing as not having your deceased loved one at home with the family for a day or two before the funeral.

Olivia shook her head. "No, I don't think I could stand it. Besides, Mr. Henninger and Mr. Royer assured me that most folks hold their viewings right in the funeral parlor these days. It's much more convenient, being right there next to the chapel, and all."

Martha didn't say what she was thinking, which was that it all sounded pretty cold to her. Instead, she said, "I'll go with you, if you'd like."

"Thank you, Cousin. That would comfort me a bunch. I'd rather Mama didn't go down there 'til later in the day, after I've seen to everything. She's got enough on her mind, what with Daddy and all."

"I think you've got plenty on your mind, too, Olivia. I know it would do your ma's heart good to know she was helping you, just like you help her."

"Oh, I expect you're right. I guess I'm just so used to taking care of Mama. That was what me and Daddy always did, both of us together. That was our job, he said, to take care of Mama. I guess it'll just be my job from now on." Her face clouded, and tears started to her eyes and spilled down her cheeks. Martha handed her the handkerchief that she had stuffed up her sleeve, and Olivia dabbed her face with it, one-handed.

It was true, Martha thought, that Uncle Lester had always taken care of Aunt Ruth Ann like she was a hothouse flower, and had recruited his only daughter to do the same for as long as Martha had known anything about it. Aunt Ruth Ann seemed to think that was just the way things were supposed to be. Odd. Ruth Ann was her mother's sister, and unless the laws of natural inheritance had been turned on their head, Martha was sure that Ruth Ann was as capable of being as competent and tough as any of the Gunn women. Yet Ruth Ann and Olivia had developed their dynamic long ago, and would probably have trouble seeing each other differently. Now that their lives were changing so fundamentally, would they surprise each other?

Like Alafair was surprising Martha?

Martha shook her head tightly and came back to the moment. "Well, I couldn't find anything out of order with the books out at the well. But they had some excitement out there last night. Somebody about wrecked the place, searching for something, Mr. Nickolls reckons."

Olivia pulled herself and little Ron up straight. "I declare! I was just about to tell you exactly the same thing about the office! Somebody got in last night and tore it up top to bottom. They even managed to open the safe and go through all the papers that were in there. Mike Ed called Chief Burns right away, of course, but what could he do? Funny thing is, as near as I can tell, the burglar didn't take anything. Didn't even touch the petty cash."

"What about the warehouse? The crates and merchandise?"

"Not touched, that we could see. And we sure looked. Could be that whoever it was didn't have time to search anywhere but the office. What I can't figure is how they got in and out of there without being seen. We have a night watchman."

"It's a pretty big warehouse. Could someone have managed to sneak in and out without being seen if they were watching the guard's movements?" Martha pondered a moment before she offered, "Or it could be that Mike Ed hired somebody who's in cahoots with the thieves. In any event, the fact that they only searched the office may mean that they're looking for papers, and not some other kind of loot."

"Was anything missing from the drilling operation?"

Martha hesitated. Would it help Olivia in any way if she knew about the missing nitroglycerin right this minute? "A thing or two. Like your break-in, though, they seemed to be most interested in the papers and records, and Mr. Nickolls said there was nothing missing from those."

"Oh, Martha, what is happening here? Kenneth must have done something awful bad. He must have crossed somebody with a mean streak a mile wide, and I'm putting my money on Buck Collins. But what can it be? Why doesn't Collins just ask me for it, whatever it is? I'll give it to him if he'll just leave us alone. He killed my Kenneth. What else could he possibly threaten us with that would be half as bad?"

Olivia started to cry again. Concerned, Grace abandoned her dolls on the porch and draped herself across Olivia's knees just as Martha seized her cousin's arm to comfort her.

Olivia wiped her eyes with the handkerchief again, and little Ron sagged dangerously in her lap. "I want to go home, Martha. I don't want to stay here at Mama's anymore."

"Oh, now, Mr. Burns thinks you and Ron will be safer here at your folks' for a spell, at least until he can figure out who's behind this frightful business."

"He knows who's behind it as well as I do. Can he prove it—that's the question? Collins is slick as a gut. There's a dozen dirty deeds that everybody in town knows to lay at his feet, yet not a one has ever been proved against him. I'm afraid. I'm so afraid that he's going to get away with it again, and my poor Kenneth will go unavenged."

"Still," Martha said, "I think it would be better if you didn't stay at home by yourself just yet."

"I know. Don't worry. I wouldn't do anything to put Ron in danger. But I want to go home, anyway. Just for a little bit, just to check on things and to sit in my own house for a few minutes." Olivia shifted Ron to her shoulder, took Grace's hand, and stood up. "Come with me."

"Right now?"

"Don't look so surprised. Supper's not for another couple of hours, and I could use the exercise, not to mention the distraction. We'll walk down there and sit for a little while, then walk back. It's broad daylight. Nothing's going to happen. Grace, you want to take a walk?"

"Yes! Can we ride the fair's wheel again?"

"The fair is over, sweet pea," Martha said, then to Olivia, "Just let me run up and tell Mama where we're going."

◇◇◇

By the time his visitors left, early in the afternoon, Pee Wee and his men had gone over the field, buildings, and well with meticulous care, and had restored everything to its original order as best as they could. Aside from a quart or so of nitroglycerin, they had found nothing missing. But that one missing quart of explosive was worrying Pee Wee something awful.

They had lost almost an entire day's worth of drilling, and Pee Wee didn't feel he could afford to delay blasting the well obstruction any longer. He and his crew checked every inch of the derrick and drilling machinery for booby traps before he felt comfortable enough to proceed.

The men drew three hundred feet of tubing out of the well, section by section, while Pee Wee himself transported the remaining can of nitro from the magazine to the well. When the well was ready, Pee Wee sent the crew off to safety while he prepared the torpedo himself.

He poured water into the canister, which immediately separated the nitro from the alcohol it was mixed with, causing the explosive to sink to the bottom. He siphoned it out of the can into a smaller copper vessel, and then carefully poured it into the shell which had been positioned at the mouth of the well. The torpedo was armed with a blasting cap and a battery-powered timer, and lowered gingerly at the end of a wire down the hole, all the way to the bottom, where it detonated.

The blast went off satisfactorily and cleared the obstruction, though Pee Wee was a little disappointed that he hadn't opened up a gusher. He smiled at his own folly. He knew that it was very unlikely the well was deep enough to strike, but the enterprise had been plagued with so much trouble lately that he thought he was owed a little luck.

It seemed to take forever for the twisters to hook up a new drill bit and replace the tubing in the well. When the rig was finally, finally ready, Pee Wee, Zip, and Deo Juarez, the Texican mechanic, walked the twenty feet from the derrick to the engine house. Muddy the dog followed on Zip's heels at a misaligned trot, his tongue lolling out of his sideways mouth, as relaxed and hideously ugly as ever.

"Engine house" was a grand appellation for the three-walled shack that surrounded the enormous, gasoline-powered generator that powered the drill. The building opened toward the derrick, and served no purpose other than to keep rain, snow, and windblown dirt out of the engine. The fact that it afforded the drillers some protection from the elements was entirely incidental. They fired up the generator and it roared into action. Pee Wee stood at the open end of the engine house and watched with satisfaction as the drill began to rotate. The twisters prepared to attach another length of pipe to the drill as the well deepened.

Deo appeared at Pee Wee's side. He hadn't heard him come up, but the noise of the engine was such that he wouldn't have heard the blare of the trumpets announcing the Second Coming.

Pee Wee might have said he liked Deo, if he had known him well enough to form an opinion. With the single exception of Zip Kolocek, Pee Wee made a practice of keeping his distance from the crew. Oil field workers were too transitory, generally unsavory, and usually too short-lived to waste emotion on. Deo was a good-natured little guy, though, and good at his job, which put him higher than most in his boss' estimation. He had told Pee Wee that he was born in El Paso. He had such a thick Mexican accent that he was hard to understand, which in itself didn't mean that he wasn't American-born. But coupled with the fact that Juarez, Chihuahua, was attached to El Paso at the U.S.–Mexican border, Pee Wee had about decided that Deo was calling himself after the hometown he had fled after some unknown trouble. Pee Wee didn't really care. Deo was good at his job.

Deo sidled up close enough to be heard over the noise and Pee Wee skewed him a curious glance.

"Where's the oil can, boss?" Deo yelled into his ear. "One a'them journals, she getting hot. Not workin' all day, it makes her stiff."

Pee Wee glanced back over his shoulder at the tool shelf, where the lubricants usually were, then leaned back in toward Deo. "Well, there it is, right there, you dingbat. I reckon that in all the commotion, it either got put back on the second shelf instead of the first, or you've done gone blind."

Deo's gaze followed Pee Wee's pointing finger, and he laughed. "I gone blind, I reckon, boss." He retrieved the roundish, long-spouted can from its unaccustomed place on the shelf before he returned to the generator.

Deo and Zip put their heads together so the older man could explain the procedure to the younger. Pee Wee couldn't hear a thing, of course, so he watched with interest as Deo used one finger and his opposite fist to pantomime a shaft turning jerkily in a bearing.

Most of the men on the crew had adopted Zip as a kind of pet, and it wasn't unusual to see someone giving the boy a lesson. After all, that's how most of them had learned the business, themselves. Pee Wee smiled as Zip leaned in as best he could, considering that a one-eared dog was lying across his feet, and listened earnestly.

Pee Wee was feeling much better, now that the effects of the vandalism were righted and they were back in production. Whatever Collins' gang had been looking for, it apparently hadn't been on the oil field property. Collins would probably leave him alone, now.

As for the nitro, well, whatever mischief the thief intended didn't seem to have anything to do with the well, because they hadn't found a trace of it anywhere on the property.

I reckon we dodged a bullet, he thought, and blew out a sigh of relief.

Deo handed Zip the oil can and pointed to the rapidly spinning axle. Zip gently shoveled the dog off his boots with one foot. He stretched his lanky body across the machinery, being careful not to touch any moving parts, and tilted the oil can carefully over the journal. For a tenth of a second, a thin stream of viscous yellowish oil descended through twelve inches of air toward the pounding engine.

Not long enough for Pee Wee's thinking processes to engage, but it didn't matter. There was no gap between the instant he saw that the oil was cloudy and not clear and the instant he knew that he was looking at disaster.

He just about had time to lunge forward and yell "Stop!" as the familiar, acrid smell of nitroglycerin hit his nostrils.

It was an easy walk to Olivia's house, on oak-lined and graded streets, protected from the sun by the mature summer foliage that overhung the sidewalks. Martha noted that the afternoon was cool, which was a blessing. She wasn't used to nice weather yet, after such a hot, dry summer. Grace was maniacally dashing up and back along the sidewalk, full of energy after an afternoon of inactivity. She paused once or twice to pull a flowering weed from a yard, and Martha kept a close eye on her to make sure she didn't help herself to someone's carefully tended peony.

There were some nice neighborhoods in Enid, she thought. *Perhaps if I ever have a home of my own, I'll steal a decorating* tip or two from some of these houses. She pointed at the large red brick house they were passing. "Look yonder at the blue trim around the windows. Isn't that unusual? And see how she's got flowers and vegetables together in pots on the porch? What a good idea!"

Olivia shifted the burbling Ron to her other shoulder. "That reminds me. Don't let me forget to water the sweet potato vine on the porch. My poor violet in the living room hasn't had a drink in days. It's probably drooping bad by now, if it isn't dead."

They turned onto Elm and approached Olivia's white, brick trimmed house. "Your hydrangea bush in the front yard looks good," Martha observed. "But that sweet potato vine might could use some water."

Grace dashed up onto the front porch and pounded all around, followed more sedately by Martha and Olivia. Olivia pulled open the front screen and froze, a perplexed expression on her face.

"What is it?" Martha asked.

"The front door is ajar."

Olivia reached for the doorknob, but Martha stepped forward and grabbed her hand.

"No, don't! Somebody could be in there waiting for you. Let's go back to your ma's and call the police."

Olivia shook her off, annoyed. "I'll be blamed if I'm going to be afraid to enter my own house. Here, hold the baby. Y'all wait out here until I call you."

She thrust Ron at Martha and went inside before her cousin had time to protest. Startled, Martha jiggled the baby in her arms and stood nervously waiting for Olivia's signal, half prepared to make a run for it. "Grace, hush up that singing for a minute and come here," she hissed.

Grace swallowed her song, wide-eyed at Martha's tone, but didn't move from her spot at the end of the porch.

Olivia stuck her head out the door and gestured at them. "Come in here."

Martha sagged with relief before she followed her cousin inside with the kids in tow, but they stopped dead just inside the door, stunned.

The place was wrecked. The furniture was splintered and the upholstery shredded. Books and papers were strewn over every inch of the parlor floor, and all the rugs had been tossed into a heap. The curtains and rods had been torn down. The bookshelves in the parlor had been ripped off the wall and lay in a pile of broken wood.

Down the hall, they could see bedclothes piled on the floor outside the bedroom doors. The kitchen looked like a bomb had gone off, blowing every dish, utensil, and cabinet to shards. What was left of the counters was white with flour and sugar, and the ice box had been emptied onto the floor in a mess of mashed food and glass.

For a moment, nobody said anything. Olivia's face was so red that Martha feared she'd have a stroke right then and there.

Grace lifted her hands and squeezed her cheeks between her palms. "Oh, my goodness!" she exclaimed.

"Now, when last we left Mr. Pudd'nhead Wilson, he had just showed the jury how he could tell Count Luigi from his twin brother Count Angelo by just the marks of their fingers on windowpane."

"How's the murder investigation going?" Lester asked.

Alafair lowered the book into her lap and looked up at her brother-in-law. Lester was turned on his side, his skeletal frame almost swallowed up by the big feather mattress and pillows and the pile of quilts that covered him. How that body could still keep hold of his soul was a wonder to her, but the eyes that stared out at her were quite alive and bright with curiosity. "I think that Pudd'nhead aims to show that it was Tom who done the judge in."

"I mean, has Chief Burns made any progress in finding out who killed Kenneth?" His voice bore a trace of irony. He knew perfectly well that she was trying to put him off the topic.

"Lester, what good is it going to do you to fret yourself over something you can't do anything about?"

"It'll fret me a lot more to go to my reward without knowing whether or not justice has been done."

Alafair closed the book and took a breath. She almost said that after he passed, he'd know everything. She didn't want to upset a dying man, but when anyone tried to keep things from her "for her own good," she was annoyed beyond enduring. She didn't want to inflict that condescension on Lester. "It's early days, yet, though I think the chief is of the same mind as everybody else that Buck Collins is behind Kenneth's death in some way or another. But if he has found any proof positive, I ain't heard about it. I'm still thinking that Collins didn't have much of a reason to kill Kenneth, anyway."

"He knows I'm dying."

Alafair blinked. "What?"

"Buck knows I'm dying. He knows he doesn't have much time left to do me one last bad deed."

Alafair was incredulous. "Do you mean to tell me that you think Collins killed your son-in-law just to cause you grief? Send you to your grave in misery? Ruth Ann told me something of the bad blood between you, but that's going some, Lester! What monster would go to such lengths to cause pain to a dying man? Can anyone be so cruel?"

Lester shook his head, pitying her naiveté. "You don't know Buck like I do. There's nothing he wouldn't do to spite me. I'm guessing he wants me to know that he manipulated poor old stupid Kenneth and now he's poised to take everything I built after I die."

"Dear me! I can't hardly credit it. It does seem that somebody is hunting for something, though whether it's Buck Collins or not I don't know. Seems burglars broke into the office at the warehouse and the office at the oil well, too, and tore both places up looking for something." She didn't tell him about what had happened at Olivia's house. There were limits to how far she was willing to go in the interest of full disclosure.

Lester's sunken eyes widened. "I'll swear! Was anything stole?"

She hesitated before she said, "Nothing of any value. Mike Ed and Pee Wee reckoned that the vandals were looking for some papers, or something written down. We looked over the books at both places this morning and didn't find anything out of place, but I think the boys plan to go through everything again with a fine-tooth comb. If they just took a page out of a ledger, or a contract, that won't be so easy to spot."

"Lord, Lord," Lester breathed. "I sure didn't plan on Olivia having to deal with anything like this after I'm gone. Old Buck is one step ahead of me, this time."

"I've never found that our plans bear much resemblance to what actually happens to us."

Lester sniffed a laugh. "That's the truth."

They fell silent for a long moment. The trees outside the open window behind Lester's bed were noisy with birds that had gathered in the branches to plan their upcoming trip south for the winter.

"I only want one thing more before I lay my burden down, Alafair," Lester said.

"What's that?"

"To see this thing through to the end. To make sure Buck can never have power over Olivia. I mean for her to have that shipping business free and clear before I go."

"Can you pay off the debt, Lester?"

"Only if I sell off part of the business, which I don't want to do. Me and Russ have been putting our heads together about it, though. I only hope I have enough time."

Every comment that passed through Alafair's head was too trite and meaningless to be spoken aloud, so she simply leaned forward and squeezed Lester's arm.

"You want me to read to you, now?"

"I'm feeling pretty tired, Alafair. I think I'll sleep."

Alafair walked away from Lester's bedroom with Mark Twain in her hands, hardly aware of where she was going as she pondered Lester's remarkable comments about Buck Collins. She had heard nothing but awful tales about Collins, and it truly seemed that most people in town feared or hated him. Yet she'd not exchanged more than two words with him. The picture she had of him was painted by others, not her own personal experience of the man. Maybe he was the monster everyone made him out to be, or maybe not. If he was so completely evil, why hadn't he been run out of town on a rail long ago?

He was a pillar of Enid society, after all. Parks and buildings were named after him. Many people worked for him of their own free will. He had a wife and family who must love him.

No one is all bad, she thought, or all good, either. And unless he's insane, even when a man does bad things, he usually thinks he has a good reason.

She walked down the stairs and caught sight of Lu, dusting the furniture in the parlor. She watched the housekeeper for a moment before interrupting her.

"Lu, if anybody comes looking for me, tell them I've gone to call on Mr. Collins at his house."

Lu straightened and eyed her like she had just grown two heads. But she said, "Yes, Miz Tucker."

Martha and Streeter McCoy, with Grace in tow, trudged up the porch steps and into Ruth Ann's parlor in exhausted silence. Martha plopped herself down into the plush sofa and stretched her legs out in front of her. Ike the cat had met them at the door and was presently weaving about the parlor floor, waiting for everyone to settle before he chose the most likely lap.

"I'm hungry," Grace told her.

"I expect you are," Martha admitted. "In all the excitement, none of us got any dinner. Run out to the kitchen and see if Lu will fix us some sandwiches. Come get me if Lu isn't there...." She raised her voice, because Grace was gone in a blur with Ike hot on her heels. Martha chuckled and looked up at McCoy, who was still standing in the middle of the parlor floor.

"Sit down for a spell, Streeter," she invited.

He didn't have to be asked twice.

Martha had telephoned him at his office an hour earlier from her cousin's house, alarmed and excited and full of news about the break-in. She hadn't exactly asked him to come, but the moment he rang off, he had attached the sidecar to his motorcycle, jumped on, and sped over to Olivia's to offer whatever assistance he could.

The police were there, questioning Olivia in the kitchen. Martha and her aunt Ruth Ann were following along behind the detective who was surveying the damage and cleaning up anything he told them they could.

McCoy had spent an hour hauling large pieces of broken furniture into the backyard, until Grace had had enough of being good and staying out of the way, and Martha had asked him to give them a lift back to the Yeager house in his sidecar. The trip had been quicker than walking, but it hadn't done much to calm down an already overly excited three-year-old.

Martha withdrew her hatpin and took off her hat and put it on the side table next to her. "Wonder what he's looking for, this burglar?" she finally said.

"Apparently he hasn't found it."

"That we know of," Martha corrected him. "Olivia hadn't been back to her house in a couple of days. Nobody really knows when her house got broken into. None of the neighbors heard anything that got their suspicions up. It could be that Collins sent someone to search Olivia's house the same night as the warehouse and the oil field, or maybe it was earlier and we just didn't know about it until now. What I'm hoping is that the burglar, or burglars, found the mysterious item and delivered it to his boss...."

"Collins, we presume...."

"We presume. I'm hoping he found the item and delivered it to his boss. And now the boss is happy and intends to keep his counsel and not bother Olivia anymore."

"That's a happy thought, but if it's so, then why hasn't Collins withdrawn his claim on Kenneth's estate? If Collins is indeed our culprit."

Martha shrugged. "Well, he wouldn't want to tip his hand. But like you said, it's just a happy thought."

Grace came in from the kitchen, clutching a bamboo serving tray in her two hands and stepping carefully to avoid spilling napkins and cutlery across the floor. Ike preceded her at a saunter, and Lu followed, carrying a large platter piled with thick pork roast sandwiches. Grace set the tray on the tea table next to the sandwiches and straightened with a grin, extending her arms with a flourish, rather like a magician who had just pulled off a particularly difficult trick.

"Good job, cookie," Martha said. "Pull up that footstool and sit down at the table, here, and let's eat some of these good-looking sandwiches."

Grace was more than ready to eat and snatched a sandwich off the platter, but she had her own ideas about seating arrangements and hoisted herself into McCoy's lap. He settled the child on his knee with a delighted grin at Martha. She grimaced back. Another vote in his favor. Ike jumped up onto the settee beside them, marginally more interested in the roast pork than in being companionable.

"I bring pitcher of milk and some glasses," Lu told them.

"Lu, is my mother still upstairs with my uncle?" Martha asked her. "I'd like to talk to her."

"No, Miss. Your uncle asleep now. Your ma, she left."

"Left? When?"

"Maybe a half hour ago."

"Did she go to Olivia's?" Martha looked at McCoy. "We must have just missed her."

"No. She tells me that if anyone asks, she's gone to visit Mr. Collins at his house."

Martha's forehead wrinkled and she stared at the housekeeper silently, unable to process this information. "Collins? Are you sure she said Collins?"

"Yes, Miss."

"Did she say why she…" McCoy began, but Martha jerked herself to her feet and he swallowed his words mid-sentence.

"Streeter!" she exclaimed.

Grace delicately picked a piece of fallen roast pork off of McCoy's trouser leg and fed it to Ike before she looked up. But McCoy's eyes widened at the urgency in Martha's voice.

"Take me uptown—right now!"

His lips parted, perhaps to speak, but Martha didn't give him a chance.

"Your motorcycle! Take me to the Collins mansion!"

He asked no questions. He stood and handed Grace to Lu and went into the parlor with Martha two steps ahead of him. He snatched his leather helmet and goggles off the hat rack with one hand and grabbed Martha's arm with the other, and hustled her out the front door.

Ike remained with the sandwiches, but Lu walked to the screen with Grace in her arms and watched the young couple hurry down the front sidewalk toward McCoy's motorcycle.

"Where's Martha going?" Grace had not yet decided whether or not to be upset by Martha's sudden departure, and eyed the housekeeper for a clue.

"Time for your mama to come home." Lu patted the child's leg. "Your sister give her a ride."

Martha flung herself into McCoy's sidecar without worrying about propriety, giving him a glimpse of her white-stockinged calves. He caught his breath and tried to concentrate on adjusting the helmet on her head and tightening the goggles so they wouldn't slip down her nose.

She batted his hand away. "Stop fussing, Streeter. Let's go, let's go. I need to find Mama right quick."

He shook the numbness out of his fingers, flung a leg over the cycle and stood on the starter, and they roared off down Washington.

He had no idea what was happening. He had had no idea of what was happening from the moment he got off the train at the Enid railroad station, retrieved his cycle from the baggage car, and went calling at the Yeager house. He was getting rather used to it. McCoy was a man who had always been in charge of his life. There was something surprisingly exhilarating about having no control whatsoever.

He glanced at his passenger. Her hair had come completely undone and was streaming out behind her from under the helmet. He squeezed the accelerator.

It was a long walk from Ruth Ann's to the Collins house off of Van Buren. The sky was covered with fluffy white clouds that floated serenely across the blue. The weather was fairly cool, but Alafair was hot from her brisk walk as she mounted the steps onto the spacious porch of the grand, golden-brick, Spanish-style mansion. She knocked, and was fanning herself with her handkerchief and admiring the wrought iron detail around the windows, when the big, oak-plank front door swung open. She found herself eye to eye with an elegant, liveried Negro butler.

"May I help you?" he said.

"I'd like to speak with Mr. Collins, please."

"Mr. Collins is not at home."

Alafair changed tack at once. "Is Missus Collins to home, then?"

The butler examined her critically, rather like he might an unusual bug he had just found on the porch. She wasn't worried about passing muster. She knew she looked quite presentable in her navy blue skirt and white blouse, and what was now her second-best hat with the cherries on the band.

Apparently the butler thought so, too. "I'm sorry, Madam. Mrs. Collins is not at home at present, either. She has gone to the railroad station to meet Mr. Ellery Collins on his return from Baltimore this afternoon. I expect her back before supper, however. If you'd like to leave a calling card, I'll see that Mrs. Collins receives it."

Alafair felt an ironic smile tug at her lips. A calling card, indeed. "Thank you, but it was Mr. Collins I actually came to see. No need to bother the lady."

"I expect you will find Mr. Collins at the Agriculture Exhibit in the basement of the Collins Building, Madam. Today is the last day of the exhibit, of which he is the sponsor."

Alafair sighed and thanked the man. She was girding herself for another lengthy walk when she caught sight of a streetcar coming toward her down Van Buren, heading in the direction she wanted to go. She sprinted to the curb and flagged him down.

◇◇◇

Alafair was long gone by the time McCoy and Martha pulled up to the curb in front of the Collins manse. Martha leaped out of the sidecar and dashed up the sidewalk and porch steps, and was urgently knocking on the door by the time McCoy trotted up behind her.

"Is my mother here?" she demanded of the man who answered.

The butler didn't say anything at once. He was too startled by the sight of the young woman in goggles and a leather helmet standing before him, looking frantic and windblown. He glanced at the tall man behind her, who gazed back at him.

"Your mother, Miss?"

"Mrs. Tucker. About yea big, dark hair. I was told she was coming here to talk to Mr. Collins. Is she here?"

After a moment's thought, the butler nodded. "She was here, Miss, maybe half an hour ago, but Mr. Collins is not at home and she didn't tarry."

"Where did she go?"

The butler struggled not to let his expression register disapproval at this unladylike insistence. "I believe she intended to go to the Collins Building in order to speak to Mr. Collins at his place of work."

"Thank you," Martha called back over her shoulder, already halfway down the steps.

McCoy added his own thanks and followed Martha back to the motorcycle. He threw his leg over the saddle and glanced at his passenger. "To the Collins Building, I presume."

"Yes, Streeter, and let's hurry, please."

"Martha, my darling, I expect it's time you told me what this is all about."

"I will when I have time. Can we go now?"

But he just stared at her, determined to understand what she was thinking, for once.

She puffed impatiently. "She's always doing this. She's going to confront Collins about something or other, about some idea she's come up with about how he's involved in Kenneth's death. She's like to get herself killed, Streeter."

"What do you think he's going to do, sugar? Pull out a gun and plug her right in his office? He seems more like the type who would send someone to smother her in her sleep."

His attempt at making light of the situation didn't work. "Streeter! Don't even joke like that. Her snooping around has got her hurt before, and I aim to keep her from it this time."

Her distress was very real, and McCoy was instantly sorry he had teased her. He stepped on the starter without another word.

Buck Collins was taking a turn around the special Founders' Jubilee display of farm products in the enormous exhibition hall in the basement of the Collins Building. With his man Hanlon close at his elbow, he was spending the afternoon glad-handing the dignitaries and gracing the ordinary citizens with his attention one last time, before the display was dismantled. The splendid exhibit consisted of samples of just about every kind of agricultural product grown in the entire northwestern part of the great state of Oklahoma. The hall was filled with varieties of corn, wheat, head feed, potatoes, and garden vegetables, proudly displayed by every local man, woman, boy, or girl who had put a seed in the ground over the previous season. One end of the hall was taken up with schoolchildren's artwork—drawings, paintings, maps, and essays by the hundreds, on the walls and on easels. The children's art was very popular, and that end of the hall was crowded with proud parents and grandparents, exclaiming over their darlings' work before it was returned to them to be displayed at home in a place of honor. Many people had congratulated Collins for hosting the exhibit. He had spent much of the afternoon here, enjoying the warmth of the crowd and taking advantage of the opportunity to think about something other than the events of the past few days.

A middle-sized woman in a white blouse and blue skirt put out her hand and he shook it, but her grasp tightened when he attempted to withdraw.

"Mr. Collins," she said.

He looked up into her face. "It's Mrs. Tucker, isn't it?"

She smiled. "You have a good memory, Mr. Collins."

"What do you want?" His tone was more curious than abrupt. "I'm truly sorry for your niece's troubles, and I wish her nothing but well, but I don't intend to discuss my business affairs with you, Madam. That's a thing should be left to the lawyers. Besides, this is not the place…"

Alafair squeezed his hand, then released it. "I'm not here to talk business, Mr. Collins. I wouldn't understand it if we did. I want to ask you what this bad blood is between you and Lester."

When she mentioned Lester's name, any human warmth that may have been in his eyes drained away, and she found herself staring at gold-flecked blue eyes as hard as ball bearings. She took an unconscious step backward, startled.

"Ask him," Collins said, brittle as ice.

Alafair had felt no fear of Collins, the Enid founding father who had given a speech at the Jubilee opening ceremonies. She couldn't say that about the Collins who stood before her now. She swallowed. "I did, sir. But I'd like to hear your side of the story."

He gazed at her for a silent moment, assessing. He looked over his shoulder at the man standing behind him. "Hanlon, drive the lady home."

Alafair didn't even consider arguing as Hanlon stepped forward and offered her his arm.

Collins shook off his black mood and moved on to greet a knot of people who were admiring a large pumpkin at a table close to the door.

He didn't spare any indignation for the woman who had interrupted him. In fact, he was already forgetting what she looked like. But she had thoroughly spoiled his good mood by uttering that hated name.

Lester Yeager.

Damn his eyes.

He had just about completed his circuit of the hall when he became aware of a commotion near the main entryway. He turned back toward the women he had been talking to and excused himself before moving toward the noise, feeling irritated. He couldn't imagine why anyone would be making a fuss about a bunch of corn and potatoes. Probably some reveler who had had one too many nips with the carnies as they dismantled their tents. Collins was annoyed that the security guard at the door hadn't discretely taken care of the unruly wretch before anyone could become aware of him.

A woman screamed, and Collins elbowed his way through the crowd, alarmed now, just in time to see a strange gargoyle of a figure smash the security guard in the jaw and knock him cold. A couple of men lunged toward the fray, but the gargoyle turned on them with an inhuman noise rather like a hiss, and leveled a .44. The crowd backed off and melted away to relative safety, scurrying out the doors and squatting behind tables, just as Collins stepped forward.

"What..." he began. He hesitated when he recognized who was pointing a gun at his head. "Nickolls! What in the name of Jesus and all the saints happened to you?"

Pee Wee wasn't that easy to recognize. He looked like something that Satan himself had dragged out of the bowels of hell and thrown into a pig wallow. He had probably been wearing a shirt at one time, since he still had cuffs around his wrists, but the rest of it was gone. His corduroy trousers were shredded, one foot booted and the other bare. Where it wasn't lacerated, his skin was black with soot, or dirt, or burns, or something else that didn't bear thinking about. His hair stood straight up in spikes, wild as the wildest Celt to ever run screaming at the Roman legions. His good left eye was rimmed around with white and bulging with an unnamable animal emotion. The right eyepatch was gone, exposing the scarred and puckered eyelid around a blind eye, which added to the horror of the bare-fanged snarl that distorted his face.

"Zip is dead." Considering that he looked inhuman, Pee Wee sounded remarkably calm and civilized.

Collins' eyes narrowed. He had no idea who Zip was, but now was not the time to ask. What an ironically bad time to send Hanlon on an errand. He caught sight of one of his employees peeking out from behind a painting on an easel and jerked his head toward the exit. The man slipped out a side door, and Collins turned back to Pee Wee.

"I'm sorry to hear that," he said.

"I'll bet you are. They ain't even enough left of him to send home to his ma for a funeral."

"What happened?"

"Deo Juarez is blowed to hell, too."

"Now, just calm down, Nickolls. I don't know what you think happened, but it won't help anything to go off half-cocked, here. Whatever you're aiming to do with that pistol..."

"I aim to shoot you with it, you son of a bitch."

And then Pee Wee shot him. Collins went down with a shriek, clutching his shredded left shin.

"I know he was just a *frijole*, but Deo was a damn good worker." Pee Wee fired again, hitting Collins in the right thigh.

The second shot galvanized the few men who were watching this drama from their hiding spots behind the pillars and furniture. There weren't that many people in Enid who cared whether or not Buck Collins got kneecapped by his latest enemy, but just in case things were about to get out of hand, several men charged out of their hiding places and tackled Pee Wee before he could shoot off anymore of Collins' body parts.

Hanlon settled Alafair into the backseat of Collins' black brougham, walked to the front of the auto and cranked the engine, then leaped into the driver's seat when it turned over. He put the auto into gear and eased out of the parking area at the rear of the Collins Building, steering around a bridled but unsaddled horse which was wandering aimlessly across the street. He was inwardly cursing idiots who didn't know how to hitch their mounts when Alafair spoke to him.

"How long have you worked for Mr. Collins, Mr. Hanlon?"

Hanlon eyed her in his side mirror before he spoke. "Three years."

He had pronounced it "t'ree years."

"Are you from Ireland?" Alafair asked.

"I am."

"Where in Ireland?"

"County Kerry."

"My father-in-law is from Ireland. County Tyrone. Is that anywhere near where you're from?"

"No, ma'am. Kerry is a long way from Tyrone."

"Is Mr. Collins from Kerry?"

"No, Mr. Collins is from Antrim. Also a long way from Kerry," he added, hoping to forestall further grilling.

It was a vain hope. "So you met Mr. Collins here in America."

Hanlon's tone conveyed his long-suffering patience with her. "Aye."

Alafair had about decided that Hanlon was the least talkative Irishman ever born. "In Kansas?" she asked.

No reply. She stared at the back of his head. Well, she didn't expect he was proud of the fact that Collins had found him in Leavenworth. She persevered.

"Do you like working for Mr. Collins?"

He said nothing, but the bitter snort that he emitted told her what she wanted to know. She decided to stop annoying the man and leaned back into the leather seat.

Hanlon was checking traffic to his left before pulling onto Randolph when an eruption of running people spewed out into the street from the entrance of the Collins Building and scattered in every direction. Startled, Alafair reached forward and grabbed Hanlon's shoulder.

"What's all this commotion, Mr. Hanlon? Do you reckon it's a fire?"

Crowds were pouring out of the building in a panic, dragging sobbing children by the hands and pushing spouses before them. Hanlon got out of the auto and seized a fleeing passerby before he could streak away.

"What's happened, man?"

The man looked up at Hanlon, his eyes popping, and tried to shake free. "Let go, I've got to get to the police! Some hellhound just shot Buck Collins!"

Alafair found herself out of the car and on the sidewalk beside Hanlon without entirely remembering how she got there.

Hanlon dropped the man's arm like it was on fire. "Shot?" he repeated.

The man grabbed his boater off his head, waved it around a bit in wild excitement, then plopped it back on before he ran off, hollering over his shoulder, "He's a crazy man! He keeps yelling, 'Zip is dead'!"

Alafair emitted a cry of distress. "Oh, no! Can it be?"

She looked up at Hanlon, who was frozen to the sidewalk, white as chalk. Suddenly he ripped off his chauffeur's cap, threw it to the ground, and spewed forth a string of curses that would have caused Alafair to faint dead away had she understood a single word. Then he took off for the Collins Building at a run, with Alafair right on his heels.

Hanlon hesitated at the bottom of the stairs leading into the exhibit hall, and Alafair ran into his back. He absently pulled her around to his side by her arm, and they stood there for a long moment, trying to make sense of what they were seeing. A .44 pistol lay discarded next to the wall. Buck Collins was writhing around on the floor, wailing in agony, clutching his bloody legs. Four or five burly farmers were holding down a flailing, manlike creature who kept howling, "You killed my dog!"

In her desperation to reach her mother, Martha nearly leaped out of the sidecar while McCoy was still roaring toward the crowd milling around the ambulance parked askew in the street in front of the Collins Building. McCoy grabbed her hand and snatched at the brake, alarmed.

"Look, honey! You can relax," he yelled over the engine noise, "there's your mother right there. She's all right!"

Alafair was standing on the sidewalk, alone, watching men carry Pee Wee out on a stretcher and load him onto the ambulance. Hanlon was nowhere to be seen. Martha rushed up and threw her arms around Alafair's neck, nearly weeping with relief, but Alafair was too distracted to take much notice of her distress. "I'm fine, sugar. I'm fine. Where's Grace? Is she behaving herself?"

Martha ripped off her helmet and goggles, and her dark hair cascaded over her shoulders. "She's fine. Lu has her. What's happening?"

"Good. Oh, kids, it's such an awful thing! There was a big explosion at the well and Zip Kolocek and some other poor fellow were killed. Pee Wee got it into his head that Mr. Collins was behind the blast and galloped all the way in to Enid on a horse, hunted Collins out, and shot him in the legs!"

"Good Lord!" McCoy exclaimed, and Martha said, "Did you see the shooting, Ma?" But Alafair was unaware of the interruption and plowed on.

"They took Collins off a while ago. I don't know how bad he's hurt. Pee Wee's hurt, too, in the explosion. He got himself all the way here from Garber on horseback, but he looks like he's been gnawed on by wolves. Zip! That poor child! I can't hardly believe it."

Martha seized her mother's arm and urged her away from the scene. "Mama, come on. Let's get out of here."

"Come on, Mrs. Tucker," McCoy said. "Why don't we go sit down at the Owl Drug for a minute and catch our breath? Get something to drink. Tell us all about it from the beginning."

The look in Alafair's eyes was still distracted, and her cheeks a hectic red, but she seemed to approve of McCoy's suggestion. Her head bobbed up and down. "Yes, that's a good idea. I could use a few minutes to catch my breath."

Martha shot McCoy a grateful look as they each took one of Alafair's hands and steered her down the street toward the drugstore.

By the time Alafair had related the events of the afternoon to the two young people and to several ravenously interested drugstore employees, she had calmed down considerably. In fact, she was feeling subdued, depressed by the thought that happy, innocent Zip Kolocek was blown to bits. She hoped against hope that Pee Wee was so rattled by the blast that he was imagining something that wasn't true.

"Why is Pee Wee so sure Mr. Collins blew up the well?" Martha asked.

Alafair shrugged. "I guess he's been convinced by the popular opinion that Mr. Collins is behind every unlawful event that has occurred in Garfield County since the Run."

"But you don't think so?" McCoy asked.

"Of course she doesn't." Martha struggled to keep the sarcasm out of her tone.

She didn't entirely succeed, because Alafair gave her an ironic smile. "Here's the question, hon. Who stands to gain something from these deaths? Now, Kenneth owed Mr. Collins a lot of money. Mr. Collins will get his money back one way or another whether Kenneth is alive or dead. Seems to me that killing Kenneth and then pressuring Olivia to repay the debt just makes life a whole lot more complicated for Mr. Collins than it needs to be." She gave her Coca-Cola a desultory stir with her straw. "And what earthly benefit would it be to him to blow up a couple of innocent drillers and a dog? He might be as spiteful as your uncle says, but he's sure smart enough not to make unnecessary trouble for himself."

"I'm guessing those drillers getting killed was an accident. I'd bet that if anybody was supposed to get killed, it was Pee Wee," McCoy offered. "And as for Kenneth, maybe he knew some awful secret about Collins and threatened to tell, and Collins had him killed to shut him up."

Alafair nodded. "That could be. It'd have to be a pretty awful secret to scare somebody as cool as Buck Collins."

McCoy took up the position of devil's advocate. "What about Nickolls? Could he have a reason to want Kenneth out of the way?"

"Well, I might just be persuaded that Pee Wee wanted Kenneth out of his hair, but I'll never believe he had anything to do with killing Zip. It was plain as a pig on a sofa that he loved that boy."

"Maybe one death didn't have anything to do with the other," Martha said. "Could be one person killed Kenneth and somebody else altogether murdered the other fellows."

Alafair turned her head and regarded Martha thoughtfully. "Now, there's an idea."

"Here's what I'm thinking," McCoy stated. "I'm betting that Collins' bodyguard, Hanlon, had a hand in one or both murders. He's always lurking around in the background. He made friends with Zip, who he'd never cross paths with in the normal course of things. Maybe he was sent to spy out at the oil field."

"I like what Streeter said about Pee Wee being the target of that explosion at the well, Mama. Him and Kenneth were partners. Maybe the idea is to get rid of the owners of the oil well."

Alafair pondered this before she responded. "All right, sugar. Say somebody wanted to do away with Kenneth and Pee Wee both—the co-owners of the well. Who stands to gain?"

There was a moment of dead silence.

The two women stared at each other, wide-eyed.

"Don't even think it," Alafair said.

McCoy was confused. "What?"

Martha ignored him. "Since Kenneth died," she said to her mother, "and after her daddy passes, she'll own Yeager Transport and Storage outright. And if Pee Wee was to die, she'd own the well outright, too."

McCoy got the picture. "You can't imagine that your cousin…"

Martha cut him off with a look. "I imagine that the sheriff and the chief of police will put their heads together and come up with the same thought, if they haven't already."

"It's a ridiculous idea," Alafair said. "In fact, this brings us back to Collins, to my way of thinking. Doing away with Kenneth and Pee Wee would just make it all the easier for him to wrest everything at once from one bereaved, inexperienced, twenty-one-year-old girl. The only problem is, I happen to know that Lester is leaving controlling interest in the business to my brother George, so if that's Collins' plan, his game will be knocked into a cocked hat."

"Uncle George! Does Olivia know this?"

"I don't think so. And don't you go telling her, now. Lester may want to change his will yet."

"Well, then, Ma, if she doesn't know, that's no alibi for her, or for anybody else, either."

"I know, Martha." Alafair leaned back and sighed. "Thank you for buying me a pop, Streeter. I feel better now. I think I'll walk on over to the hospital and see if the police will let me sit with poor Pee Wee for a spell. Streeter can take you back to Ruth Ann's, Martha."

"Let me sit with you, Mama."

"No, I'll be fine, sugar. I need you to take Grace off of Lu's hands. Tell everybody what's happened and where I am. I'll take the streetcar back to the house in an hour or so."

Olivia and her mother were alone in the vandalized house. The police had finally left after an interminable search, endless questions, and instructions to Olivia to make a list of missing items and contact them instantly if she found anything of interest in the wreckage.

Ruth Ann slumped in an armchair, the one upright piece of furniture in Kenneth's study, looking tired and deflated. She was holding a cheerful, bouncy Ron in her lap. Olivia stood in the middle of the floor with her hands on her hips, surveying the damage. She felt unnaturally calm about the whole thing. She wondered briefly if the sheer number of disasters in the past few days had completely used up her supply of emotions. If so, she was grateful for the respite.

She bent over and righted a side table before returning a dented lamp to its place on top.

"Olivia," Ruth Ann admonished, "leave all that, now. It'll be dark soon. Pack up anything you want to take with you and let's get on back to the house. You can come back in the morning, after we visit Kenneth at the funeral home."

"Just a minute, Mama." She slid the center drawer back into Kenneth's desk. "I'd feel better if I could at least get the rest of the furniture standing upright. Then it won't look quite so hopeless tomorrow."

She squatted down and grasped the toppled bookshelf, but it was heavier than she had thought and she couldn't budge it.

Ruth Ann stood up with Ron in her arms. "That's too much for you, shug. Give it up. Tomorrow we'll have Mike Ed send out some men from the warehouse and they'll have everything back in place in a blink. Besides, you're all rear end over every-which-way with that bookshelf. That's the bottom you're lifting, see? You're trying to set it upside down."

But Olivia wasn't listening. She stood up and kicked some of the scattered books out of the way. "Look here, Ma. What's this?"

Ruth Ann peered at the second shelf, where Olivia was pointing. "What? That? It looks like a piece of brown paper."

Olivia stepped over the disarray of books and papers on the floor and leaned over to feel the small paper square that had been appended somehow to the bottom of the shelf. "It's been glued to the shelf. I can feel something underneath the paper here, something hard. Wait. This paper is only pasted on three sides. It's like a little pocket, open toward the front. I can scoot this out...."

She straightened and held up a small metal object pinched between her thumb and forefinger.

"It's a key, Ma. A little key."

Ruth Ann's eyes widened. "I'll be switched! You didn't know that was there?"

"No."

"What do you suppose it's to?"

"It looks like a safe deposit box key, Mama. But it's not the same as the one for the box we have at the First National. It must be for one at some other bank."

Ruth Ann began to bounce Ron on her hip, and he laughed, unaware of his grandmother's agitation. All of a sudden, Ruth Ann wanted to get out of that house in the worst way. "What does it mean, Olivia, him hiding a key like that from you?

Maybe it's nothing. Come on, let's go home right now and call Mr. Burns."

Pee Wee dragged himself up out of the darkness by sheer will. The last thing he remembered was flailing around on the floor in the exhibition room of the Collins Building with a two-hundred-pound, overalls-clad farmer sitting on him and another pounding his gun hand on the floor. He blinked at the white, pressed-tin ceiling above him and struggled to remember just what had happened before the farmer took a seat on his sore ribs, then heaved a satisfied sigh when the vision of Buck Collins' calf exploding replayed itself in his mind.

His vision was a little foggy, and it took him a second to realize that the specter hovering over him to the right was a person. His first thought was that he was dying, and his mother was come to fetch him to heaven. "Ma?" he whispered.

The blurry apparition moved closer. "It's Miz Tucker, honey. How're you doing?"

He blinked to clear his vision, and Alafair's face came into focus.

"Miz Tucker…where am I?" he croaked. He swiveled his head enough to see a beige wall and the corner of a wooden nightstand.

"You're in the hospital, Pee Wee. The chief had you brought here after you passed out. Do you remember what happened?"

"Zip is dead," he said, before he could catch himself.

Alafair's sharp expression was replaced by a look of such startling tenderness and concern that he caught his breath. Tears started to her eyes, but didn't spill over. Pee Wee swallowed back his grief before her compassion could unman him.

When she answered him, her voice was steady. "I heard that's what you said. The sheriff has gone out to Garber to see what happened." She paused. "You sure shot the dickens out of Mr. Collins."

"I did," he confessed. "Why ain't I in jail?"

"Well, now, you are under arrest. There's a policeman standing right outside the door."

Pee Wee snorted. "I should have figured. No other way I'd have a hospital room all to myself."

"Why'd you shoot Mr. Collins, son?"

"Somebody put that missing nitro into the oil can. Blew that boy to pieces when he went to oil a sticky journal. Killed the machinist, too."

Alafair took her handkerchief out of her sleeve and gently dabbed the tears that were running from Pee Wee's good eye. He hadn't even realized that he was crying.

"And you think Mr. Collins done it?"

"Killed the dog, too," he continued, as though he hadn't heard her. "That boy loved that heejus critter."

"I know he did, Pee Wee."

"About the only thing he didn't claim for that dog was that he was a musical instrument."

"He was a fine specimen, that dog."

"What are you doing here, Miz Tucker?"

Before she answered, Alafair poured a little water into a glass from a pitcher on the bedside table. She carefully raised Pee Wee's head from his pillow with one hand and held the glass to his lips. After he had taken a few sips, she put the glass down and settled back into her chair.

"I was there, honey. I came down to the Collins Building to talk to Mr. Collins before you showed up."

Pee Wee's forehead wrinkled. "Yes, ma'am. But why are you here?"

"Oh. I asked Mr. Burns if I could sit with you for a spell. I thought you might be needing…well, I hear your folks passed on some time ago." She didn't give him time to ponder this statement. "Looks like you've been through a mangle. How are you feeling?"

"Hurts some to breathe, and I'm a mite swimmy-headed, but I reckon I'll live 'til tomorrow, if a tree don't fall on me."

"The doctor says you have some broken ribs and a big knot on your head, among other things. I'm surprised you can feel anything at all, considering the size of the needle full of pain-killer they stuck you with. I've seen the vet use needles like that on mules."

She was trying to use his physical state to distract him from his emotional state, but it didn't work.

He lay back on his pillow and stared at the ceiling before he began to muse aloud, talking to himself more than to her. "The generator is blowed to hell. The well is sure enough out of production until I can scare up the money to build a new one. The old one can't be fixed, that's for certain. The engine house is nothing but splinters, the derrick is about to fall over, and I think the well head was damaged. Don't know how I'm going to get the money to get it going again. I've bought plenty of lumber and supplies from Herb Champlin's hardware stores over the last year. Maybe he'll hire me on as a tankie at his new skimming plant. Guess my drillers are out of work." His single eye glanced her way. "Them as ain't killed, that is."

"Pee Wee…"

"I think old Deo Juarez had himself a couple of little ones down in El Paso."

"Pee Wee…"

His eye widened, and she could see gooseflesh rise on his burned arms. "Lord have mercy! What am I going to say to Zip's ma?"

Alafair reached forward and put her hand over his mouth. "Hush, now. Hush, now. It's a terrible thing that happened, but there's nothing you can do about it other than get well, so you help the law bring whoever done this to justice."

Chief Burns was standing outside the door to Pee Wee's room, talking to the officer on duty, when Alafair emerged into the hall. She seemed calm and businesslike, he thought, even though she was wiping away the tears that were dribbling down her cheeks.

Burns gestured at the room with his chin. "He awake?"

"No, he's finally asleep."

"How is he? Is he making any sense?"

She shrugged. "He's pretty shocky yet. How's Mr. Collins?"

"They're operating on his legs, now. Don't know the prognosis. His wife and sons and all the rest of them are here, though."

Alafair nodded. "I'm interested in how everybody just takes it for granted that Collins is behind all my family's recent trouble."

"Well, there's good reason to think so. Lester Yeager and Buck Collins have been bitter enemies as long as I've known anything about it. And, if your niece's late husband really was involved in some kind of shady business with Collins, that's a thing that don't often turn out well."

He paused, wondering if Alafair was still listening to him. She had shifted her weight to one foot and folded her arms, and was staring at the hospital-beige wall of the hallway. When he stopped speaking, she looked at him.

"Do you expect Sheriff Hume still has that empty nitroglycerin can from out to Pee Wee's well?"

Burns didn't answer right away. Instead he was wondering why he was even talking to this perfectly ordinary-looking woman with the disconcerting gaze, who was a stranger to him, to boot. None of this had anything to do with her, except in the most perfunctory way. She was just one of the extended family which hung around like a tableau in the background of any tragedy. But she kept turning up, asking odd questions and making observations in as straightforward a manner as any man he had dealt with. Burns was finding it hard to dismiss her in the polite and cursory fashion he normally used to deal with family. He wondered if her unassuming presence and sharp eye actually might be of some use in this situation. He gave an unconscious shrug and decided to go with it.

"I don't know, ma'am. I expect he does. Why?"

"Mr. Burns," she said, "have you ever read *Pudd'nhead Wilson*?"

Hanlon waited until the very last minute to buy his train ticket. After watching his boss being hauled away in the ambulance, he had gone back to his little attic room over the garage behind the Collins house just long enough to shuck out of his chauffeur's uniform and change into the most common, nondescript clothes he had. He took what cash he had from the drawer in the dresser and stuffed it in his pocket, and pulled a worse-for-wear cowboy hat down low on his forehead. He wasn't supposed to have a pistol, since he was on parole, but he did, of course, wrapped in a ratty blanket and stashed on the top shelf of his closet. It was small, but it fit in his jacket pocket just right, along with the razor. He would have liked to take a change of clothes, but he didn't want to be carrying anything or have anything on him that might be memorable in the slightest. He considered stealing something of value from the house that he could hock later. Nothing portable that he could get to quickly came to mind. He managed to get down the back stairs and into the alley behind the property without being seen, and walked through side streets until he reached the train station.

He meandered around the street for a long time, sticking close to back entrances and alleys, hovering close to the station and watching closely for any sign that the law was about. If he had had a choice, Hanlon would have preferred to leave town on a horse, or by hitching a ride on a delivery truck or wagon. The fact that it was Saturday made it easier. There was a lot of activity on the streets at this hour on Saturday, since the stores were open late and a lot of folks came out to shop and stroll, or just to watch people. He preferred a crowd. It was easier to be unseen in a crowd.

It was right about dusk, just before the lamps are lit, when it's hard to be absolutely sure of what one is seeing, when a train pulled into the station from the east. Hanlon waited until arriving passengers had disembarked and he began to see those who were departing begin to board before he made his way into the station. He stood near the entrance for a few seconds and checked out the other people in the room: a woman with two middle-sized kids, a couple, a cowboy asleep on a bench with his hat pulled down over his face. Satisfied, Hanlon walked up to the counter and eyed the schedule posted next to the window to see where this train was bound. Not that it made any difference, as long as it was out of here.

"One for Woodward," he said to the clerk.

"Better step on it, mister," the man said. "Train's leaving in a couple of minutes."

Perfect. Hanlon paid for his ticket and walked immediately out onto the platform, where he could survey the situation one last time before he got on. The conductor beckoned to him from one of the passenger cars. He boarded and made his way down the aisle of the as-still-unlit car, finally taking a seat near the exit in the back. The train had not begun to move, but Hanlon could hear the chug of the engine firing up.

He leaned back and closed his eyes, already planning his route out of Woodward and to the west. California, maybe. There were a lot of Irish in California. A good place to get lost.

He felt someone sit down in the seat beside him and opened his eyes. It was the cowboy he had seen sleeping in the station. The cowboy smiled before reaching into his coat pocket, drawing out a sheriff's deputy badge, and holding it under Hanlon's nose.

"Why, Mr. Hanlon," the cowboy said, "are you leaving town without letting anyone know? I believe that's a violation of your parole."

Sunday, September 19, 1915

Martha could hear Grace's piping laughter coming from the backyard as she approached her aunt's house on the sidewalk. It was a pretty morning, but Martha wasn't in a very pretty mood. She had just spent two hours with Olivia and Ruth Ann at Mr. Henninger's brand spanking new funeral home, viewing Kenneth's artfully displayed body and discussing funeral details.

It had all seemed incredibly macabre to her. The entire time she was there, she kept thinking that Kenneth looked rather like he had painted his face like a blowsy saloon girl and then stretched out and gone to sleep on one of the display counters at Klein's. But Olivia seemed happy with the arrangement, so she bit her lip and kept her opinion to herself.

Finally, she had had enough, so she had left Olivia and Ruth Ann to commune with the dearly departed for a while.

She headed back to the house alone, and as she walked up the driveway and into the backyard, she found Lu hanging bedsheets on the line with Ron on a quilt at her feet. Grace had created a cradle out of a small wooden crate and some rags, and was in the process of hauling Ike over to it in order to serve as baby. She was carrying him with both arms clutched around his generous middle, right under his front legs, the bottom half of him swinging precariously in front of her. He was so big that she could barely manage his weight, and his back paws were only a fraction of an inch off the ground, his toes splayed in alarm. He looked over at Martha, the picture of long-suffering resignation, in the forlorn hope that she might rescue him from this indignity.

Grace called out a greeting to Martha, but was too intent on her task to come over, so Martha left poor Ike to his fate and walked to the clothesline. Lu moved a hanging sheet aside and gave her an appraising look as she approached.

"Everything okay at funeral place?"

Martha shrugged. "Olivia seems happy."

Lu's expression didn't change, but Martha thought she detected an ironic glint in the black eyes.

"Have you seen my mother lately, Lu?"

Lu indicated the house with a lift of her chin and stabbed a clothespin over the end of a pillowcase. "Since church, she been up with Mr. Yeager, reading. Mr. Yeager says he likes your ma's book."

Martha nodded. "Thank you. Would you like for me to take the kids off your hands?"

Now all she could see of the housekeeper was two slipper-clad feet peeking out from under an enormous white sheet. "No, Miss. Maybe later, when Miz Yeager and Olivia come home and I fix luncheon. You go rest now."

Martha opened her mouth to make a polite protest, but in the end she just said, "Thank you," and didn't argue. She entered the house through the back door and walked through the parlor, pausing to hang her hat on the rack in the foyer before she mounted the stairs. The house was quiet. When she reached the second floor, she threw a glance at her uncle's bedroom, and was surprised to see the door was standing open. She could make out Lester's outline under the quilts, and an empty chair standing beside the bed. Even from the stairwell, she could hear her uncle's ragged breathing.

Curious, she walked down the hall to her mother's bedroom and looked in. Alafair was lying on top of the bedspread, staring at the ceiling, her hands folded over Mark Twain's book on her chest.

"Ma?" Martha said, and Alafair's head turned on the pillow to look at her.

"Hello, honey. How does Kenneth look?"

Martha walked into the room and sat down in one of the side chairs under the window. "Pretty good, considering that he was dead for a week before he got found."

"It helps if somebody puts you in a cold storage unit." Alafair's tone was dry.

"You know, it did occur to me that Kenneth got himself so doped up that he just walked into that locker and stretched himself out for a little nap."

Alafair sat up and propped herself against the headboard. "Me, too. Except that you've got to have a key to get in them lockers, and he didn't have a key on him." Alafair crossed her ankles and moved her book from her lap to the bed. "Speaking of keys, when is Olivia going out to the bank in Garber to see if that little key she found fits anything?"

"Oh, it'll fit. Sheriff Hume telephoned the banks out there yesterday and found out that Kenneth did rent a box at the First Bank of Garber back about a year ago. The sheriff said he'd come pick us up and take us on out there on the train early this afternoon. The bank manager will meet us there and let us in. The sheriff was going to see a judge this morning and get a warrant. Unless Kenneth had told the bank that Olivia could get into the box, which he didn't, they aren't going to let her open it without a court order."

"So you're going, too?"

"She asked me, so I said I would."

"How about Streeter McCoy?"

"How about him? There's no reason in the world for him to come." Martha suddenly realized that she sounded unduly acerbic, so she changed the subject. "Isn't it just the awfullest thing about poor Zip Kolocek? I sure liked that boy."

Alafair's face crumpled and she looked away. She took a deep breath before she replied. "That poor child. That poor innocent boy. What critter would do something so mean that would blow a couple of fellows to pieces like that?"

"I reckon Pee Wee Nickolls is convinced he knows what critter."

Alafair looked back at Martha. "I hate it that Pee Wee took the law into his own hands like that. Now he's not only lost everything, he's under arrest."

"I expect that any jury of folks from around here will be on Pee Wee's side."

"How is he doing this morning, have you heard?"

"I understand he had an operation early this morning to pick chunks of wood out of his body and set some bones."

"What about Collins?"

"I haven't heard about him. I don't think he's expected to die, though."

Alafair gave a thoughtful nod. "Pee Wee's lucky the blast didn't take out his other eye. I hope he decides to go into another line of work, after this."

While Martha was discussing events with her mother, Sheriff Hume and Chief Burns were sitting in the chief's office, drinking coffee and bringing each other up to speed on their respective murder investigations. Neither was in a hurry to question Hanlon, who was currently on the second floor of the courthouse, handcuffed to a chair, in the dim, airless, converted janitor's closet that currently served as an interrogation room for the Enid police department. John Burns had been the Chief of Police for the City of Enid for only a few months, but he and Elsworth Hume had worked together quite a bit already, mostly raiding illegal drinking establishments and seizing contraband booze. Hume was competent and serious about his work, and Burns liked that. He also liked the fact that, even though Hume appeared to be grim and humorless, he had a ready, dry wit which was so subtle as to be almost undetectable.

The death of Kenneth Crawford from an overdose of opium in Enid had occurred in Burns' jurisdiction. The deaths of Deo Juarez and Zip Kolocek from an overdose of nitroglycerin outside of Garber had happened in an unincorporated area, and thus were the purview of Hume, the Garfield County Sheriff. Given the fact that everyone involved with these three murders was unshakably convinced that Buck Collins was responsible for both incidents, the Sheriff's Office and the Enid Police Department were working together on their cases.

Until Hanlon had made a break for it the night before, there had only been the sketchiest of circumstantial evidence connecting Collins to any of the deaths. There was an undercurrent of carefully repressed excitement in the room as the two lawmen prepared to question Hanlon. No one dared say it out loud, but the possibility existed that Buck Collins had finally made a mistake that could be used to bring him down.

Hume glanced at his pocket watch and set his mug down on the corner of Burns' desk. "Well, I reckon we'd better get on with this, before Collins' lawyer shows up and goes to interfering with our interrogation techniques."

Burns laughed. "I expect that Collins ain't thinking quite as sharp as usual right about now, thanks to old Pee Wee Nickolls." He stood up and pulled on his suit jacket, and the two men walked down the hall to the stairwell leading to the second floor.

"You think this little ruse of ours is going to work?" Burns was taking the stairs two at a time in an effort to keep up with the longer-legged Hume.

Hume shrugged. "It's worth a try. If Hanlon goes for it and spills the beans, we won't have to make good."

"Well, I hope we don't. That lawyer of Collins' is slicker than spit on a glass doorknob." He signaled to the guard standing outside the interrogation room to unlock the door.

Hanlon looked up when the door opened, but said nothing. Burns turned the only other chair in the small room around backward and straddled it. Hume leaned back against the wall in the corner and crossed his arms over his chest.

"I hear you tried to leave town under cover of night, Mr. Hanlon, with a firearm and a razor in your pocket, to boot," Burns said. "Now why would you go and do something stupid like that? That's a violation of your parole, after all. Are you so eager to go back to the clink?"

"I've got nothing to say."

"Collins might have something to say about your attempting to leave his employ without his permission, when he finds out about it."

"It was Collins sent me on an errand. You can ask him about it."

"Collins is not in any condition to answer questions right now, Hanlon, as well you know. I figure the sheriff and I will just have to ask you. Where were you on Friday night? Anywhere near Yeager Transfer and Storage? How about the home of Kenneth Crawford? Or maybe you took a little trip out toward Garber that night, and while you were ransacking the Crawford well buildings, you decided to replace the machine oil with nitroglycerin. Considering what happened, I believe we could convince a judge that that little stunt constitutes murder."

"I was with Mr. Collins all evening on Friday, and I retired late to my room, which is above the garage at the back of the house. I spoke to Cletus, Collins' butler, when I came in. His room is next to mine. He can tell you right when I came in. You can't charge me with anything, Burns. Collins will vouch for my whereabouts as soon as he's up to it. You've got nothing."

"Is that so? You spent several years enjoying the hospitality of the State of Kansas, didn't you, Hanlon?"

"You know damn well I did."

"I believe that whenever a con checks into Leavenworth, he gets to leave his fingerprints on a card, which the prison keeps forever. I expect you've had that honor, so you're familiar with the idea of fingerprinting. Really helps with identifying repeat offenders, I hear."

Hanlon reddened, but had nothing to say to this. He glanced over at Hume, who was still standing silently in the corner. Burns reached into his pocket, withdrew a tobacco pouch and papers, and proceeded to roll a cigarette. He offered it to Hanlon, who took it.

Burns struck a match on his leg and leaned forward to light Hanlon's smoke before he continued. "So, you know that whenever a person touches anything, he leaves behind the marks of his fingers, and those marks are like nobody else's. In fact, it seems that some eggheads think that you can prove without a shadow of a doubt which exact man out of all the men in the world touched any particular article you care to study. And did you know, too, that the forward-looking and progressive city of Enid, Oklahoma, has just come into possession of a fingerprint kit?"

Hanlon exhaled a long plume of smoke. "My heartiest congratulations."

Burns' mouth twitched. "And did you further know, smart ass, that we are in the process of testing several items taken from the scenes of all three break-ins, including an empty nitro can, and we have discovered some very nice fingerprints that we are going to photograph? Our plan was to send those pictures to the penitentiary in Leavenworth, Kansas, where the Feds have agreed to compare them with their collection. In fact, we've requested that they start their comparison with one particular set of prints that we think highly likely to match up with some of ours."

Hanlon looked unimpressed.

"But you know what?" Burns continued. "Since you decided to violate parole and get yourself arrested, I don't think it's going to be necessary to send those photos all the way to Kansas. We now have those very fingers of interest right here in our custody."

Hanlon shifted in his chair, irritated at Burns' chipper tone of voice.

But the chief wasn't done yet. "Seems there are another couple of fellows who weren't interested in hanging around to help us with our investigation, either, Hanlon. The man that Mike Ed Burns hired to be watchman at Yeager Transfer and Storage tried to take a powder not two hours after I questioned him. Bull Heath, the old boy who was supposed to be watching Crawford's well the night it was broke into, he did give us the slip. He was a booger to track down, but the sheriff's men finally caught up with him yesterday. Both of them have provided us with their prints."

"Be interesting to hear what them two have to say." Sheriff Hume spoke for the first time.

The lawmen eyed Hanlon expectantly. He took a final drag on the cigarette, tossed it to the floor, and ground it under his heel.

Burns looked at Hume. "Collins has made a bunch of fellows do a bunch of things to a bunch of folks, you know, Sheriff."

"So I hear," Hume said. "But damn if we've ever been able to catch him at it. I'd be willing to do a lot for the man who helped us nail that slippery scoundrel."

Hanlon said nothing, but he did look like he'd love to leap out of his chair and throttle both men at once.

Burns stood up and moved over to the door. He put his hand on the knob, but before he opened it, he looked back at Hanlon one last time. "You know, before he departed this life, Zip Kolocek told the sheriff that you and him had become acquainted some months back, and that you have been out to the Crawford well site more than once. Zip considered you a friend."

Hanlon looked away and sighed.

"It's not much of a friend that protects whoever blows his pal to smithereens, Hanlon." Burns opened the door. "Mattingly," he said to the officer posted outside, "take Mr. Hanlon back to his cell."

Hanlon stood up. Burns stepped aside to let him pass, but Hanlon didn't move. He stared at the floor for a long minute before he sat back down.

Burns cast Hume a glance before he closed the door.

"I'm not goin' down for a goddam bastard from Antrim," Hanlon said.

"Tell us what you know, and we'll see what we can do for you."

Hanlon shook his head. "If I didn't do what he said, he'd tell my parole officer that I'd done something I shouldn't and get me sent back to prison. You see?"

"What did he tell you to do?" Hume asked.

"We were looking for something. Collins said while we were at it, we should bust the place up. Do some damage."

"Which place?" Hume asked.

"It'll be my prints on the can."

Hume nodded. "It was you at the well."

"Me and Bull. I didn't want nobody to die, though. Especially not the boyo. I didn't know that little bit of nitro would kill anybody. I figured it'd just make a nice pop and give 'em all a fright, maybe damage the machinery. Bull wanted to shoot the watchdog, but I wouldn't let him. I liked that ugly cur. I fed him a hamburger mickey with some sleeping draught I got at the drugstore in Breckinridge, and he went out like a light. You were right, Burns. That kid came into Enid regular to buy supplies for the outfit, and Collins had me sidle up to him and get to talking. I was supposed to pretend I wanted to work on an oil field. I went out there a few times. I'd report back to Collins what I saw, what was happening out there. Strange thing, though. I got to like that kid and his mutt. He was my friend, and for me, those are in short supply."

Burns took over the questioning. "What about Kenneth Crawford's home and the office at the Yeager warehouse?"

"I had nothing to do with those. He sent somebody else to do them, all on the same night, after Crawford's body was found."

"You said you were looking for something. What was it?"

Hanlon shrugged. "A log book, Collins said. A business ledger with his name in it. He said Crawford would have it stashed away somewhere, hidden."

"But you didn't find it?"

"No. Can't say about the other places, though."

"What was in this ledger, besides Collins' name?"

"Shipping records, he said. Sales figures. Don't know what for."

The sheriff stepped in. "Did you kill Kenneth Crawford?"

"I did not. I don't know anything about that. Collins didn't send me to do the deed, nor did he tell me his plans in that regard."

"So..." the sheriff began, but Hanlon spoke at the same time.

"I didn't want to go back to prison," he said.

"I'm afraid we can't help you there, Hanlon," Hume told him. "But considering your cooperation, I reckon we can try to get the charge reduced considerably."

Hanlon nodded, resigned. "As long as you nail that son of a bitch."

Hume showed up at the Yeager house in his Garfield County Sheriff's Department vehicle early in the afternoon to pick up Olivia and Martha for the trip to Garber. He ushered the ladies into the backseat and drove them to the train station in time to catch the 1:15, for even though the road between Garber and Enid was well graded and maintained, it was still twenty miles of dirt and they didn't have all day to drive.

Martha had never been to Garber, and looked around with interest as she, Olivia, and Hume made the short walk from the station into the main business district. The towns in the

Cherokee Strip seemed to be more unruly than those in the Indian Territory, she thought. Garber was another of the towns that hadn't existed as such before the run of '93. Oil was bringing a big influx of new growth to the area and all the buildings looked shiny and rather raw. In spite of all the bustle and prosperity, Martha detected a whiff of disreputability in the air.

Commerce was the order of the day in Garber, Oklahoma. It was a much smaller town than Enid, but plenty active. During daylight hours, banks and stores were kept busy by farmers and oil businessmen, and at night, several bars prospered under the patronage of drillers, roustabouts, cowboys, and bindlestiffs.

Manager Martin Church was standing on the boardwalk, waiting for them, as they walked up to the First Bank of Garber. He was a thin, pale man with thin hair and a thin smile on his face, dressed in his Sunday best. They made their introductions pleasantly enough, but Church insisted on inspecting the warrant before he unlocked the door and ushered them inside the bank building. Church lit a gaslight on the wall and adjusted the flame until it was bright enough to suit him, then invited them to sit.

"If you don't mind, Mr. Church," Hume said, "we're anxious to get on with this and get on back to the station in time for the 2:55 back to Enid."

"As you wish, Sheriff." He turned to Martha. "Miss, if you'll wait here in the lobby, please. Mrs. Crawford and the sheriff, only, allowed in the vault."

Martha acquiesced and made herself comfortable in one of the big padded armchairs by the front door while Olivia and the sheriff disappeared with Church into the nether regions of the bank. For fifteen minutes or so, she contented herself with watching the passersby through the front window and imagining what it would be like to work for Mr. Church instead of Mr. Bushyhead at the First National Bank of Boynton. She listened for any sounds from the vault, but all she could hear was the familiar, homely hiss of the gaslight on the wall next to her. The idle thought crossed her mind that the bank in Boynton was already electrified.

The click of heels on the wooden floor roused her and she stood as Olivia reappeared from behind the tellers' cages and smiled at her. Hume was close behind, clutching a leather-bound ledger under his arm.

"Did you find something important?" Martha asked.

Hume looked positively cheerful. "Looks like Buck Collins will have more to worry about for the rest of his life than bum legs."

"You're a hard man to get in to see," Ruth Ann said.

Collins shifted in his hospital bed, sitting up as straight as he could for a man with two legs in traction. "That's what happens when you're under arrest, Ruth Ann." His tone was dry, and he seemed as cool and in control of his emotions as he always did, but Ruth Ann could tell by his pinched expression that he was in pain, as well as more than a little amazed that she was here.

"Mr. Burns wasn't keen to let me in. They took my handbag and my hat, of all things, and made me turn out the pockets in my skirt. I suppose they thought I came to shoot you again. And I figured your lawyer was going to have a stroke."

"That's what I pay him for, to have a stroke instead of me."

"Anyway, thank you for agreeing to see me. Why did you agree to see me, anyway?"

"Why did you come, if not to shoot me?"

"I want you to tell me why you did it, Buck. I know you and Lester have had your differences, but this! How could you?"

Collins nodded. "I figured that's why you're here. I told them to let you in because I want to tell you that I had nothing to do with the death of Olivia's husband."

Ruth Ann looked skeptical. "Mr. Burns allowed as how you'd say that."

"It happens to be true."

"And what about the rest, Buck? Are you going to deny that you sent your henchmen to break into those buildings and do damage? Olivia's home! That you're responsible for the death of that young man and the machinist out at Kenneth's well? That you've been working mighty fast and furious to get your hands on property that is going to be Olivia's before long? Is that what you're trying to tell me, Buck Collins?"

Grief and fury had transformed the sweet and retiring Mrs. Yeager beyond recognition. Collins gazed at her for a moment before he attempted a reply. "I never…"

"Don't bother, Buck," Ruth Ann interrupted. "Olivia and Sheriff Hume found the records of the little absinthe shipping business that you and Kenneth were in together. How'd you get him to do it? Did you threaten to foreclose on that loan you made him to start the well? Or were you just going to have somebody break his arm if he didn't cooperate?"

Collins looked away. He could see the back of the guard who was posted outside the door to his room. Ruth Ann's sister was sitting in a chair across the hall, next to one of Buck's sons, who had left the room when Ruth Ann came in. He heaved a sigh and returned his gaze to the pale-faced woman sitting in a chair next to his bed.

"If you tell Burns I said this, I'll deny it, but I want you to know that I never wanted it to turn out this way. I wouldn't knowingly cause you or your daughter grief. I just wanted that ledger back after I heard that Crawford was dead. Those boys were only supposed to search for the book, not vandalize and commit mayhem. That explosion shouldn't have happened."

"Yet you thought this was a real good opportunity to get your hands on Lester's property."

"Lester's dying, Ruth Ann. It'll be Olivia's property soon."

Ruth Ann drew back in her chair, appalled. "You don't need to point that out to me."

"No, you don't understand. I don't want to take Olivia's property from her. I offered to be her partner."

Ruth Ann stood up. "Buck Collins, you're a man who has spent a lifetime doing exactly what you want and getting away with it, no matter who you hurt in the process. You'll pay, in this life or the next."

She turned on her heel and walked out of the room as Buck grabbed the bar above his head and pulled himself up. "I could have made her rich," he called to her retreating figure.

While Ruth Ann was in with Collins, Alafair sat in her chair outside the hospital room-cum-jail cell and waited. She could see the two people through the open door, and could tell that the conversation was heated, at least on Ruth Ann's part, but she couldn't hear what they were saying. The young policeman stationed at the door leaned back on his hands against the wall, an unhelpful expression on his face.

The young man in the chair next to her stared off into space, holding a newspaper in his lap. He was in his early twenties, Alafair reckoned, a slender young man with a long nose and close-cropped hair the color of dark honey. He looked a bit bedraggled, dressed in a wrinkled linen jacket and plus-fours. There was something familiar about his looks, the way he held himself, and Alafair wondered if she had seen him somewhere before. In the street on some previous visit, perhaps. That was a possibility, if he was who she suspected he was.

"You're Ellery Collins, I believe," she said to him, "Kenneth's friend."

He turned his head to look at her, his eyes widening. "Yes, ma'am."

She nodded. "I'm Miz Yeager's sister. I heard you were coming back to town. I expect it was a shock to arrive and find out that your dad had been shot."

He gave a rueful laugh. "I haven't even been home yet. My mother and sister-in-law met the train and brought me directly to the hospital. We were here all night."

"Is your mother still here?"

"My brother took the women home to get some rest. I volunteered to stay here until he gets back."

"It's good of you to spell your mother like that. How's she taking all this?"

He shrugged. "She's all outraged. Can't believe he'd be mixed up in anything shady, of course."

"You don't sound so sure about that," Alafair observed.

He eyed her, then asked, "Why did Mrs. Yeager want to see him?" His curiosity seemed more idle than intense.

"She didn't tell me. When Chief Burns told her your dad was under arrest, she declared she had to talk to him, and off we went."

"Ah. About Kenneth, I suppose. I'm surprised he'd see her."

"They've known each other a good long time. It sure is lucky that you decided to come back to Enid when you did. What made you decide to come home?"

Ellery leaned back in his chair and crossed his legs. A brief smile crossed his lips. "It's Mrs. Tucker, is it? For a minute there, I got the feeling that I was talking to Chief Burns again. I believe he asked me exactly the same question."

Alafair reddened. "Sorry if I sound like I'm accusing you of something."

"It's all right. I don't mind telling you that I came back because I heard what happened to Kenneth. He and I were friends, once, and I'm sorry about what happened to him. I wanted to tell Olivia."

"Did you and Kenneth have a falling-out?"

"No, not exactly. We just went off in different directions, more or less. He had big ideas, and I'm not very ambitious." His rueful smile reappeared. "Just ask my father. I just wanted to get out of here. I've been back in Baltimore, working for a newspaper."

"You look awful familiar to me, son. Have we met before?"

The idea intrigued him, and he studied her face for a moment before he answered. "I don't think so, ma'am. But we know a lot of the same people. We may have crossed paths at some time."

"That must be it." Alafair wanted to ask him straight out if he thought his father had anything to do with Kenneth's death, but she expected that would be going too far. Ellery's comments made her think that he and Buck had some differences, but they were still father and son. She was trying to think of some other way to worm information out of him when Ruth Ann strode out of Collins' room, her expression thunderous.

She caught sight of Ellery, who stood. "Ellery," she said. "I heard you were back. This is all your fault. If Kenneth hadn't got mixed up with you, he'd have never gone astray."

"I'm sorry you think so, Mrs. Yeager." His bland expression didn't communicate anything of what he was thinking. But Alafair noticed that he didn't argue with her.

"Let's go, Alafair." Ruth Ann stormed off down the hall without looking to see if Alafair was behind her.

Ellery didn't appear to be upset by the confrontation. He sat back down and retrieved the newspaper from where he had put it on the side table. He reached into his jacket pocket, withdrew a pair of spectacles, and slid them onto his long nose.

Alafair stood so suddenly that he looked up at her, startled. "Are you all right, ma'am?"

"Oh, no! I mean, yes," she sputtered, struggling to think of something to say that made sense. "I better catch up with Ruth Ann. Goodbye. Hope everything works out." She could feel his eyes on her back as she hurried off down the hall.

The two women were back at the Yeager house within fifteen minutes. Or it could have been even less than that. Alafair couldn't actually remember the trip. They walked into the parlor to find Martha, Olivia, and Streeter McCoy sitting in a circle and talking quietly. Alafair's gaze immediately sought Olivia, whose slender body lounged easily in one of the armchairs, her waves of hair like dark honey pinned up in a casual arrangement on her crown. She absently pushed her glasses up on her nose with a finger.

"Mama!" Olivia caught sight of them and turned in her chair. "Have y'all been at the hospital all this time? You missed supper."

"We were beginning to wonder what happened to y'all," Martha said. "I was just about to ask Streeter to go to the hospital and fetch you."

"Were you able to talk to Collins, Mrs. Yeager?" McCoy asked.

Ruth Ann moved into the room and sat down with the young people, bristling with news, but Alafair didn't move from the entryway. "Is Grace asleep?" she wondered to Martha.

"Yes, I put her down near to half an hour ago."

"Reckon I'll look in on her." Alafair withdrew her hatpin and turned to go upstairs.

"You want something to eat?" Olivia called after her.

"No, sugar, no, thank you. I'll be down directly."

Grace was sound asleep, curled up in the middle of the big bed in Alafair's room with Ike the cat draped across her feet, like a fat, furry foot warmer. He didn't seem to bother the girl any, because she did no more than sigh contentedly when Alafair bent over her and kissed her on the cheek. Ike reared his head and blinked at her.

"I'm obliged to you for babysitting, Ike, but I don't fancy brushing cat hair off my nightgown in the morning, so do me a favor and get yourself off the bed."

He considered her request for a minute before settling himself back down. Alafair picked him up, intending to feel annoyed, but not quite able to manage it. Ike hung in her two hands like a deadweight, gazing at her ruefully as she started to put him on the floor. She ended up sitting down in the rocking chair under the window with the cat in her lap.

"Oh, my heavens, Ike." She spoke softly so she wouldn't disturb Grace. "Why didn't I know? Why didn't Ruth Ann tell me?" She stroked the cat's soft fur as she considered the epiphany she had experienced at the hospital. Maybe she was wrong. Maybe she was seeing something that wasn't there at all.

But she didn't think she was wrong. She knew she would never ask Ruth Ann. If her sister had kept such a secret all these years, she obviously didn't want it ever to be known. What made Alafair feel horrible was that Ruth Ann had been all alone, far from her family, and probably humiliated, terrified, and ashamed.

Alafair stopped rocking. Of course she hadn't been alone. She had had Lester, who loved her, and loved her daughter, and made them his own.

Monday, September 20, 1915

"Once Hanlon spilled the beans, it was all over for Buck Collins." Sheriff Elsworth Hume spooned a pile of fried tomatoes onto his plate and gave Ruth Ann a benign smile.

Kenneth's funeral was over, and Lu had done more than her usual masterful job with the funeral dinner. Ruth Ann had invited both the sheriff and Chief Burns to dine with them, along with Mike Ed Beams and his wife and boys, and Streeter McCoy. The dinner had begun with a tureen of vegetable soup, followed by the most sumptuous tenderloin of beef that Alafair had ever seen. Lu had simmered the gorgeous piece of meat in a big roasting pan in the oven, surrounded by onions, carrots, turnips, and celery, and then added allspice and butter to the resulting juices. The tenderloin had been presented on a serving platter, surrounded by tiny fried meatballs and the vegetables, all drenched in gravy.

Lu had shaped mashed potatoes into balls as well, then brushed them with egg, browned them in the oven, and served them alongside the late summer tomatoes which she had breaded and fried. Also served were buttered lima beans, fresh-baked rolls, a mixed salad, iced tea, and pots and pots of strong, black coffee. On the sideboard, peach pudding, apple tarts, slices of cheese, and a bowl of whipped cream waited, in case any of the mourners managed to retain any appetite at all after the feast.

Olivia had begged off dinner, and was now lying down in her room upstairs with little Ron. The funeral had drained all the emotional strength she had left and Alafair expected that the idea of being pleasant and hospitable for another minute was more than Olivia could bear.

Lu was attending Lester upstairs, while Alafair and Martha did any necessary waiting on table and Ruth Ann acted as hostess.

"Why would Hanlon admit anything?" McCoy asked. "He looks like somebody who's had enough experience with the law not to let himself be tricked or intimidated into implicating himself so easily."

Chief Burns answered. "We spun him a tale about being able to lift fingerprints off of some of the things we collected from the scenes of all three break-ins, including the empty can of nitro from the Crawford well, so he figured he was caught anyway, and he might as well make the best deal he could."

"A tale?" Martha repeated. "You tricked him?"

"I'm afraid we did." The chief shot an amused glance in Alafair's direction. "I got the idea from Mark Twain himself, and Mr. Puddin'head Wilson."

Alafair made no indication that she knew what he was talking about. "You mean you really can't lift fingerprints?"

"Oh, we might have been able to get some kind of useful information off that can, if it hadn't been cleaned out, or if a dozen people hadn't handled it after it got picked up. Or maybe if we sent it to an expert in California, all wrapped in cotton wool, and had a couple of months to wait for an answer, or best of all, if we actually had a fingerprint kit and anybody at all in Garfield County had the slightest idea how to use it."

"Besides," Hume said, "I got the feeling that after the Kolocek boy got killed, Hanlon finally decided he hates Collins more than prison."

Alafair looked back up at Hume after helping Grace navigate a couple of little meatballs with gravy. "I feel kind of sorry for poor Mr. Hanlon."

Hume's eyes widened and he made an incredulous noise.

"Well, I think he's right sorry that Zip got killed. I expect he doesn't have a bunch of friends."

"He didn't have to do Collins' dirty work, Alafair," Ruth Ann pointed out. "He could have gone to the law."

"Men like him probably don't much trust the law, Mrs. Yeager," Mike Ed Beams said.

Hume nodded his agreement. "Hanlon is just the latest in a string of muscle men that Collins has used to squeeze and scare people into doing what he wants. Collins gets 'em fresh out of Leavenworth. When he needs a new bully boy, he sends up there to Kansas and has some low critter paroled out to his custody with the promise of a job. If the fellow has grown some scruples while he was in prison and don't want to knock heads and break legs any more, all Collins has to do is say the word, and he's back in the pen quicker than you can spit. After a while, the fellow disappears, and I doubt if he moves on to a more fulfilling situation, neither. Collins ain't a thoughtful and tender employer to his enforcement squad. I reckon it is almost enough to make you feel sorry for the murderers, Miz Tucker."

"I'm surprised one of these characters hasn't turned on Collins, if what you're saying is even half true!"

"I guess he's managed to keep his abuse less disagreeable to the thugs than going back to prison, at least to now. Buck covers his tracks better than anybody I ever seen. He owns a whole stable full of lawyers, any one of which can twist the law around 'til it's plumb standing on its head." Hume gestured with his fork. "Whether he meant to kill the boy or not, Hanlon is still responsible for his actions. I reckon we've got him for manslaughter, at least."

"What about Buck Collins?" Ruth Ann asked.

"Oh, we do owe Hanlon for helping us get Collins," Burns informed her. "Seems Collins bought the absinthe by the carload and brought it into the country from Mexico. Crawford then arranged through Yeager Transfer contacts to have the cases shipped all over the southwestern United States. Collins was making thousands of dollars a year on it and giving Kenneth a cut, which he was using to keep his well in business."

"The business really picked up after Congress outlawed the use of absinthe in this country," Hume added. There was a hint of irony in his voice.

"But what about Kenneth and those other folks?" Ruth Ann demanded. "Buck killed them sure as he did them in himself."

"Oh, we're charging Collins in the deaths of Zip and the Mexican," Burns assured her. "Your son-in-law, too, but all we have is circumstantial evidence in that case, ma'am. Maybe it's enough, I don't know. He insists long and loud that he didn't have anything to do with Crawford's death. If Collins' lawyers are good enough, that murder charge may not stick. But don't worry. Between the smuggling, the break-ins, and the other deaths, he'll go away for a good long time."

Alafair wiped Grace's hands while she studied her sister's face across the table. He has a lot more to answer for than Burns knows, she thought.

Alafair did her best to act as intermediary hostess and to look after Lester while Olivia and Ruth Ann entertained callers after the funeral dinner. As the day wore on, Alafair's already favorable opinion of the remarkable Lu grew to high admiration. The housekeeper not only did everything that needed to be done elegantly and excellently, she managed to do it invisibly as well.

Early in the afternoon, a boy in a gray Western Union uniform and cap rode up on a bicycle and delivered a telegram for Ruth Ann. Alafair felt a slight trepidation as Ruth Ann opened it. She wasn't sure if her sister would be able to handle another catastrophe.

She was relieved to see Ruth Ann's expression lighten as she read the message.

"It's from Daddy. Him and Mama are in Fort Smith. They should be here in the morning."

Alafair felt her shoulders relax and she emitted a relieved sigh. Their mother's presence was never anything but a comfort. Their father would take over, now, like the patriarch he was. Had it been Alafair in her sister's position, she and her father would spend the next week butting heads, but Ruth Ann would be quite happy to defer to his judgment. She felt a brief pang for Olivia, but decided that contending with her grandfather's benign tyranny would at least keep her mind off of her grief. And it would be good for Lester to know that Ruth Ann's parents would be here to see to her for as long as necessary.

Alafair walked out onto the porch and found Martha and McCoy sitting together in the swing, talking quietly and watching Grace entertain Ike with a feather on a string. Ron was burbling on McCoy's lap, waving his arms and doing his best to be the center of attention and interrupt the young couple's conversation.

"What was in the telegram, Ma?" Martha asked her.

"It's from Grandpa, honey. Looks like they'll be here tomorrow morning."

"Oh, that's good! I was beginning to wonder if they were going to make it before…"

Alafair sat down in one of the Adirondack chairs and unburdened McCoy of the baby so he could be free to wipe the drool off of his trouser leg. "Looks like they'll be here while Lester's still with us. Too bad they didn't quite make it in time for Kenneth's funeral. Still, Ruth Ann will be mighty glad to have them, and I'm glad we'll get to see them before we have to leave."

"When are you planning on going home, Mrs. Tucker?" McCoy asked.

"Well, I'm thinking maybe a day to visit with my mama and daddy. Then we can leave on Wednesday."

"So we won't be here for Lester's funeral?"

"There's no telling how much longer Lester will live, Martha, honey. I think it's better to do for the living. There will be plenty of folks to attend the funeral without us. Now, why don't you two go get yourselves something to eat, or take a little walk for a few minutes? I'll watch the kids. Then when y'all come back, I'll go up and check on Lester. I've been doing a lot of thinking, lately, and I've got a thing or two I want to talk to him about."

After Martha and McCoy left, Alafair took their place on the porch swing with Ron in her arms, just as Grace decided to decorate the protesting cat with the feather.

"Grace, don't squeeze Ike like that. He doesn't like it."

Grace loosened her grip and crawled up onto the swing next to her mother while Ike made his escape into the yard.

Grace snuggled down at Alafair's side. "I want to go home, Mama. I miss Daddy and all of them."

"So do I, baby girl. We'll go home pretty soon, don't worry. You'll get to see Grandma and Grandpa Gunn tomorrow. That'll be nice." She shifted the wiggly baby in her lap.

Grace brightened. "Grandma?"

"Your other grandma, sweet pea. Grandma and Grandpa Gunn from Arkansas."

The girl deflated. "I want *my* grandma. I want to go home."

Alafair felt a pang. Grace hadn't seen her Gunn grandparents in over a year. She probably didn't remember them at all. "You've had fun at Aunt Ruth Ann's, haven't you?"

"I like Ron. I like to play with Lu and Ike. Can Ike come home with us?"

"No, sugar. Ike lives here. He'd be homesick at our house. Besides, he might not get along with the other kitties."

"Ike's not like our kitties."

Alafair laughed. "He sure ain't! He thinks he's a person."

The idea tickled Grace and she gave Alafair a pearly grin before continuing. "I like Zip."

Alafair had not told Grace that Zip was no more. She hadn't seen the point. "I like Zip, too."

"Zip showed me his big new house."

"Does Zip have a new house? When did you see his big new house?"

"Last night, up in the sky. He's real happy there. He has a real good dog, too. His name is Junior."

"Is that so? I'm so glad to hear that! What's his dog like?"

"Oh, Ma, he's beautiful!"

Alafair was almost overcome by a sudden urge to cry, profoundly moved to think that Zip and Muddy were well and happy together somewhere. Muddy deserved to be beautiful. She swallowed the lump in her throat. "Tell me, sugar, have you seen Mr. Wing-Neck lately?" She figured that since she had the opportunity to make use of a little child's direct line to heaven, she might as well check on Kenneth.

"Oh! I forgot about him. He got tired of waiting and went away." Grace sat up, round eyed, and returned to a topic of more interest to her. "Zip went sky high," she said.

Alafair's heart skipped a beat. "Where did you hear that, darlin'?"

"The man in the hat said it."

The man in the hat? Chief Burns, maybe? Grace could have been talking about any number of men. There had been so many people coming and going, discussing the parade of events that had occurred over the past week, none of them paying any attention to one little pair of ears that heard a lot more than anyone credited.

Grace lifted her arms over her head. "He went so high he never came down, right up to heaven, and the sky took him!"

With Ron in one arm and Grace by the hand, Alafair stood to go into the house just as Martha walked around from the direction of the garage. She was alone, and looked rather forlorn. Alafair paused and waited for her to approach.

"Did Streeter go back to the hotel?"

Martha took Ron from her mother before she replied. "Yes, he's got to pack. He's leaving out to go to the City tomorrow afternoon."

"Grandma and Grandpa will be here in the morning, but I don't see why you shouldn't go ahead and see him off at the station when he leaves."

"We've said our goodbyes, Ma."

"Well, I expect you'll see each other again when we get home."

Martha bounced the baby in her arms and gazed off into space, but didn't comment. Alafair looked down at Grace, who was standing quietly at knee-level, holding her mother's hand and listening to the conversation with unusual interest. "Grace, go on inside. Look at your picture book that's on the hall table. I'll be right in."

"Okay," she said, instantly distracted, and banged into the house.

Martha was eyeing her warily when she turned back. "I don't want to go over this business about Streeter again, Mama."

Her attempt to stave off her mother's questions did her no good.

"So y'all haven't gotten anything settled?" Alafair asked.

"Nothing has changed that I can see."

"But you love him."

Martha laughed, but she didn't sound very happy. "Maybe I do, Ma, but this isn't a fairy tale. Love doesn't make everything turn out all right. In fact, it makes things pretty complicated, in my limited experience."

"I know it's your life and all, and you have to make your own choices about it. But you've said straight out that you love him, and he's told you that he wants you to do whatever will make you happy. I think something else is bothering you that I don't know about. What else do you want? Do you want to live with me and Daddy for the rest of your life?"

Martha smiled. It didn't escape her notice that her mother had never considered the possibility that an unmarried woman might live on her own. But that was never her plan. "Well, why not, Ma? I could work for as long as I wanted to, then. And when you and Daddy got too old to work the farm, I'd have a bunch saved up, and it'd be no problem for me to quit and take care of y'all. You'd never have to worry about anything, ever. I'd take good care of you."

Alafair had just drawn a breath to argue, when it dawned on her what Martha was saying. Her eyes widened, and she stood there for an instant with indrawn breath, stunned. "Do you mean to tell me that all this is because you think you have to take care of me and Daddy?"

Martha looked away, suddenly struggling not to cry. "I worry about you, Ma. Y'all are doing fine right now, but you're not getting any younger. I mean, I know you aren't going to live forever, but I had always figured I wouldn't have to deal with that for a long, long time. But anything can happen, can't it? Last year, when you got so hurt trying to protect Mary…why, it's a miracle you healed up as well as you did. You could have been crippled, or lost your sight! What's going to happen when you can't do for yourselves anymore? Who's going to see to things, then?"

Alafair was speechless for a moment. When on earth did this happen? When had the daughter become the mother? And why had Alafair not even noticed? "Martha Tucker," she said gently, "I don't know whether to be touched or to be insulted within an inch of my life. First of all, me and Daddy don't hardly have one foot in the grave. It's going to be a bunch of years before we have to have somebody mash our food and change our drawers for us. And second of all, if something does happen to one of us before our time, we do have nine other children who will bear some responsibility for us. It's not all going to be on you. In fact, I expect you'll be no spring chicken yourself when it comes to it. You might do better to be having me some grandkids right about now who can take care of both of us."

Martha blinked. She had never actually considered her siblings. "Who knows what the other kids'll be up to, by then? Why, they could all be living in Texas, or Europe, or China."

"Daddy and me could be rich as Midas, with a bunch of servants to carry us around on their shoulders all day, too, and not need y'all kids at all. You don't know what'll be going on in thirty years, Martha. Your pitiful old parents know enough to make arrangements before we're too feeble to think straight. Besides, where did you get the idea that this is all up to you, anyway? I know I've always counted on you when I've needed some help with the other kids, or with the house or some such. More than the others, now that I look back on it. But if I've given you the idea that you have to sacrifice your life and happiness for us, I sure didn't mean to, and I'm sorry for it."

Martha gripped Ron and leaned forward, earnest and intent on making her mother understand. "It's not a sacrifice, Mama.

I want to do it. I've wanted to take care of you for as long as I can remember. Since little James died and you were so upset that we had to go live with Grandma while Daddy stayed out on the farm, building the house. I was scared that if I didn't do something to help somehow, the family would never get back together. And then we did move home, and everything was just like it should be, until Bobby died. Then I was scared that both you and Daddy would go crazy or die of grief, and I'd be raising all the kids myself, me and Mary."

"Honey, you were fourteen years old when Bobby died! Your grandfolks may have had something to say about what happened to the rest of you if something had happened to me and Daddy, too."

"You're right, of course." Martha had to raise her voice to be heard over Ron's vigorous and noisy fist-sucking. "Funny, Ma, I've never talked about this to anybody before. When I say it all out loud it sounds kind of ridiculous, doesn't it?"

"No, it doesn't. I had the same kind of feelings about my folks when I was young. Your Grandma Gunn was always kind of frail, and Grandpa didn't look to me like he particularly noticed that she might need some help. I spent a lot of time worried that something might happen to her, and planning how I was going to look after my daddy and my brothers and sisters. I'm wondering why I never saw your plight, sugar, considering that I was the same way, and probably had a lot less reason to be than you do. All I can say is that sometimes grown-ups don't realize how much the things they do affect their children, sometimes forever. I did wrong by expecting too much of you when you were just a little girl. It was so easy and natural, since you were always right there without my having to ask you."

She put her hand on Martha's cheek. "I'll tell you this, Martha, my darlin', darlin' girl, my beloved. That was a long time ago. You're not a child anymore. No, you're not, not by a long shot. Believe me, we are always going to want you around. But if you give up having a life of your own for us, especially since there's no reason in the world for you to, your dad and I are going to be mighty unhappy about it. So you've got to let it go, Martha. Just drop it like a hot rock, simple as that. It's time for you to leave your mama and daddy and go make your own life, just like your brothers and sisters are going to do. That's how Daddy and me will know we've done our job."

Sometime in the middle of her mother's discourse, Martha began to notice a strange sensation growing in the center of her chest. A lifelong weight that she hadn't even known was there had begun dissipating into the ether, and a glorious feeling of lightness was filling her body. For a minute or two, she sat still and enjoyed the unfamiliar feeling before she said, "Maybe I will go to the train station with Streeter tomorrow."

Alafair didn't notice that Martha was a new woman. She opened the screen and stood back. "Good. Now, let's go inside and you can take care of the kids for me. It's about time for me to go up and sit with Lester a bit."

"Did Ruth Ann tell you that she got a wire from Fort Smith a little while ago?" Alafair asked as she settled herself in the chair beside Lester's bed. "Looks like our folks are on their way. They ought to be here by tomorrow morning."

"She told me. That'll be good for Ruth Ann," Lester said. "Kenneth's funeral was hard on her. She's been wanting her mama."

"I'm glad they'll get to see you again, Lester."

"Well, me too." He fell silent for a moment and his eyes drooped. He seemed to be struggling this afternoon, and Alafair felt a pang of grief. His end couldn't be far.

As she thought it, though, his eyes opened and he looked at her, his gaze sharp and clear. "I'm glad this murder business is solved before your folks have to be troubled with it."

Alafair turned her head and looked out the window. The sky was clear and brilliant blue. It was much warmer again, but the oppressive heat of the summer had been broken. It felt like fall.

She looked back at Lester. "To tell you the truth, I'm surprised that it really was Collins who was behind Kenneth's death."

He smiled at her. "Why? It was plain as day to me."

Alafair shrugged. "I know. Everybody—the police chief, the sheriff, and certainly you Yeagers—believed right from the get-go that Collins was the culprit. Nobody else was even considered. Well, in my experience, things aren't usually that straightforward."

"Alafair, sometimes things really are exactly what they seem to be."

"I reckon." A hint of a smile appeared on her face and she shook her head. "Still, if all Collins was after was that ledger, then why would he have one of his thugs kill the one person who knew where it was before figuring out some way to make him give it up?"

Lester was growing impatient with her refusal to be convinced. "A snake don't have to have a reason to kill. He kills because it's his nature. Maybe they were feeding Kenneth dope to get him to talk, went too far, and he died before they got the information. Then it occurs to Buck that since I have one foot in the grave, this might be just the opportunity to get control of everything I love, all I've built."

She considered this a moment, then nodded. "Sounds reasonable. Me and Martha and Streeter were talking about this earlier on, trying to figure out who would benefit the most from Kenneth's death. You know, we got to thinking that it would be Olivia."

Lester snorted. "How does it benefit Olivia to be a widow?"

"It sure doesn't benefit her heart. But it does make her rich in her own right."

"That's ridiculous. Olivia would never even think of such a thing."

"I agree. There's not a mean or deceitful bone in that girl's body. But someone else might have thought to remove Kenneth on Olivia's behalf."

Lester turned his head on the pillow to look at her.

"But who would do such a thing?" Alafair continued. "Ruth Ann sure loves that girl enough to do murder for her. But you said yourself that Ruth Ann is just too blamed good. Besides, she loved Kenneth, and didn't see his weaknesses. So, who else, I wonder? Who would do anything to protect Olivia and keep her out of the clutches of Buck Collins? Who'd have the power—and the will—to do it? I can only think of one person who fits that description, Lester."

Lester said nothing. They gazed at one another for some moments.

It was Alafair who broke the silence. "But what I want to know is how you did it? How could you do it, laying there in that bed, weak as a kitten?"

He actually grinned, an awful rictus that made him look like a death's-head, which gave Alafair a start.

"That's the interesting part, Alafair. I just set things up, and Kenneth did himself in." Lester nodded toward the dressing nook. "Laudanum. Every time he came to visit me, he took a swig of that laudanum. I put raw opium in it. I had a little ball of the black tar that I bought on my last trip to San Francisco, early this year. Opium is easy to come by up there. Lamerton had just told me I was sick. I'd heard this ain't an easy way to die, so I figured to keep the dope hid until I couldn't take the pain anymore and then end it quick. But I found another use for it. I put so much of it in the laudanum that one good swig is all it took to kill him. He'd come over late in the evening two or three times a week after I got down. He told Ruth Ann he wanted to visit me, bring me up to speed on the warehouse or the shipping. I can't see that dresser direct from here in this bed, and he knew it. But look yonder at the dressing table."

Alafair looked toward the small table next to the wall. All she noticed at first were the bottles and knickknacks, the lacy crocheted runner, the silver comb and brush set. She turned back to Lester, perplexed.

"The mirror."

She swiveled in her chair and saw instantly that the large mirror on the wall over the table was angled perfectly to see into the alcove, with a full view of the tall dresser with the brown glass bottle of laudanum on top of it.

"As soon as we were alone, he'd get up to leave me something on the dresser. Some contract or report or some such. Just an excuse to put something on the dresser. He'd lay it down, grab up that bottle, pull out the cork and take a swig. Then he'd come back in here and sit down in that chair and visit for a half hour or so, getting happier and sleepier all the while. So I sent him a message to come up to see me Sunday morning, between Sunday school and church, so I could tell him about this trip I wanted him to take to Guymon. There wasn't anyone else in the house at the time, just as I knew there wouldn't be. He made his usual detour for a snort, then sat down to give me some cock-and-bull story. I kept him talking long enough that he fell into a stupor and died right in that chair. I told Olivia and Ruth Ann that he left from the house to go to Guymon."

Alafair listened calmly, fascinated by the idea that he had managed to pull it off, and more than a little worried that she wasn't more horrified by Lester's tale of cold-blooded murder. She shook herself.

Lester turned his head to stare out the window again. "I was disappointed in Kenneth from the beginning. I was mighty disappointed that Olivia chose him in the first place. He wasn't near good enough for her."

Alafair straightened, but said nothing.

Lester continued. "If I'd have let him, Kenneth would have run the business into the ground. I should have given up trying to teach him a long time ago. I sure never should have put his name on the property title. But it's easy to say you shouldn't have after it's too late. If he hadn't been Olivia's husband, I'd have kicked his behind across the Kansas line back in '13, after the first time he let down a solid customer for a crackbrained scheme that lost us near to $500. I never let him negotiate or fulfill a contract on his own after that. And he wasn't just a bad businessman. He was a dope addict. He got worse and worse over the years. Olivia kept it a secret as long as she could, but I found out soon enough."

"I had no idea."

"Neither did most folks. Ruth Ann didn't, for sure. Mike Ed knew what he was like, and Olivia, too, of course. It's been her good sense that has pulled his fat out of the fire more times than I could count. She'd have never left him. She's too honorable. But she'll be much better off with him gone. What else could I do? I couldn't let my daughter go down to ruin with that pea-brain, or Ron, my only grandchild."

"Did you really leave part of the shipping business to George?"

"I did in an earlier will. After Kenneth met his end, I changed it so that Olivia gets everything."

"So you planned to get rid of Kenneth for a long time?"

Lester didn't even bat an eye. "Since I found out I was going to die. Then, once I heard he was going around with Buck Collins' son, I knew Buck would figure out some way to use my knuckleheaded son-in-law to get to me some way or another. Of course, I hatched the plan before I knew that Kenneth had already mortgaged Olivia's future to my worst enemy."

"Did you mean to pin it on Collins?"

"I figured the police would find a connection between them, and they did. And like you said, everybody's plenty willing to believe he did it."

"You sure hate him, don't you, Lester? Even if he got his hands on everything you own, you know he'd never do anything that would hurt Olivia."

He took a breath to speak, stopped to consider the implication of what she had said, and swallowed his comment. "You been talking to Ruth Ann?"

"No. Not about Buck Collins and Olivia."

"Then who told you?"

"I figured it out myself, Lester. I saw Ellery Collins at the hospital. There's a family resemblance."

"Olivia is the light of my life."

"No one will ever find out anything from me," she swore.

"It's justice, Alafair, that he should pay for what he did to Ruth Ann, the finest, purest woman ever born."

"Ruth Ann has a wonderful life, thanks to you. She's loved and cared for beyond most women's wildest dreams. Olivia, too. I know you hate the man, but Buck Collins is like to hang for a murder he didn't commit," she pointed out. "That isn't justice."

Lester shrugged. "He won't hang. He's got too many lawyers for that. But he'll go to jail for sure. And maybe he didn't kill Kenneth, but he's still a murderer. He was responsible for doing in those fellows out to the oil field, and there's half a dozen others met an early end thanks to Buck Collins."

"Why the meat locker?"

"So he'd get found eventually. I didn't want anyone to think he had just run off and was still alive. I didn't expect it'd take so long, though. I didn't know the man who rents that particular locker was out of town."

"How did you get him out of here and over to the warehouse? You had to have help. Was it Mike Ed, or Doctor Lamerton? Not Olivia or Ruth Ann, surely! It couldn't have been little old Lu. I've seen Ruth Ann dose you out of that bottle a score of times. Why don't it kill you? Are there two bottles?"

"Let that rest, Alafair. Some things I ain't telling. It was my idea to get shet of Kenneth, and I did it all by myself. Doesn't matter anymore. There isn't anything they can do to me now."

"But murder, Lester," she said. "That poor boy was foolish, but he didn't deserve to be murdered. Aren't you afraid to stand before God?"

Lester smiled at the thought. "I've made hard, bad choices all my life, Alafair. I've chosen my family over God every time, and would again. Besides, God has already seen to my punishment by keeping me alive for so long. And I've done my penance as best I could, too. There's nothing in that bottle on the dresser but colored water. I got rid of the poisoned bottle. There's a bottle of the real stuff here in the bedside table. I only take it when I have to, when I need to be clear in the head to help my family."

"Lester, for heaven's sake!"

"There's no reason for you to tell Chief Burns, Alafair. It won't help Collins much, and it'd just cause trouble and heartache for Ruth Ann and Olivia."

She had no idea what to say. She shook her head, which Lester took as agreement.

"You know, Alafair, I never was much of a deep thinker. I was too busy making a living to be a philosopher. But for the last while, since I've been lying here helpless as a babe, I've had a lot of time to ponder on things I never cared to think of before. Like dying, for one. The oddest thing is that it's a relief, in a way, to know that there's nothing more you can do. All them burdens you've borne all your life are taken from you, and you've got nothing to say about it. It's funny." He sighed. "I hate to boot you out, but I'm not feeling so well right now. Hurting pretty bad."

She stood and made a move to retrieve his medicine from the drawer in the bedside table.

"Don't trouble yourself, please, Alafair," Lester said.

It seemed to Alafair that she stood and gazed at Lester's drawn gray face for a long time, but it was probably only a few seconds. She felt a strange sense of dislocation, as though she was watching herself watching Lester.

He smiled at her. "Thank you, Alafair, and good night."

She turned and left without another word.

Alafair walked down the stairs, numb. How could she complicate her sister's already sad situation by volunteering the truth to the law? She knew that she couldn't possibly let Collins die for killing Kenneth, yet he should go to prison for his involvement in the deaths of Zip Kolocek and Deo Juarez. Unless she had to save Collins from the noose, or unless she was asked point-blank if she knew who killed Kenneth Crawford, she knew she would keep silent.

She paused on the next-to-last step. Martha and the kids were nowhere to be seen, but Ike the cat was sitting at the bottom of the stairs, staring up at her. Was that accusation she saw in his yellow eyes, or sympathy?

"What else can I do?" she asked him. "Only God can punish Lester now, and we have to protect Ruth Ann and Olivia, if we can."

The cat's tail swished across the floor.

"Wish I knew how he managed it, though."

Ike got up and trotted into the parlor. Alafair followed absently and made her way toward the settee, but the cat turned around and wove himself around her ankles, nearly tripping her. She huffed and moved him out of her way with her foot. He took a couple of steps and looked back at her before he jogged off toward the kitchen.

Alafair had no idea why she followed him.

The cat got right up to the kitchen door before he slewed off down the hall, and Alafair was about to go after him when she heard the sound of laughter behind the closed door. Curious, she pushed it open enough to peek in.

Lu was standing at the stove, stirring some wonderfully aromatic concoction in a big pot on the stove. Her son, the laconic Arnold, clad as before in his Birk Equipment Company uniform, leaned up against the cabinet with his arms crossed over his chest. The laughter stopped abruptly as they turned to see who had interrupted.

"Oh, sorry," Alafair said, startled. "Hello, Arnold."

"Mr. Yeager all right?" Lu asked.

"He's resting."

The housekeeper turned away from the stove and wiped her hands on the tail of her apron. "Oh, Miz Tucker, glad to see you. Come in, please. Don't mind Arnold."

Arnold had already picked up his cap and was heading for the back door. "I'm just leaving, Miz Tucker. Got deliveries to make. Nice to see you."

"Don't let me…" she began, but he was gone before she could finish the sentence.

"Come in, come in," Lu repeated. "I make a chocolate pie for Miz Yeager, like your recipe. Come taste."

"Chocolate pie? Oh, yes, I gave you my recipe. I forgot about that. Ruth Ann will be so pleased." She stepped up to the stove, took the proffered spoon, and dipped it into the filling that had just come to a languid boil in the pot. It was as black and thick and smooth as Arkansas River mud. The smell was mouthwatering. She closed her eyes and took a taste, and grew faint with ecstasy.

The taste was so familiar, so like home, so reminiscent of the special, rainy Sunday afternoons with her children, when she would let them help her make their favorite treat.

"Miz Tucker, what's wrong?"

Lu's anxious voice brought Alafair back to the present, to her sister's kitchen. She realized that tears were running down her cheeks, and she brushed them away with the back of her hand, embarrassed.

"Oh, nothing, Lu, don't fret yourself. This is so wonderful, just like home. I reckon I'm wearing my feelings on my sleeve because of poor Lester."

Lu nodded. "Mr. Yeager, he's very brave."

"I always admired him so." Alafair's tone was wistful. The words "until now" hovered unspoken in the air.

The housekeeper's expression changed. She assessed Alafair for a moment before she spoke again. "Miz Yeager ever tell you how I come to work here?"

"No," Alafair admitted, curious. Why would this secretive woman suddenly want to enlighten someone she barely knew about her personal history?

"My husband was merchant, very rich. He brought me to California long time ago, when I was young girl, before president passes the 'no Chinese' laws. My husband was a cruel man. I was very pretty once." Lu smiled. "He beat me a lot, so I'm not so pretty now. I had six children, all boys except one girl. All died but two sons. My husband says I am a bad wife. He would sell me to pleasure house, but broken nose spoils my face, so maybe he will kill me and get another wife."

Alafair sat down in a kitchen chair, still clutching the wooden spoon. How many times had she heard similar stories from women in Arkansas or Oklahoma? It sounded like Chinese wives didn't have it any better.

"When my boy Arnold is nineteen, he works at big hotel in San Francisco. He is footman on fancy hotel carriage. Mr. Yeager, he comes every year to San Francisco for business, stays at hotel. Arnold helps with his luggage all the time, and Mr. Yeager likes Arnold, talks to him, asks about his family, about what Arnold wants to do with his life.

"One day, my husband beat me bad, nearly kill me. Break my nose again, ribs, arm. Arnold, he sneaks me away that night, but they don't take Chinese at San Francisco hospital. So Arnold hides me in his room, in loft at garage for fancy carriages."

Lu turned to check on the pie filling before she continued her tale. "Arnold never told me how Mr. Yeager finds out. Maybe he sees that Arnold is upset. Arnold, he speaks perfect English. Maybe he asks Mr. Yeager for help."

Lu paused, and sighed. "All I know is that Mr. Yeager goes with Arnold to Chinatown, gives my husband money to leave me alone. He pays a doctor to fix me, pays hotel so I stay with Arnold in his garage room until I'm better. Afterwards, Arnold tells Mr. Yeager that my husband has sold me to him."

"He bought you!"

"He did not know. He tells me to go away, be safe, but where can I go? So, he tells me I can have job in his home, in Enid, if I want. Miz Yeager, she is kind as her husband. I am honored to take care of them for as long as I live."

"What about your children? Did Arnold suffer for defying his father?"

Lu's eyes widened. "Oh, no. His father loved him very much. Arnold is eldest son, very promising. When my husband died, Arnold took his father's money and brought his brother and families here. He wanted to take care of me so I never work, but I would never leave Yeagers. I would do anything for Yeagers. So would Arnold. You understand?"

"Even if it was a very bad thing?"

"Even if anything. I owe my life."

The two women gazed at each other in silence for a long time, Lu standing in the middle of the kitchen floor, so small that she was almost eye to eye with Alafair, who was still sitting in a chair with a spoon in her hand.

There was no figuring this one out, Alafair was thinking. Best leave it to God. A thick bubble in the pie filling plopped softly, bringing her around. She stood up. "Thank you for telling me your story, Lu. Now, do you have a pie crust ready?"

It was late when the pies were done. Alafair wanted to go to bed, to sink into oblivion and sleep a dreamless sleep. But when she left the kitchen, she only got as far as the darkened parlor before she sank into one of the armchairs and closed her eyes. She huffed when what felt like a furry cannonball leaped into her lap, and she looked down to see Ike's yellow eyes reflecting the dim light coming from the foyer. He gave her a soft "yowp" and began to purr when she rubbed the back of his neck.

"Tell me, Ike," Alafair murmured, "does one horrible act wipe out all the many wonderful things a good man does in his life?"

If he maintained a philosophy about such things, he wasn't inclined to share it with her. He turned over on his back, demanding a belly rub.

Tuesday, September 21, 1915

Olivia, Alafair, Martha, Grace, and Ron were on the platform to meet Grandma and Grandpa Gunn when the train pulled into the station from Tulsa. The family rushed to greet Grandma and Grandpa before they were properly off the train, creating such an obstruction that the conductor had to usher them out of the way so that the other passengers could disembark.

It took several minutes for the grandparents to exclaim over the children's growth and the young women's beauty, and to relate the progress of their journey. Alafair hadn't seen her parents in over a year, and she looked them over critically while they commiserated with a solemn but composed Olivia over the unexpected loss of her husband. They were their familiar selves, as completely opposite in appearance as any two people could be, and yet just as perfectly complementary. Elder Robert Gunn was huge—immensely tall and broad, hard and wiry and disjointed as a scarecrow. Sister Selinda Gunn was tiny, soft, and deceptively frail looking. He was fair and ruddy and blue-eyed to her olive complexion and dark eyes. And their personalities matched their looks, as well, since Robert was a giant presence, white-hot and overwhelming as a sunny day, while Selinda was quiet, cool, and gentle as a starlit night.

Grandpa Robert engaged a porter to carry their bags and the group moved in a knot through the station and out onto the street, where they piled into Lester's Oldsmobile. Olivia took the wheel, with her grandfather and Grace beside her. Grandma Selinda, Alafair, Martha, and Ron squeezed themselves together in the backseat.

"You look tired, Ma," Alafair said to her mother, raising her voice over the engine roar and the rush of the wind.

"I could say the same about you, Alafair."

Alafair grimaced. "It's been a mighty long and upsetting week."

"Oh, such a shock about Kenneth! I'm so sorry we couldn't get here before now. How is Lester holding up? Did Ruth Ann stay home to tend him?"

"He wasn't looking so good this morning, Ma. We could barely rouse him. I'm glad y'all finally made it. Ruth Ann sure needs you."

In the automobile, the trip from the railroad station straight to Ruth Ann's house took less than ten minutes. Olivia pulled up into the driveway and came to a halt outside the garage at the back of the property. Lu was already standing quietly beside the drive. As soon as they piled out of the car the diminutive servant began to hoist the luggage out of the back. Only Alafair cast her a glance as the family trooped in to the house through the back door.

Alafair left everyone downstairs in the parlor, removing coats and hats and settling down to the refreshments Lu had left on the sideboard, and went upstairs to retrieve Ruth Ann and perhaps help her prepare Lester for a visit.

As soon as she reached the top of the landing, she could see through the open bedroom door that Ruth Ann was standing beside the bed. She couldn't see Lester over the pile of quilts covering him. Alafair paused at the end of the hall, and Ruth Ann looked up at her. Her face was pale as ash, except for the bruise-colored circles around her eyes.

"I heard y'all come in. Mama and Daddy make it all right?"

Alafair released the breath that she didn't know she was holding before she walked up and paused in the bedroom door. "Yes, everybody is downstairs. They're anxious to see you and Lester. Do you want me to bring them up, or would you rather I sat up here with him while you go down for a spell?"

"Lester's gone, Alafair." Ruth Ann's voice was calm.

After an instant's stunned pause, Alafair crossed the room to her sister's side. Lester was lying on his back with his hands arranged over his heart. He looked as small and dry and brittle as a corn-husk doll, she thought, but peaceful.

"Oh, Ruth Ann." It was all Alafair could manage to say.

"It's all right, Sister. He went real easy. It's a relief, really. He suffered so much."

"I guess he figured his work was finally done."

"Yes, there was nothing more he could do here, so I reckon the sky took him, like little Grace would say." Ruth Ann gave a little hiccup that could have been either a laugh or a sob.

"Are you all right?" Alafair asked. "Do you want me to leave you alone for a while?"

Ruth Ann's eyes left the figure in the bed and looked at Alafair. "I'm fine. He's safe with Jesus," she said, all business now. "And Daddy's finally here to take care of us for a while 'til we get things all arranged. We'd better go down and tell the folks."

Alafair followed her sister down the stairs, not quite knowing how to feel. Ruth Ann was going to be all right. She felt good about that. She also felt good that Lester wasn't suffering anymore and that Olivia would retain control of her life and fortune. She didn't feel so good about the secret she and an unobtrusive little Chinese woman would probably share for the rest of their lives.

◇◇◇

Martha walked to her aunt's front door from the train station after seeing Streeter off. They had taken their leave of one another on the platform and agreed to have luncheon together in a week's time, after both had settled into their respective routines. They didn't discuss any further future than that, but neither minded. They had taken a mutual step in the same direction. That was enough for now.

Martha found her mother, aunt, cousin, and grandmother sitting together in the parlor, discussing the quirks and traits of their lost loved ones with nostalgic good humor and eating chocolate pie. Grandpa was at the Henninger-Royer Funeral Parlor, taking care of Lester's final arrangements with Mr. Henninger. Lu hovered around the ladies, refreshing tea glasses. Ron was napping in his great-grandmother's lap. Grace, sitting on the floor at Alafair's feet, was amusing herself in some other world that included a piece of cheese, her rag doll, and Ike, who was more interested in the cheese than the game. Martha stood for a moment in the foyer and watched them talk, thinking it was very interesting how the Gunn women were different ages, sizes, and complexions, but they all had the same face.

"Hey, darlin'," Alafair called, when she spotted Martha lurking in the hall. "Did Streeter get off all right?"

"Come on in and have a sit-down," Grandma Selinda said.

Martha stepped forward into the doorway with a smile. "Yes, Streeter got off just fine, Mama. Just let me throw my hat on my dresser and change my shoes, Grandma, and I'll join you directly. Be sure and save me some of that pie, now."

Martha climbed the two flights of stairs to the attic bedroom, withdrawing her hat pin and removing her hat on the way. She tossed it on a chair and went to the mirror over the dressing table to straighten her hair. Her hand paused on the brush as she studied her reflection.

She leaned forward a little to scrutinize her image more closely. The same face she had just seen on the women downstairs was staring back at her.

"It's like we're all the same woman," she said aloud. Suddenly, she was struck with the idea that she was standing at the very end of a long, unbroken line of women that went all the way back to Eve, all with one great soul, moving forward through time.

This was her time. And her responsibility, too, to the line of women who would come after her, to move that woman's soul into the twentieth century.

She tucked in a stray curl and went downstairs to eat some chocolate pie and talk about the weather.

Sunday, October 1, 1916

Shaw Tucker conceded that Martha had chosen a beautiful day for her wedding to Streeter McCoy. After the ceremony, he took full advantage of his position as father of the bride to hold forth and entertain the many guests that milled around in his house and yard. This was the fourth time in four years that he'd married off a daughter, two just this year, and he had to admit that it was more enjoyable for him each time. He still had six kids to go, and he figured that by the time he walked Grace down the aisle, he'd be the happiest daddy in all of Christendom.

It occurred to Shaw Tucker that he hadn't seen Alafair for a good long while. It wasn't like her to neglect her hostessing duties, and he found himself not exactly concerned, but at least curious as to her whereabouts. He made his way over to a corner of the yard where his three other married daughters, laughing Mary, beautiful, headstrong Alice, gentle Phoebe, were sitting under a tree and enjoying a lively conversation about something.

"Y'all seen Mama lately?" he asked.

Mary reached up and brushed something off of her father's waistcoat. "Not lately. Last I saw, she went back into the house with Martha to help her change into her traveling duds."

"Martha's changed now," Alice said. "I see her over there by the food table with Streeter and Gee Dub."

"Y'all look like you're having a good time," Shaw observed.

"We were just reading this letter that Mama got from Aunt Ruth Ann yesterday, Daddy." Phoebe held up the missive. "Did you read it yet?"

"Your mama read to me that your cousin Olivia's well came in a gusher a couple of weeks ago. I reckon her and that one-eyed partner of hers are rich as Croesus, now."

"Did Mama tell you that now that he's been acquitted of attempting to murder Buck Collins, Olivia and Pee Wee Nickolls expect to get married?" Mary said.

"She did. She said your Aunt Ruth Ann is mighty happy about it, too."

"It's about time," Alice decided. "All Olivia has been able to write about for the last few months is 'Pee Wee this' and 'Pee Wee that,' how good he is to her, and how he loves that boy of hers. She should have just married him and had done with it ages ago."

"Not everybody is as sure about everything as you are, Alice." Phoebe patted an empty chair next to her. "Sit down, Daddy. You must be run off your feet."

"No, thanks, girls. I reckon I'll see if I can figure out where Mama went to."

He checked around the yard before he went into the kitchen from the back porch. The counters and table were sagging with dishtowel-covered food, but Alafair was not there. He walked into the parlor and noticed at once that the door to their bedroom was closed. He blinked, surprised, and unconsciously smoothed his floppy black mustache with the back of his index finger and brushed the shock of black hair off his forehead with the flat of his hand. He had forgotten that the bedroom had a door that closed.

When he opened it, the seldom-used door squeaked, and Alafair, dressed to the nines in her fashionable suit, looked up from her seat on the bed. Her eyes were wet and red, and she looked away quickly, embarrassed to be caught weeping. Shaw strode across the room and sat down beside her before draping his arm across her shoulders.

"Alafair, why in the goat beard are you crying?"

"Oh, Shaw, I feel like an idiot child. It's nothing. Just don't you worry about it. Here, I'll wipe my eyes and go splash some water on my face and get back to the doings."

"Well, now, Alafair Gunn, that's just not good enough. You're not one to cry over nothing, especially on such a happy day as this one, so you'd better tell me what's bothering you."

She gazed at him a minute, looking miserable and red-nosed, before her eyes flooded again and she ducked her head. "You'll make sport of me," she warned. "But the truth is, well, I've spent the last twenty-five years wishing that Martha would find her a good man that she could love, run her own house and family. I was beginning to wonder if it was going to happen for her at all, but it did. Streeter is all that I could have wished for her, and more. But now that it's finally happened…oh, Shaw, I feel so bereft. I feel like somebody's died. I'm going to be so lonesome without her."

"Oh, honey. It's not like she's moving to Arabia. Her and Streeter have that real nice place above their business right downtown, not two miles from here. She'll be here or you'll be there near to every day. Why, you'll probably see her just as much as ever."

She sniffed and smiled at his attempt to cajole her out of her mood. "I know it. But there's something different about Martha leaving home than there was with the others. Her and me, we've been through a lot together. She's not just my daughter, Shaw. She's my best friend. Oh, we'll always be close, but it'll never be the same around here now that she's gone."

They both stood up and she started out of the room, but he seized her arm and she turned toward him, surprised. He reached out and placed his hands on the wall, trapping her between his two arms with her back to the wall. He leaned down so that his face was inches from hers.

"Well, sugar, I reckon I'll just have to be your best friend, then. Just like I was before Martha came along and just like I will be after Grace is long gone." To her amazement, he kissed her, and her knees turned to water.

"Shaw," she chided, breathless, when he drew back, "what if somebody comes in?"

He laughed. "They'll just have to be shocked. Now, come on and eat a bite of cake. I think the newlyweds are getting ready to go."

They walked out together, just in time to join in the festivities as Martha climbed into the sidecar of Streeter McCoy's Harley-Davidson Model 11-F three-speed twin and they roared away toward Boynton.

Alafair waved them away with her handkerchief, holding Shaw's hand and feeling curiously elated.

Recipes

Alafair's Chocolate Pie/Pudding

Powdered cocoa was widely available in 1915, even in the wilds of the Cherokee Strip. This pie is quite simple to make, but potent. You must be an extreme chocolate lover to eat this. Some family members have indicated that this pie is too rich for a normal human being.

¼ cup powdered cocoa
2 cups sugar
2 cups milk
1 egg
¼ cup flour
¼ tsp. salt
1 tsp. vanilla

Mix dry ingredients thoroughly. Beat one egg well and mix into milk before adding to dry ingredients. Cook over medium heat, stirring constantly, until mixture thickens and boils with a dull "plop." Remove from heat, add vanilla and mix well. Pour into 8-inch prepared pie shell. Alafair would have let the pie stand at room temperature but it can be refrigerated until set. Top with meringue or whipped cream. Leave out the egg for chocolate pudding.

Meringue

3 egg whites
3 Tbsp. sugar

Beat sugar and egg whites together until stiff. The mixture will be white and be able to hold a peak. Spread the mixture over the top of the pie and put in a medium oven until the meringue sets and browns slightly.

There is a colorful country name for meringue, but we are far too refined to repeat it here.

FANCY CITY FOOD

In 1915, many foods would be available to a cook in a well-to-do city the size of Enid that would be harder to come by on a farm or in a smaller Oklahoma town like Boynton. Alafair's pantry would have been filled almost exclusively with meats, fruits, and vegetables that she and her family had raised and preserved themselves. However, her sister Ruth Ann Yeager would have had the resources and the opportunity to try foodstuffs imported from all over the United States and the rest of the world. Having a live-in cook to create elaborate meals from exotic ingredients is also very helpful.

One note about cooking: times and temperatures given in the following recipes are approximate. Ovens vary, and even the dish you use will affect the cooking time. For instance, a glass baking pan will cook a dish faster than a metal one. So keep your eyes peeled.

Beef Tenderloin

In Alafair's time, a cook would have had the butcher specially cut the tenderloin from the side of beef for her. Tenderloin of beef is available these days, but it isn't cheap, to say the least. This dish is gorgeous and delicious, as well as expensive. It might be the perfect entrée to serve next time you have the president of the United States over to dinner.

1 beef tenderloin (about 3 lbs)
2 Irish potatoes, cubed
4 medium carrots, sliced into 1-inch chunks
2 turnips, cubed
4-6 large stalks of celery, with leaves
1 or 2 large onions, quartered
2 cups water
1 tsp. allspice
1 Tbsp. butter

Put the meat in a roasting pan with 2 cups of water and the vegetables. Simmer in the oven for about one hour and 15 minutes at 400 degrees, or until done to your liking. When nearly done, add the allspice and butter to the meat juices. For serving, arrange the vegetables and meatballs (recipe follows) around the tenderloin on a large platter and pour the meat juices over everything.

Meatballs

You may certainly use ground beef to make the meatballs, but this is the fancy way. Boil a nice 1-pound hunk of lean beef until done through, then finely chop it and mix with ½ beaten egg, ¼ onion, minced, and salt and pepper. (Alafair likes 3 or 4 shakes of salt and 7 or 8 shakes of pepper.) Roll it into small balls, brush with beaten egg and roll it in fine bread crumbs or crushed cracker crumbs. Fry until brown in enough fat to cover the bottom of the skillet.

You can save the broth that will be created from boiling the beef to make soup.

Gumbo Soup

This is not the same as Creole gumbo, which is spicier and more complex. This soup is quite simple, very nutritious and savory.

1 medium onion, sliced
2 cups thinly sliced fresh tender okra
4 cups fresh or home-canned tomatoes
1½ quarts of broth

Luckily, you now have some very nice broth on hand from boiling the beef for meatballs. If you are using fresh tomatoes off the vine, scald (dip in boiling water for just a few seconds) and peel them and chop them up. Fry the onion in meat drippings until beginning to brown. Combine all the ingredients in a large pot and simmer slowly for three hours.

Okra will thicken the soup and is very good for the digestion.

Mashed Winter Squash

Winter squashes are heavier and denser than summer squashes, and have a hard shell. Most varieties of winter squash can be used for this recipe, but good, sweet, firm butternut or acorn squashes are ideal. Squash can be boiled or baked. Boiling is fast, but baking intensifies the flavor and sweetness. Baked squash is much easier to deal with, too. To boil a squash, you should peel and seed it, cube it, and cook it in a small amount of water for 15 minutes or so. To bake, halve the squash, scoop out the seeds, and place the pieces cut side down on a baking sheet or shallow baking pan. For a nice, three-pound butternut, bake at 350 degrees for half an hour, then turn it over and bake for another 15 to 20 minutes, or until the squash is very soft. Remove from the oven and allow to cool enough to handle, then scoop the flesh out of the shell with a spoon into a pot and mash like potatoes. Over a medium low flame, add a scant quarter cup of milk or cream, a quarter cup of maple syrup, and 2 tablespoons of butter, and mix well. Stir constantly until hot, then turn out into a serving dish. Make a well in the top of the mound of squash and plop a big spoonful of butter into it.

Succotash

Anyone who has only eaten succotash out of a can has no idea what the real thing is like. One can make a quite passable succotash from frozen baby limas and frozen sweet corn kernels, but if you want the authentic succotash experience, this is the way to do it.

2 cups fresh shelled baby lima beans
about 12 ears of young sweet corn (makes 2 cups of kernels)
⅓ cup butter
½ cup cream

Place the beans in a pot and barely cover with cold water. Scrape the kernels from the ears of corn and put aside. Boil the beans with the scraped cobs for about 30 minutes. Then remove the cobs, put in the corn kernels, and boil for 15 minutes more. Add the butter and cream and salt and pepper to taste. Do use real cream. Milk just isn't the same in this dish.

Fried Parsnips

Northerners tend to be more familiar with parsnips than Southerners, and this would be especially the case in 1915. Many recipes call for the parsnips to be boiled before frying, but if you choose young, tender parsnips and not big old woody ones, this is absolutely not necessary. Simply wash and scrape 3 or 4 medium-sized parsnips, cut into coins, like a carrot, and fry in enough fat to cover the bottom of the pan. When one side is brown, turn the parsnips with a spatula and brown the other side. Parsnips can be fried *au naturel,* but for a nice variation, dredge the coins in flour before frying. Salt and pepper to taste.

Fried Tomatoes

Frying is a great way to use green tomatoes, but red ones can be fried as well. Just cut firm, ripe tomatoes into thick slices, season with salt and pepper, dredge in cornmeal, and fry in meat drippings until they are brown on both sides.

Mashed Potato Puffs

This is a lovely side dish, and easy to make, especially if you have leftover mashed potatoes. Shape hot mashed potatoes into egg-sized balls and place them on a buttered cookie sheet. Brush with beaten egg and brown in a 400-degree oven for 10 or 15 minutes.

Grace's Little Almond Cookies

¾ cup butter
2 cups flour
¼ cup sugar
½ tsp. almond extract

Cream the butter and sugar together, then work in the flour. If the dough is crumbly, mix in another tablespoon or two of butter. Roll out the dough about ½-inch thick and cut with a cookie cutter, if you like pretty shapes. Or the floured mouth of a small drinking glass will do just as well. Place the cookies about ½ inch apart on an ungreased cookie sheet and bake in a moderate oven for 15 to 20 minutes, until they begin to brown around the edges. This will make about 2 dozen small cookies.

Peach Pudding

- 1½ cups stewed peaches
- 4 eggs
- pinch salt
- ¼ tsp. nutmeg
- 2 cups cream
- ½ cup sugar
- 1 Tbsp. flour

The first thing to do for this delectable dish is to peel and slice 5 or 6 peaches and stew them for about 40 minutes in a little water, ¼ tsp. cloves, and a cinnamon stick. Drain off the liquid and reserve for another use, then arrange the peaches over the bottom of a 2-quart baking dish.

Beat the eggs and sugar together well, then add the flour and nutmeg. Slowly add in the cream, stirring constantly. Pour the custard over the peaches in the baking dish and bake for 45 minutes at 350 degrees.

Serve with whipped cream. And in the name of all that's holy, not that stuff you spritz out of a can. If you've never whipped your own cream, here's your chance. The following is an easy way to do it: To 1½ cups of whipping cream, add ¼ cup of powdered sugar and 1 tsp. vanilla, and beat until soft peaks form.

Alafair would have used a whisk to whip the cream, but if you have neither the patience nor the wrist strength to do it this way, use an egg beater. Or an electric beater, if you must.

Historical Notes

Absinthe was the LSD of its day. It is a potent type of spirits, distilled from herbs and wormwood, which in the late nineteenth and early twentieth centuries was popular with the Bohemian set in the United States and Europe. Absinthe had the undeserved reputation of being highly addictive and hallucinogenic, and was banned for sale in this country in 1912. To this day, traditional absinthe cannot be imported into the U.S. for human consumption.

The **Garber Pool** was located five miles south of the town of Garber, Oklahoma, in Garfield County, on a farm belonging to one George Beggs. The original oil lease on the land was owned by the Sinclair Company, but when Sinclair allowed the lease to lapse, Mr. Beggs sold the mineral rights to Enid banker and businessman **Herbert Champlin**. Champlin was hesitant to invest in the risky business of oil, but his far-seeing wife insisted that he take the step. It was a good thing for Champlin that she did. The field struck big in September 1916. Champlin rapidly changed his mind about the advisability of getting into the oil business, and immediately bought Victor Bolene's small refinery in Enid, which was still under construction at the time. Champlin built a pipeline from his field in Garber to his greatly expanded refinery, and so was born the Champlin Refining Company.

John Burns, hired in 1915, was the chief of police for the City of Enid, and **Elsworth Hume**, elected in 1910, was the sheriff of Garfield County at the time of this story. I borrowed their names, but since I have no idea what these gentlemen were actually like, the characters are pure invention. One interesting historical tidbit, though, is that Mr. Hume and two of his sons bought the Overland Automobile Company in Enid in 1919 and manufactured cars for a few years.

Eugene V. Debs ran for president of the United States five times on the Socialist ticket. In 1912, he garnered more votes in Oklahoma than in any other state. He was the keynote speaker at the 1915 Founders' Day Celebration in Enid. Debs was one of the founders of the International Labor Union and later of the International Workers of the World, and was a peace activist. Founding labor unions and being a peace activist was frowned upon by the government during World War I, and in 1918 Debs was arrested for un-American activities and sentenced to eleven years in the federal penitentiary in Atlanta. In 1920, he made his final run for president from prison.

Marquis James, whose mother rented a meat locker from Yeager in this novel, grew up in Enid and worked on several Enid newspapers in his youth. In 1915, he was in his midtwenties and working as a reporter for the New Orleans *Item.* He went on to become a well-known and respected newspaperman in New York and the author of several books, including biographies of Sam Houston (1930) and Andrew Jackson (1938), both of which received the Pulitzer Prize. He also wrote a wonderful book about growing up in Enid after the Cherokee Strip Land Run in 1893 and through the early 1910s entitled *Cherokee Strip: Tales of an Oklahoma Boyhood*, which was republished by the University of Oklahoma Press in 1993.

The **Cherokee Strip** is a tract of land fifty-eight miles wide which starts where the panhandle joins the body of the state and stretches 226 miles across the top of Oklahoma at the Kansas border. The Cherokees never actually lived in the Strip. Their nation is in the northeastern corner of Oklahoma. The Cherokee Outlet, as the Strip was properly called, was given to the Cherokee Nation by treaty in 1836 as an outlet to western hunting grounds. Unfortunately, the Cherokees backed the losing side in the Civil War, and in 1866 Congress "persuaded" the Nation to sell parts of the Strip to several other tribes. After the war, Texas cattlemen drove their herds to Kansas railheads by way of several trails through the Strip, the most famous of which, the Chisholm Trail, runs right through Enid. Many ranchers decided that it was a lot more profitable and a lot less tiring to lease land from the Cherokees and raise cattle right on the lush grass in the Strip, and between 1865 and 1890, the land was covered with huge cattle ranches.

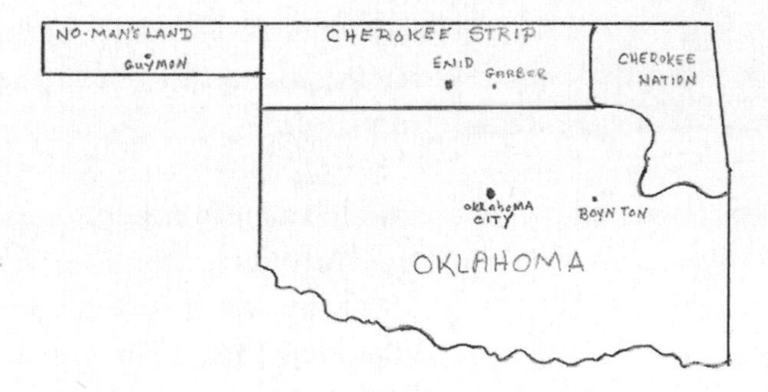

The **Cherokee Strip Land Run** was the fourth and the biggest of the five great Oklahoma land runs. In 1890, one year after the original Oklahoma Land Run, the president and Congress decided to open the Strip for settlement. They made the ranchers remove their cattle, divided the land into seven counties, imaginatively named K, L, M, N, O, P, and Q, and opened four land offices at Enid, Perry, Alva, and Woodward. A prospective homesteader was allowed into the territory before the run to scope out the land, decide on a section he liked, and pay his filing fee. But in order to officially claim the land, he had to line up at the starting line and make a run for it when the gun was fired at noon on September 16, 1893. If he was the first to reach his chosen section and drive his stake into the ground (*stake a claim*), he then went to the land office to file the claim. A racer might reach his prospective claim to find that a *sooner* had *jumped the gun* and illegally planted a stake before the run was officially started. Filing the claim was an ordeal, as well, since the land offices did a *land office business*, and the lines of weary homesteaders waiting to file were unbelievably long. Over 100,000 people made the run, on horseback, in wagons, on foot, and even by bicycle. Several times, some wag shot a gun into the air ahead of time, causing overexcited racers to take off, only to be chased down by cavalry troopers and hauled back behind the line. One poor soul jumped the gun at 11:55 and was chased by soldiers for nearly a mile before they shot him dead, which turned out to be the only way they could get him to stop.

The 1910 United States Census lists one person of **Asian** descent living in Enid, Oklahoma.

Founders' Day Jubilee was a very big deal all over the Cherokee Strip, but the multi-day Enid event topped them all for many years. Founders' Day is now called the Cherokee Strip Celebration and is still celebrated in Enid and several other towns in northern Oklahoma.

Puddin'head Wilson was written by Mark Twain in 1894. The novel is set in the little Missouri town of Dawson's Landing in the year 1830. Puddin'head is a small-town lawyer whose hobby is collecting the fingerprints of any amenable person he can persuade to cooperate. Over many years, Puddin'head collects the prints of nearly every soul in town, and is eventually able to utilize his collection to solve a murder and establish the identities of two men who were switched in the cradle as babies.

Oil Field Terminology

Bindlestiff—A man who traveled from job to job with all his possessions in a bundle, or *bindle*, which was often tied to the end of a stout stick and slung over the shoulder.

Boweevil—A general flunkie, who ran errands for the drillers and did whatever unskilled job needed to be done around the field. Nowadays, he would be called a "gofer."

Doodlebugger—The owner of a doodlebug machine, which resembled a wheelbarrow. This fabulous piece of equipment ostensibly was able to excite the molecules of the earth, rendering them transparent and enabling the operator to see through hundreds of feet of rock and soil right down to an oil deposit. During the oil boom years of the late nineteenth century and early twentieth century, these enterprising gentlemen traveled around the West, offering a "foolproof" way for eager landowners to determine exactly where to drill in order to strike oceans of oil and become wealthy beyond reckoning. For a handsome fee, the doodlebugger promised to run his machine over the property in question, find the oil pool, and save the landowner the expense of sinking a *duster*, or dry oil well. Needless to say, a doodlebugger never stayed in one place for very long.

Journal—This is a machinist's term for any rotary shaft that turns in a bearing.

Roustabout—A general oil field worker, more skilled than a boweevil.

Shooter—An explosives specialist, who knew the proper techniques for blasting open an obstructed oil well with nitroglycerin or dynamite. This was an extraordinarily dangerous job, especially in the early days of oil drilling, and a shooter was paid a high premium for his services. He was often short-lived, however.

Skimming plant—The old name for an oil refinery.

Tankie—A man who works on the giant oil storage tanks at a refinery. Tankies were considered the roughest, most unsavory sons-of-a-gun in the entire oil business.

Twister—Works the drill at an oil well. Twisters are the archetypical filthy, sweaty, shirtless guys who attach length after length of pipe with a giant wrench to the enormous rotary drill as it descends deeper and deeper into the ground.